THE NEWS FROM DUBLIN

ALSO BY COLM TÓIBÍN

Fiction

The South

The Heather Blazing

The Story of the Night

The Blackwater Lightship

The Master

Mothers and Sons

Brooklyn

The Empty Family

The Testament of Mary

Nora Webster

House of Names

The Magician

Long Island

A Long Winter

Non-fiction

Homage to Barcelona

Bad Blood: A Walk Along the Irish Border

The Sign of the Cross: Travels in Catholic Europe

Love in a Dark Time: Gay Lives from Wilde to Almodóvar

Lady Gregory's Toothbrush

All a Novelist Needs: Essays on Henry James

New Ways to Kill Your Mother

On Elizabeth Bishop

Mad, Bad, Dangerous to Know: The Fathers of Wilde, Yeats and Joyce

A Guest at the Feast

On James Baldwin

The News from Dublin

STORIES

———

COLM TÓIBÍN

PICADOR

First published 2026 by Picador
an imprint of Pan Macmillan
The Smithson, 6 Briset Street, London EC1M 5NR
EU representative: Macmillan Publishers Ireland Ltd, 1st Floor,
The Liffey Trust Centre, 117–126 Sheriff Street Upper,
Dublin 1 D01 YC43
Associated companies throughout the world

ISBN 978-1-0350-3073-6 HB
ISBN 978-1-0350-3074-3 TPB

Copyright © Colm Tóibín 2026

The right of Colm Tóibín to be identified as the
author of this work has been asserted in accordance with
the Copyright, Designs and Patents Act 1988.

All rights reserved. No part of this publication may be reproduced,
stored in a retrieval system, or transmitted, in any form, or by any means
(including, without limitation, electronic, mechanical, photocopying, recording
or otherwise) without the prior written permission of the publisher.

Pan Macmillan does not have any control over, or any responsibility for,
any author or third-party websites (including, without limitation, URLs,
emails and QR codes) referred to in or on this book.

1 3 5 7 9 8 6 4 2

A CIP catalogue record for this book is available from the British Library.

Typeset by Palimpsest Book Production Limited, Falkirk, Stirlingshire
Printed and bound in the UK using 100% Renewable Electricity by CPI Group (UK) Ltd

This book is sold subject to the condition that it shall not, by way of
trade or otherwise, be lent, hired out, or otherwise circulated without
the publisher's prior consent in any form of binding or cover other than
that in which it is published and without a similar condition including this
condition being imposed on the subsequent purchaser. The publisher does not
authorize the use or reproduction of any part of this book in any manner
for the purpose of training artificial intelligence technologies or systems.
The publisher expressly reserves this book from the Text and Data Mining
exception in accordance with Article 4(3) of the European Union
Digital Single Market Directive 2019/790.

Visit **www.panmacmillan.com** to read more about all our books
and to buy them.

For Vivienne Guinness

Contents

The Journey to Galway 1

Summer of '38 12

Five Bridges 33

Sleep 60

The News from Dublin 74

Barton Springs 93

A Sum of Money 98

A Free Man 122

The Catalan Girls 156

The Journey to Galway

She remembered an unusual silence that morning – a stillness in the trees and in the farmyard, and a deadness in the house itself, no sounds from the kitchen, and no one moving up and down the stairs. But she wondered if the silence had been real, or, instead, if it had been something she had merely imagined afterwards. She was unsure if getting the news had not actually changed her memory of the hours that came before. At times she thought that it hardly mattered, but at other times, especially when she woke to dawn light and dawn birdsong, the details of how word of Robert's death came, and precisely what the period before was like, belonged to her life as much as her breath did, or her heartbeat. It came to her as a story that had been told and retold rather than a brutal single fact, as though placing it in time and remembering how the news had spread would come to soften what had happened, ease it, edge it away. The details of her journey to Galway to tell Margaret, for example, and what she thought about on those two trains. Or where she was sitting when the word came, and what went through her mind in the seconds before she saw the telegram.

She lay in bed some mornings living it all from moment to moment, knowing that she would go on doing this until she died and that nothing she could do would make any difference. For her, there was a line between the time before she heard of her son's death and the time after. In the time before, she had wondered, if bad news were to come, where she would be, what room she would be in, at what time of the day it would come. She had even pictured herself receiving the news, her own face in shock, her voice gasping. And every evening, as she walked upstairs to bed, she had marked the day just ended as another one that had come and gone without news and thus a day to be savoured, to be thankful for. These thoughts seemed as different from the thoughts of later as land was from ocean, as air from water, as a death in a play in a theatre from a real dead body lying in a pool of blood in the real street outside.

When Robert had written letters, they had been read with care and attention. She knew that there was much he could not say, which meant that a stray phrase carried weight, perhaps even hidden meanings. But how much was often unclear because his letters were written in haste. Perhaps he had intended his letters to mean nothing more than what they said. Yet it must be true, she thought, that unintended words gave away something. But when he wrote, 'I sometimes awake feeling as if some part of me was crying in another place' it hardly mattered whether he had meant to alarm her or not, whether he had meant or not to let her know how afraid he was despite his efforts to be brave, and, as an airman in a war, how much daily fear he lived with and how much he masked. The other place where he was crying, she thought, was here, where she was now, the house which he owned, which his father and grandfather had also lived in. If the crying was hidden, then it was hidden here and in the woods and fields around here. The thought almost satisfied her as she read the letter again and again.

It struck her afterwards that what he did in those few years when he was a fighter pilot was merely an exaggerated version of what we all do as we live: we swagger, we are full of pretence that there is no real danger coming towards us, we talk as though the enemy is in flight, or under control. As time moves, however, it drags us with it until the time for pretending ends and the body lies spent. When she saw him in London, and later when he came home to Coole, she noticed the swagger. She made sure that she gave no sign that she was watching all the time for a break in it, gave no sign that much of it might have been closer to bravado than bravery. He could hardly have put his fear on display for her when he came home. He had not come home to frighten them but rather to reassure. She hoped he believed his own pose some of the time at least, but she wondered when night fell for him and he was alone, how much he knew, how much he could foresee, and how little peace he got when the prospect of being helpless in a burning plane thousands of feet above the earth insinuated itself into his waking time as much as into his dreams.

She wondered about luck. He would need to be lucky; but not everyone could be lucky. Forces no one could control, or almost no one, decided which pilots died or survived. Each morning it occurred to her that this might be the day, the day when Robert's luck ran out, and then she thought that the very act of thinking this meant that it would not happen, this would not be the day. It would never be the day she imagined it would be; it would be some other day. Thinking would, or might, or should, keep it from happening.

When she wrote letters to him, she thought too about chance. This letter, she imagined as she wrote to him, might be the last word he will read from me, or it might be the letter from me he will never read; it will arrive too late and it will be returned. It will be the special letter, written in hope, maybe even confidence, written to be read by someone who was alive, who would recognize the writing and know that when she referred to Margaret and the children, she meant his wife and Richard and Catherine and Anne. These things would not need to be spelled out for him, since they were written in the quickened spirit of being alive, but they might be words that came too late.

The days before she heard the news were days that seemed to have passed in slow time and lodged in her memory with sharpness and perseverance. What hopes she felt then that the war would come to an end and Robert would survive later became bathed in irony, almost in bitterness. How foolish she had been! And also, as she thought about it, how foolish she was now to think or imagine sometimes that if she had known he was going to die, if she had been sure, she could have done something to prevent it, she could have written a letter to some high-ranking official or stayed in London and made contact with those who decided on which pilots went out on which days. How foolish she was to think that the future could have been known, or that anyone would have listened! How hard it was to realize how powerless she was!

She had gone to Dublin, stopping off on the way at her sister's house in Galway where Margaret and the children were. Both she and Margaret were happier that Robert was now in Italy. He had written to Margaret to describe being cheered all along the line as they crossed the north of Italy, how the people brought fruit and flowers. He had loved Italy, and now, as she left Margaret and the children, the thought came to her that, if anywhere was worth fighting for, it might be Italy.

In Dublin she spoke at a meeting in the Mansion House calling for the paintings which had belonged to her nephew

Hugh Lane to be returned to Ireland, as he had wanted, or at least wanted at the end of his life, a life also cut short by the war. The meeting was crowded and there was enthusiasm about the pictures and their importance for Dublin. The pictures were things that might matter. It was always what she had said, that the struggle for freedom in Ireland was nothing compared to the struggle which would come afterwards, the struggle to build on the freedom, and that was what she had been working towards. The pictures would inspire that struggle, maybe their return would symbolize it. Helping to bring them back from London would be the least she could do. From Dublin she wrote to Robert, saying that if the pictures came back she should feel, 'Now lettest Thou thy servant depart in peace.' She was not sure she meant it, but he might see the humour of it mixed in with the sense of this effort to get the pictures returned as the last one his mother would have energy for. And she gave him news about the trees she was planting, the formal rows of larch with inlets of elm and sycamore, and then some silver birch and broom. And she put in what she thought might please him about the children without making him too sad, writing of Richard with a catapult looking quite the schoolboy. She concluded with, 'God bless you, my child.' She did not know that he was already four days dead.

When she came back from Dublin she went to the wood where she had been planting and was vexed that some timber had been given away and annoyed too that the men had cut down some of the young ash. She had imagined Robert returned and seeing the ash trees and the blue hills between them and seeing also the broom and the flowering trees. She decided that she would spend the whole next day at the wood making up for her absence, ensuring that everything was done according to her wishes. In the morning she asked for the donkey carriage made ready and, while waiting, she decided to go into the drawing room and write a letter, some letter that was urgent, or that seemed urgent then that morning. Her day ahead was fully planned, and it was easy to imagine how it might have been. She would have been well wrapped from the cold; she would have been decisive, thinking ahead to what things in the wood might look like in a year, and then in twenty years, and then in fifty years when other people, those not yet born, would walk here. That day could so easily have happened, and, if she had spent it making her wishes known and watching the work happen, it would have left her satisfied.

She was at her writing table when Marian, the servant, came in very slowly. When she looked up she saw that Marian was crying. She had a telegram. But there had been telegrams before. Twice on her last visit to London she had received telegrams and they were from friends about the breaking of some engagement. Marian could just have presumed that a telegram meant bad news. But when she was handed it and looked down and saw that it was not addressed to her but to Margaret, she knew that it was bad. If it had news of Robert's death, it was to Margaret they would send it. The first words she saw were 'killed in action' and then at the top 'deeply regret'.

She turned to Marian. 'How will I tell Margaret? Who will tell her? Who can go to Galway and tell her?' She tried to stand up but she could not. It occurred to her that she must not cry now or think about herself. She must fix her mind on one thing – on that scene she had witnessed a few days earlier, Margaret and the three children lodged with her sister, the ease and the peace in the house despite the worry. It was to be broken now. Who would break it? She wondered if she could send Marian and if Marian could hand Margaret the telegram as she had handed it to her. She asked about trains and was told there was still time to get a connection to Galway. She told Marian to order some vehicle that could meet the train in Gort. She sat there frozen until Marian came back to say that she had also had a note from Mrs Mitchell in the Post Office saying that there was only one person who should break the news of Robert's death to Margaret, and that was Robert's own mother, and that was why she had sent the telegram on to Coole, even though she knew that Margaret was not there.

She stood up then and nodded. She went upstairs and got some things for the journey, even changing her dress as though it might matter what she was wearing. But it slowed time down as she selected it. It slowed time down too as she took the other dress off and put this one on and then checked herself in the mirror and made sure that she had forgotten nothing. The carriage would be waiting. She wondered if there was one more thing she needed to do in the bedroom, but there was not. She had the telegram in her hand now, and that was really all she needed. She would have to show it to Margaret. Maybe that is what she would do, say nothing, just hand her the piece of paper.

In any case, she would have to set out on her journey. As she looked out the long window while going down the stairs she saw one of the workmen with his head hanging low walking away from the house. The news would have spread. In the carriage she thought of nothing, forced herself to go on having no thoughts, letting nothing into her mind. The effort gave her some relief, or something that was like relief. Once they arrived at the station she determined that she would not wait on the platform with others, people whom she did not know, or allow acquaintances approach to exchange pleasantries. She would stay in the carriage until the last minute. John, the driver, told the porter the news, and the porter went and got her a ticket to Galway. As soon as she heard the train coming she went to the platform. No one, she thought, no one in the world should ever have to do what she was doing now.

As she walked towards the train she saw that Frank, her brother, was at the window of a carriage and was motioning her to come and join him. She looked at him and looked away and walked further down, away from him. She did not want his company. She could not speak. She went to some other carriage where there was a woman, a stranger. As she sat down, she tried to picture the scene in Galway, her arrival, she tried to imagine what words she would use if she were asked why she had come. She bowed her head.

At one of the station stops when Frank came to her window she tried to tell him, but found that she could not speak and instead held out the telegram, which she had in her hand. For a second it struck her that if she could only have something else in her hand, then this might all be nothing, that it was the telegram itself which was bearing down on her. Frank spoke softly. 'I know all about it,' he said. He had guessed from her face when he had seen her at the station that some dreadful thing had happened; when he sent someone to ask the driver of the carriage, the worst was confirmed for him.

As the train went on, she cried, but not much, aware of the other woman, the stranger, opposite her. She forced herself to sit up straight and steel herself. So this was what Robert's life had led to then, this death! It was like an arrow hitting its target. It would hardly matter now, or in the future, how cruel and thoughtless Robert had been in the year or two before he signed up. There was no need to judge him any more. She would remember him instead when he was a boy, or a young man she was proud of.

Someone brave and talented, filled with daring. His dying meant that she would no longer have to judge him. Death would simplify him and that at least was something. Margaret could mourn him, or some idea of him, and forget how, in the time before he joined up, he had been in love with her best friend. In that time he appeared to enjoy the idea that Margaret knew that he and her friend had become lovers.

Perhaps it was easy, or too tempting, to be cruel to Margaret; she would, she thought as the train moved towards Galway, get to know her daughter-in-law better now since Margaret would inherit everything, the house, the land. There would be a struggle. Robert was already in a place where such struggles no longer mattered. She gasped for a moment when Robert's face appeared before her and the idea came that his body had been burned and that he might have suffered badly as his plane went down.

She put all thoughts of Robert away and just looked on stoically as the woman opposite her got out her lunch basket. When the woman offered her some food, she could only shake her head. She tried to smile but she was not sure it was a smile.

Yes, she thought, going to war had solved so much, it had left things in abeyance, it had meant that all discussion had been postponed, it had made compromise impossible, but in solving what it did, it had solved too much. It had solved everything so there was nothing left. All their daily thoughts, all the differences between them, all their knowledge of one another, were nothing now and would always be nothing. Despite what had happened, Margaret had wanted Robert back. But he would not be back; he would not grow old or live to regret anything at all or be forgiven. Action had given him a strange freedom, as it must have done for others, an avoidance of having to deal with his own complexity. Death, on the other hand, would give him nothing at all. From now on, it would be all absence. For her too, everything she did or said in the future would be a way of distracting herself from the stark simple fact that her son, her only child, had died in the war. There was hardly anything else to be said; the texture of what happened was reduced to a telegram, the telegram that she still held in her hand.

And he had died in a British uniform, a uniform that had seemed more and more the uniform of another country. In joining the British army, he had been his father's son; he had followed his cousins. He had not followed her, nor had she asked him to. She wondered now if he and those like him, the others who had died for this dream of empire, this large and abstract conflict between nations, would belong to the past, if they would not be shadows fading into further and deeper shadows. Their class would not hold sway in an Ireland of the future, she was sure of that. She began to imagine what it would be like instead if she were going on a train to Dublin to be with him on the night before his execution, if he had taken part in the Easter Rebellion. She thought of how proud she would be on the train, how there would be some people travelling with her who would feel exalted by her presence. But it would end in the same way. It would end in death, it would end in three fatherless children, it would end in a future in which Robert would only be a name and a memory. He would never come into a room again. It hardly mattered what cause he had fought for, or what his impulse to join had been. It was simple; he had been killed.

She was relieved that Frank kept away from her as she changed for the Galway train, relieved that he was not also going on to Galway. She looked around for Daly, the porter whom she knew. Someone would have given him the news. But there was no sign of him. She was glad that none of the strangers near her guessed.

This was an ordinary day for them; perhaps there was comfort in that, but it was not a comfort that lasted long. When the train came she sat alone and willed only that it would go slowly, or that it might stop somewhere for a while. In Margaret's mind, she thought, Robert was still alive. Maybe that meant something; it gave Robert some strange extra time. Although she knew that that idea was foolish, it helped her but it also increased her dread. She was moving westward like cruel death itself, she thought. She was the one who had the news. Until she appeared in the doorway of that house, there would not be death. But once she appeared, death would live in that house. There would be nothing else except death. She carried death with her, she thought, as she had once carried life.

When she left the train, it was already dark in Galway. She took a car across the city to the house. When a maid opened the door, she wished she were elsewhere now – in the woods, even in the train, even in the car on the way here. She asked for Margaret. The maid said that Margaret was in the study with the mistress and followed her as she walked deliberately into the room on the right, a room that was seldom used. She told the maid to ask Margaret to come to her, just Margaret. She stood there with the door open. When her daughter-in-law appeared, Margaret looked at her and asked 'Is he dead?' She handed Margaret the telegram and then turned away towards the window while Margaret read it. She had brought the news. It was done. It was over. The journey to Galway was over.

Summer of '38

Marta held the door of the lift open for her daughter and put her hand in her coat pocket to make sure that she had her keys. She would walk Ana to her car, which was parked nearby, then, once Ana had driven away, continue on the short distance to the town centre to get some groceries. It was easier like this, easier than having Ana say goodbye to her in the apartment, easier than hearing the lift door close, knowing that there was nothing except the night ahead, no other sound but the traffic outside and the birdsong, which would die out when darkness fell.

'Oh, I meant to say that the man – you know, the man from the electric company –' Ana looked at her as though the man were someone she should know. 'The one I told you about – he knew I was your daughter and he's writing a book about the war in his spare time and he asked me where you lived.'

'I don't know that man at all,' Marta said as she closed the front door of the building. 'He is mixing me up with someone else.'

She liked to sound firm and in control. It saved her daughters from having to worry about her living on her own.

'Well, anyway, he said he knows you. So if he calls on you, that will be why.'

'The war?'

'He's collecting information on the war.'

'Does he think I was in the war?'

'I don't know what he's doing exactly. He's writing a book.'

'Well, I am sure he can write it without my help.'

They had reached Ana's car. Marta saw that Ana was not even listening to her. Her youngest daughter, the one who lived closest by, took things lightly. She was, Marta thought, probably relieved that her weekly visit to her mother was over and she was on her way home.

Marta went out three times a day, even in winter. There was always something to buy, if only a loaf of bread or a newspaper. It meant that she took some exercise and saw people.

The week after Ana had mentioned the man from the electric company, Marta saw him waiting at the front door of her building when she came home with a bag of fruit. She did know him, she realized; he was someone she often saw on the street. She must have been aware, too, that he worked for FECSA, although she couldn't think how she knew this. She didn't think she knew his name or anything else about him.

Once he had introduced himself, she understood that he wanted to come up to the apartment with her. She was unsure about this. Since Paco died, she had become protective of her own space and she disliked surprises. She even asked her daughters to phone at appointed times. But there was something both eager and easy-going in this man's manner and she knew that it would sound rude if she asked him to say whatever he had to say in the hallway of the building. Also, she thought, if something ever went wrong with her electricity, it would be useful to know a man who could fix it.

'Ana may have told you what I am doing,' he said, once he was sitting in the armchair opposite hers with a glass of water in his hand.

She nodded but said nothing.

'I am trying to chart every event of the war, just in this valley and the mountains,' he said.

'I wasn't involved in the war,' she replied. 'My father wasn't even involved. And I had no brothers.'

'Oh, no, it wasn't to ask you anything, but to say that a retired general in Madrid – actually, he's from Badajoz – who was here during the war is coming back to show me where the dugouts were and exactly where the guns were positioned. He hasn't been here since then.'

'One of Franco's generals?'

'Yes, though he wasn't a general during the war. I found his name and address and wrote to him. I didn't expect a reply, but he is coming. I spoke to him on the phone and the only person he remembered here, besides the other soldiers, was you. He remembered your name and said that he would like to see you. I asked around, because I didn't recognize your maiden name. I asked around without telling anyone why.'

'And what is his name?'

'Ramirez. Rudolfo Ramirez.'

Marta looked towards the window, as though distracted by something.

'There were a few of them,' she said. 'I'm not sure I would remember him. We didn't have much to do with them, as you can imagine.'

'Anyway, he's coming here on Saturday of next week. There will be no big fuss – I've assured him of that. I've told no one that he is coming, except you. He'll show me what he needs to show me and then I'll take him to Lleida to catch the train back to Madrid. But he said that he would come for lunch at Can Andreu, and he asked if you might join us.'

'I'm here all right,' she said, 'but I don't go out much.'

'I understand. But no one will know who he is. I could collect you and drop you back if that would suit you.'

'The war was a long time ago.' She was going to say something else and then hesitated. 'It was fifty years ago. More.'

'I know. It was hard for all of you who lived through it. The more I find out about it, the clearer it is how much it divided people. I'm trying to get the facts right while there is still time. It's history now – at least, for the younger generation it is.'

She smiled.

'Anyway, yours was the name he gave me, and he seemed delighted to hear that you were well.'

'I'm not sure I would know him. In fact, I'm sure I wouldn't.'

'Shall I drop by in a few days and see what you think?'

'If you want, but I don't go to restaurants much. I've never been to Can Andreu.'

'Well, it's Saturday week at two o'clock, and, as I said, it would be just the three of us and no one any the wiser. He won't be in uniform, or anything like that.'

'I'm sure he won't, if he was one of Franco's generals,' she said, and then instantly regretted having sounded so sure, so up to date, since she wished to give the impression that she was old and living in her own world.

'It is good of him to come,' the man said. 'I was surprised.'

Marta did not reply. She hoped that it was obvious to her visitor that he should go.

Rudolfo would be over eighty now, she calculated. But he would still have something of what he had then, even if it lurked beneath sagging flesh and slow stiff movements. She pictured an old man getting out of an old-fashioned car with difficulty, his hair white, his frame frail. Maybe he would still have some trace of the effortless charm that he had exuded all that time before.

It was the summer of '38, when the prisoners had all been taken to Lleida or Tremp. Those who had avoided capture had fled to the mountains or crossed the border into France or fled south to Barcelona. The town was quiet for a week or more – no one was sure who would come back or what would happen. The dam was being protected by Franco's soldiers, that was all. Then more of his soldiers piled in, and they took over the town hall, and they put up tents on the grounds of the school. Orders were given that shops and bars were to resume their normal hours.

At first, she remembered, people were afraid and stayed indoors. There were rumours that they were all going to be taken away, every house cleared, even the houses that had nothing to do with the war. Under cover of darkness, some people made their way into the mountains or towards the border. Everyone was waiting for something to happen. But nothing happened except that ordinary life came back, or something like it. Once the shops had reopened and there was mass again on Sundays, the talk was about the dam and how carefully it was being guarded, and about a space that the soldiers had made by the edge of the water and the makeshift bar they had built and the fire they lit every night to keep the mosquitoes away. The talk was of the supplies of food they had, and the guitar playing and singing and dancing.

She did not go there at first, but girls she knew did and even some of the older people who wanted to forget about the war.

Later, Rudolfo told her that he had seen her on the street, noticed her as she went shopping with her mother and her sisters, but she did not think that that was true. However, she was sure that she had noticed him the night she first went down to the makeshift bar. It was the way he seemed to be amused by things that drew her attention, the way he smiled. His hair was cut short; he was not as tall as some of the others. He was in uniform, his shirt unbuttoned. As he sat there watching, the soldiers began to play music you could dance to, slow songs. Some of them danced with girls from the town.

There was, she remembered, a swagger about the soldiers, which faded slowly as the night wore on, and there was something uneasy, too, which meant that when the music became sad they all seemed more comfortable, even the ones who were not dancing. When the soldiers were joined by others, who had just come off duty, there were sudden bursts of gaiety – shouting and clapping and drinking. Only Rudolfo sat quietly, observing the scene.

She realized that he was watching her. Once, he nodded to her. It could have been a casual gesture, except that it was not. She knew that it was not.

After a while, when one of her friends left, she left, too. She did not go there the following night. The next time she went, he was there as before, apart from the others, watching, amused by it all. He did not stir, merely made it clear that he knew she was there; once again, he took no part in the dancing or the showing off around the fire.

He let her know by looking at her that he wanted her and that the rest – the drinking, the dancing, the boyish antics – did not interest him. He was shy, almost retiring, but appeared also entirely sure of himself. She didn't believe that anything would happen between them. She didn't think that he would move towards her or do anything to disturb his self-contained observation of the scene around him.

Yet he kept his eye on her, and she returned his glances, careful that none of her friends were looking.

One night, there was a full moon and a clear sky. When the crowd moved to the edge of the water and let the fire die down, neither he nor she moved with them. When he spoke to her, she could not hear him, so he moved closer. She realized that no one might have noticed that she had not joined the others by the water. Some of the soldiers there had stripped down and were swimming and splashing. Away from them, close to the dying embers, he touched the back of her hand and then turned it and traced his fingers on the palm.

There was an old ruined building nearby. They walked slowly towards it and when they leaned against the wall she was relieved that all he wanted to do was kiss her and smile at her in between the kisses. In all the years since, she had never forgotten the sweet smell of his breath, his eagerness and good humour.

The next night, he found them a place where they could lie together undisturbed, and that was what they did every night until September came.

Every day that summer she waited for the evening. Her friends knew that she was with Rudolfo, but most of the girls who went to the makeshift bar had found boyfriends among the soldiers. No one ever talked about it. When her mother asked her if she had been to the soldiers' parties, she shrugged and said that she had passed by once or twice, but had walked on with her friends. When her mother asked her a second time, a few nights later, she made sure to come home early for once, so that no one at home would have an idea what she was doing.

She wondered now if she remembered correctly that the weather had changed as soon as the bombardment of the villages on the other side of the river began. Perhaps the man from the electric company would know. The bombardment began, in any case, towards the end of summer. The sound came in the night but often in the day, too, the sound of heavy artillery from up the valley. The villages that had remained with the Loyalists were being attacked.

She remembered her father saying that the soldiers had spent the summer preparing for this assault, that they had been building dugouts and finding the best positions and carrying the heavy guns there. They had left nothing to chance, once they secured the dam. He added that there was no hospital on the other side and no medicine, and the soldiers were letting no one cross the footbridge at Llavorsí or the bridge in Sort. People were trapped, he said, and the injured were dying of their wounds.

It struck her that the parties by the water were where the troops who'd been working all day preparing the guns came to relax. But she did not feel guilty. Instead, she hoped that those who had noticed her presence at the soldiers' bonfires would have their own reasons to keep silent about it. In the years afterwards, everyone – even those who had been there every night – pretended that none of it had happened.

It was the change in the weather that changed everything – she was almost certain of that. It was a grey day, with the mist that came over the valley in September, when she realized that she knew nothing about Rudolfo save his first name and that he came from Badajoz. By that time he was gone, and it dawned on her that he would, in all likelihood, not be returning. The realization broke the spell that had been cast on her, by the war itself as much as by Rudolfo.

It was not until then that she began to worry that she was pregnant. She waited and hoped that she was wrong. She woke in terror some nights, but in the day she tried to behave normally. In the meantime, the war went on up the valley, and jeeps and trucks full of soldiers and supplies drove through the town, and the town was often desolate, the main square empty, even though the bars and most of the shops remained open.

When she was convinced that she was pregnant she decided that she would marry Paco Vendrell. For years at the town festivals he had followed her around, offering to buy her drinks, asking her to dance and, when she refused, standing on his own and observing her with a single-mindedness that made her shiver. He was ten years her senior, but had seemed middle-aged even when he was younger. Since he had begun working in the control room of the dam, when he was fourteen or fifteen, he had spoken of little else: the levels of water in the two rivers, or in the lake itself, or the flow of water that could be expected soon, or the difference between this year and last year. Marta's father laughed at him, and for her mother and her sisters the idea that he had been pursuing her since she was sixteen or seventeen was a source of regular jokes. She did her best to avoid him, and if she could not avoid him then she openly rebuffed his efforts to speak to her.

Now she urgently wanted to meet him. For a few days, she watched to see if she could run into him on his way to work. Since she did not see him walking to the dam, she supposed that he was taken there by military jeep now, and brought home in the same way in the evening. No one, she knew, was allowed to approach the road that led to the control tower overlooking the dam. The only time she could be sure that she would encounter Paco, she thought, was at Sunday mass. She would have to be brave and move fast and not worry about other people watching and commenting. The opportunity to meet him might not come every Sunday.

Fortunately, there was only one mass on Sunday these days,

and the church was more crowded than it had ever been, as the people of the town, even those who had no interest in religion, or who were known to have been with the Loyalists, set out to show the troops whose side they were on now. By the beginning of that winter, it had become clear to all of them who was going to win the war, and it was clear, too, that as soon as the war ended there would be many more accusations and arrests. She understood that there would be little pity for someone in her situation, no matter who the father of the child was.

That Sunday, she went to the church early, walking quietly and demurely in the street with a mantilla on her head and a prayer book in her hand. She was sure that Paco would go to mass if he wasn't working; he was not the sort of man who stayed away. But she could not remember actually seeing him in the church and did not know if he stood at the back, as many of the men did, or if he walked right up and found a place close to the altar. She would need to find a good vantage point from which she could see everyone, but she could not, she thought, sit at the back of the church by herself, as she had never done so before and might be spotted by neighbours or by her family, who would ask themselves what she was doing there.

She sat in one of the side pews and was early enough to witness the two priests arriving, the older one, whom she knew, and the younger one, whom she had never met. What she noticed, as they walked up the aisle to go to the vestry, was their bearing, how proud they seemed and severe. They could easily, she imagined, have approached the vestry from outside, but approaching it like this gave them more dignity and more importance.

Soon, they were followed by a group of soldiers in full uniform. For a second, she was startled by the idea that Rudolfo could be among them. She looked at them carefully, however, and did not see him. Even if he did appear, she thought, whatever had happened in the atmosphere between the summer and now would mean that he would not come near her or acknowledge her. She was sure that, even were she to edge close to him and try to talk, he would avoid her.

She shivered for a moment and then watched warily as the pews began to fill up with people who kept their eyes averted. She wondered when the war would be over and wondered also, as the panic that often came to her in the night returned, what would happen to her if she could not persuade Paco to marry her. It occurred to her that she would be sent away, that her father and mother would not be able to protect her, even if they wanted to.

But how would she marry Paco? How could it be done? She had been so rude to him in the past, so dismissive. How could she make it apparent to him that she had changed her mind? What reason would she give? In this uncertain atmosphere, with the chance that many more people were going to be killed or locked up, no one was thinking of romance or marriage, least of all someone like Paco, who was cautious and whose daily work at the dam was likely more and more difficult. But there was no one else she could think of who might marry her.

In the reaches of the night, one other option had come to her, and it struck her again now. There was a secluded place above the river, about a kilometre up the valley, where the current was strong and the water deep. Over the years, two or three people had used this place to kill themselves and their bodies had not been found for days. She thought that maybe soon she should go and look at that spot, check if it was guarded by the troops. She closed her eyes at the thought of it and bowed her head.

When communion was almost over, she saw Paco walking

up the aisle. She knew then that he must have been standing at the back. She studied him as he returned. His lips were moving in prayer; his hands were joined. He seemed even odder and more isolated than usual. She almost smiled at the courage, or the self-delusion, it must have taken for him to pursue her the way he had; she wondered what thoughts he must have had before going out on those evenings and how disappointed he must have been to go home alone, knowing that he had no chance with her. It struck her, too, that, since he worked at the dam with the soldiers, he would have known about the parties at the water's edge and might have heard that she was among the girls who had gone there. He might even have heard about her and Rudolfo. It occurred to her as she waited for mass to end that he might want to have nothing to do with her now. And if he, who had been so enthusiastic, did not want her, then she was sure, absolutely sure, that no one else would want her either.

She moved quickly as the ceremony came to an end. Paco was not the sort of man who stood at the church gates after mass with a group of friends. In any case, no one would want to be seen standing around now. When she walked out of the church grounds she saw that he was already some distance away. She followed him, hoping that no one would see her. She had prepared what she would say to him. It was important to make it seem plausible, natural.

When he turned, he gave her a look that was anxious and withdrawn, and then almost hostile, as if to say that he had enough problems without her chasing him down to let him know yet again that she had no interest in him. He turned his back to her before she could even smile. As he walked faster, she grew more determined. If he had wanted her before, she figured, he would still want her now. All she had to do was be careful and hide all signs of panic as she spoke to him.

Eventually, when he looked back again and saw her, he stopped.

'I have to go home to change my clothes,' he said, 'and then they'll collect me. They are very busy at the dam. Everything has to be noted and written down.'

She smiled. 'Well, I'll walk along with you so I won't delay you,' she said. 'We are all worried at home. You know, I have no brothers. And my father says that we cannot go out alone now, not even just to the shops. So I am locked in the house or that's what it seems like.'

They continued walking. She feared that if she stopped talking for one second he would tell her something about the dam and everything she had already said would be forgotten.

'If you were free some time, it would be great if you could call at the house and maybe we could go for a walk, if only through the town and then home again. But maybe you are too busy.'

'There's a new captain from Madrid and he's a stickler for notes, and they all watch me in case I decide to pull one of the levers when they are not looking. You know, I'm the only one who fully understands the switching system, though the new fellow from Madrid is beginning to get the hang of it.'

She wondered whether, if she concentrated hard enough, she might get through to him. But it was not easy.

'Anyway,' he said, 'I'd better get going. I can't use this suit in the control room. It's the only good suit I have.'

When Paco called two days later, one of her sisters answered the door and did not disguise her amusement or keep her voice down. Marta found her coat and left with him. During the weeks that followed he called every few days. Her sisters and her mother made jokes about him, at first, then expressed puzzlement, and finally grew silent. Not one of them asked her what she was doing walking around the town with Paco Vendrell and having hot chocolate with him in one of the *granjas*.

He talked to her about the dam, explaining its strategic importance and how old some of the systems were, which meant that only someone experienced could deal with the levers, someone who knew that a few of them would not respond if pulled too fast, and also that if one of them was pulled halfway it would have the same effect as pulling it the whole way.

She already knew that he lived with his mother but found out now that his father had died when he was young. She discovered that he liked routines, liked going to work at the same time every day, and disliked the soldiers' efforts to vary his timetable. Within a week, she, too, was part of his routine. Chatting to her, he seemed comfortable. She realized that he would be content to meet this way for months, maybe even years. He would not make a quick decision or want a sudden change in his life. And, like everyone, he knew that things would be very different when the war was over. He had a way of addressing the matters that interested him slowly and deliberately. Her efforts to speed things up, to ask him, for example, if he was happy living with his mother, failed completely. He did not register anything that interfered with the current of his own conversation.

When Christmas came, there were more and more rumours. Whole families disappeared, and houses became vacant. Her father said that anyone who had the slightest reason to leave should go now. She continued seeing Paco, although he was more cautious as they walked around the town, hoping not to be noticed by the troops.

One evening as she stood up from the table she saw her

mother's eyes resting on her belly. She waited until they were alone in the kitchen.

'How soon?' her mother asked.

'Five months, maybe a bit less.'

'Is Paco the father?'

'No.'

'Does he know?'

'No.'

'Is that why you are seeing him – so that he will marry you?'

'Yes, but he's in no hurry.'

'Was it one of the soldiers?'

'Yes.'

'And he has disappeared?'

'Yes.'

Her mother looked at her.

'Let me deal with Paco,' she said.

For the next two weeks Paco did not visit. The weather grew cold and there was snow. Sometimes they could hear rifle fire in the distance, even during the day. Feigning sickness, Marta stayed in bed, joining the others only for meals. She waited for her mother to come into the bedroom and tell her that it could not be done, that Paco would not marry her. She imagined then how she would have to brave the cold and avoid the soldiers, find a quiet time and move as though invisible. She tried to imagine what it would be like to jump into a deep and fast-moving river, unsure how quickly she would sink, how long it would take her to drown. As she lay in bed, another scenario came to her: she would be sent to a convent or an orphanage somewhere and the baby would be taken from her as soon as it was born. She would not be allowed home. Maybe that would be preferable.

Eventually, when the house was silent one day, her mother

appeared to tell her that the wedding was arranged. It would happen in a few days in a side chapel and Paco would take full responsibility for the child.

'His mother seemed surprised and almost proud,' her mother said. 'She thinks the baby is his. Paco said that he has always wanted to marry you, that you are the girl for him, so at least someone is happy. There is a small flat at the top of the building where his mother lives. He is transporting furniture there right now. It would be lovely, Marta, if we didn't have to see too much of him. He has a way of wearing me down with his talk.'

When her mother had finished speaking, Marta turned away from her and did not look around again until she was sure that her mother had left the room.

As soon as Rosa was born, Paco wanted to hold her. In the days that followed, Marta watched him to see if he was holding the baby merely for her sake. She saw no sign of that, however. When Paco came home from work he wanted to know what the baby had been doing. Even being told that she had been sleeping was enough for him.

As they walked through the town with the baby, Marta was aware that other men were laughing at Paco because of his devotion to the baby. She knew that her family laughed at him too. But Paco remained impervious to the laughter. When he was at home, he tried to amuse the baby; he soothed her if she cried. And, once Rosa learned to walk, Paco loved taking her out, moving as slowly as she wanted and holding her hand with pride.

Being married to him was strange. He never once asked about the father of the child. He seemed grateful and content with everything. Marta was grateful to him in return, but that did not keep her from feeling relieved when he left for work each day or when he fell asleep beside her in the bed. She was careful to disguise this, though. And then, as they had two more daughters and moved to a bigger apartment, she found that being polite to him took on a force of its own. She tolerated him, and then grew fond of him. In time, as she realized that her parents and her sisters were still laughing at him, she saw less of them. She began to feel a loyalty towards Paco, a loyalty that lasted for all the years of their marriage.

Rosa did not look like Marta or Paco, or her two sisters. Nor, Marta thought, did she resemble Rudolfo. All she had of her natural father was her way of staying apart. She had little interest in the company of other girls and yet everyone liked her. Although Paco was proud of his two other daughters, it was always clear that he loved Rosa best.

While the others settled locally, Ana in Sort and Neus in La Seu, Rosa went to Barcelona and studied medicine. She married a fellow doctor and opened a private clinic with him, using money that his family had given them. When Paco was dying, when his heart was giving out, Rosa insisted on looking after him herself. She sat with him in a private room at the clinic day and night. When he opened his eyes, all he looked for was Rosa.

By that time Rosa had three sons of her own, and it was in the sons, especially the eldest, Marta noticed, that Rudolfo appeared again. It was in their eyes, their colouring, but also in the slow way they smiled, in their shyness. Each year, when Rosa and her family holidayed close to Santa Cristina, on the Costa Brava, Marta spent two weeks with them. Once the oldest boy could drive, he would come to collect her. That journey, alone in the car with him, gave her pleasure.

When the man from the electric company came by again, she told him that she did not want to have lunch with him and the general, and that he should not press her as she was not feeling well.

'He will be disappointed,' the man said.

'Yes, I'm sure,' she replied, realizing that the edge of bitterness in her voice had given away more than she'd meant to.

'We are all old now,' she added in a softer tone, 'and we can only do what we can.'

'If you change your mind, perhaps you will let me know,' the man said. He left her a phone number.

As soon as he had gone she phoned the clinic and left an urgent message for Rosa.

'I would be really grateful if you could come here on the Saturday of next week,' she asked, when Rosa called her back. 'And if you could come on your own. If you can, I promise I won't ask you for anything for a long time.'

'Are you sick?'

'No.'

'Is it something else?'

'Don't ask, Rosa. Just come that day. Come for lunch. You needn't stay the night or anything.'

She held her breath now and waited.

'I've looked at my diary,' Rosa said. 'I have a dinner that night.'

'Great. So if you leave my house at four or five you'll be there in plenty of time.'

'Have you seen a doctor?'

'You're a doctor, Rosa. I'll be seeing you.'

'I'll bring my stethoscope.' Rosa laughed.

'Just bring yourself.'

She came not only with a stethoscope but with a device for measuring blood pressure and a set of needles to take blood samples and a cooler to keep the samples cold until she got back to Barcelona. She made her mother remove her blouse so that she could listen to her heart and her lungs. She drew blood slowly without speaking.

'I'm old,' Marta said. 'There is no point in checking me.'

'You didn't sound well on the phone.'

'No one my age ever sounds well on the phone.'

'Why did you want me to visit you today?'

'Because I thought if I gave you an exact day you might be more likely to appear than if I said just come any day. I hardly ever see you.'

'I wish my husband knew me as well as you do,' Rosa said. She seemed to be in good humour.

The table in the dining alcove was already set. Now Marta put a tray of *canelons* into the oven and brought a bowl of salad and two plates to the table and some bread. She asked Rosa about her husband and her sons.

'They are all wonderful. The only worry we have is that Oriol failed chemistry and has to repeat it.'

'Does he still have that nice girlfriend he had in the summer?'

'He does, which is why he failed chemistry.'

When they had eaten, she brought Rosa her coffee at the table near the window.

'I found a box of photographs,' she said. 'Some of them were taken before the war. They must have come from the old house when my mother died. I found them a year ago but I put them away because they made me too sad.'

She went into her bedroom, where she had the box waiting on the chair where she normally put her clothes for the next day.

'Maybe we could pick out the best photos, the clearest,' she said when she came back, 'and if one of your boys, when they have time, could make copies for you and your sisters.'

She put bundles of photographs on the table.

'This was my grandmother,' she said, holding one up. 'She lived with us until there was a falling out of some sort and then she lived with my aunt. She was originally from Andorra and my father always thought she had money, but, of course, she had none.'

'Who is the baby on her lap?'

'That's me. There was a man who would appear once a year with a camera and a booth and people would queue up.'

They began to flip through other photographs. Most of them were of Marta and her sisters, taken on summer outings.

'I have some here with no people in them – one of the river when it was flooded, which my father must have taken, and one of the dam being built. I can't remember what year that was.'

Rosa moved these aside and began to examine another bundle of photographs of Marta and her sisters and their friends.

'Those were taken well before the war,' Marta said. 'After the war I don't think people took photographs as much.'

Rosa was studying a large-format photograph of a group on an outing with mountains in the background.

'Where is my father in this? Why isn't he in any of the pictures?' she asked.

'Your father always took the photographs,' Marta replied.

She reached for another bundle.

'He might be in one of these, but he was the only one who had a camera in the years before the war and he liked taking photographs.'

She glanced at Rosa, who was nodding.

'Anyway, if you want to take the whole box and select the best ones – and if the boys had time they could make copies. It all must seem like ancient history to them, but maybe it will mean more when they have their own families.'

'I'll be very careful with them,' Rosa said, picking up a photograph of herself as a teenage girl with Paco, smiling, beside her.

'I think I took that one,' Marta said.

'I might get it blown up a bit bigger and frame it,' Rosa said.

When it was time to go, Marta carried the box of photographs to the lift and Rosa carried the medical equipment. Marta insisted on going down with her to her car.

'If that's too heavy, just tell me,' Rosa said.

The car was parked close by. They put the box and the equipment on the back seat, and then Rosa embraced her, before opening the door and getting into the driver's seat.

Marta waved as the car pulled away. She knew that she could easily be seen by anyone approaching. She looked up the street towards the town centre to check if there was a car coming. The lunch would be over around now, she thought, and Rudolfo and the man from the electric company would pass by as they drove towards Lleida. She waited a few minutes, but when she saw no car she decided to go back inside and clear away the dishes. Later, she thought, she would walk to the town centre and do a bit of shopping.

Soon, she knew, there would be an old man standing at the station in Lleida as the train to Madrid arrived. He would get on the train slowly and then walk along the aisle to find his seat. He would, she imagined, be polite to those around him as he settled in for the journey. Rosa would be on the motorway that led in the other direction, her driving steady and competent as it always was. Marta sighed with quiet satisfaction as she thought of the two of them, moving so freely away from each other; they would both be home before night fell.

Five Bridges

She promised that the climbing would be easy.

'Even for you,' she said.

'How long?'

'An hour. Or maybe two hours. Or maybe three.'

'Give or take?'

'Yes, that's right.'

Paul had told her on their last outing to Point Reyes Station that he was leaving, packing up. She would be able to come to Ireland to visit him, he said now, and they should start making plans for that.

'I'll be at my folks' house, at least at the beginning, and they really would love to meet you in person. It'll be nice when you come.'

'It's sad they never came here,' Geraldine said. 'They could have visited any time. They said they would.'

'No money, I suppose, and too far.'

They were still a mile or two from Stinson Beach. If he took the slow way back into the city, they would be late. He had to be careful to drop her off on time. She would grow nervous at the thought of her mother waiting.

'Don't text to say you'll be late. Just don't be late.'

This, which had appeared twice on Geraldine's phone a year earlier, had become a mantra for Paul and his daughter, a way of lightly mocking Geraldine's mother, during these trips in his car on Saturday afternoons.

As Geraldine fell silent, Paul realized that he should not have said that his parents had no money. Geraldine would worry about this, and it was not even true. She was almost twelve years old now, and he had resolved a while ago never to tell her anything that wasn't true.

'I spoke to Mom about you leaving,' Geraldine said, 'and she thinks you might be deported if you don't.'

Geraldine was using her adult, responsible tone.

'And Stan says,' she continued, 'that they'll be checking on all sorts of people.'

He held back from saying that he hoped someone would check on Stan.

'Would I come to see you on my own?' she asked.

'To Dublin? Yes, I suppose. Yes, you would. It would be a lovely journey. They treat young girls with great respect—'

'You said the last time,' she interrupted, 'that I could have one wish before you go and I asked Mom and she said yes, I could have one wish, within reason.'

'That's just like her, isn't it?'

'To agree, yes. But not really. She didn't actually agree. She said I had to stop asking for so many things. But I just want this. I hate her sometimes.'

She folded her arms. If this had been a normal outing, Paul would have told her that she shouldn't hate her mother. Now he could wallow in the luxury of saying nothing.

'But I think she will say yes,' Geraldine continued.

He knew that she was waiting for him to ask what the one wish was.

'Mom said if you were arrested, they'd probably come looking for her.'

'But they couldn't! She's an American!'

'They'd come looking for her to see if she could help. I mean to get lawyers for you.'

'Maybe she would help.'

'In your dreams,' Geraldine replied.

She took out her phone and began to scroll down, her attention focused. She tried, he knew, not to do this too much when she was with him. She had even asked him to tell her to put the phone away if it annoyed him. He enjoyed leaving her in peace this time. She could do what she wanted.

It was dark by the time they reached Sausalito and made for the bridge. She put her phone back in her pocket.

'What I want is this,' she said. 'I want you and me and Mom and Stan to go to Mount Tam. It's where we often go. There's a sort of hostel. Do you know the place?'

Once more, she was mimicking an adult voice. He found himself wondering if she did this with Stan, too.

'Not sure.'

'It's a lodge, a place for hikers to sleep. It's a climb.'

She told him how long the hike would take.

'To go up or go down?'

'Both. You can see everything from up there. I bet you can see the bridges.'

'All of them?'

'All five, maybe more. Isn't there one more?'

'Is your mother going to agree to this?'

'I need your agreement first.'

'Why can't you and me just go?'
'That's the point. I want all of us to go. Just one night.'
'What do you want me to do?'
'Agree.'
'I agree.'
As she reached again for her phone, he thought of something.
'You must make clear to your mother that this is your idea and your idea only and that it took a lot of time to convince me to agree.'
'Well, it did.'

As soon as Paul got back to his apartment, he texted Sandra to let her know directly from him that he really was planning to go back to Ireland very soon.

Within a minute he got her customary response: 'Txt recvd.'

The following day a text came from Geraldine: 'Tell mom u really want to go on the hike with us 3.'

And then, almost immediately, another text from Sandra: 'Was this your idea?'

He was tempted to reply 'No' and leave it at that. And then he wondered if it might be better not to reply at all, to pretend he hadn't received her text. But he knew he should resolve this now, reply while both Geraldine and Sandra were on their phones. He wondered if Stan was standing over them.

He read the text over before he sent it. He did not want to appear too friendly. 'Geraldine said she wants us all to go on this hike. Just one thing we do together before I pack up. I am happy to do it if you and Stan are.'

Sunday was his busy day. Although he called himself a plumber, he had never actually got a licence and lacked the finer knowledge of the trade. He could, however, fix a leak; he could replace a washer;

he could use a soldering iron; he could deal with most types of valves; and he could put in new taps. He had his own way of unblocking pipes. Anything more complicated he left to others. Since he had stopped drinking, he could set out immediately if there was an emergency. He didn't need to advertise; people he'd worked for passed on his number to others. He could be depended on to respond to a call from anywhere in the Bay Area.

He went into his tiny bathroom and looked at himself in the mirror. He should get a haircut before he went home, or even before he went on a hike. And get his eyebrows tidied up. And he should try to shave more often. Almost no one had been in this apartment since he had split up with Nuala Breathnach, who used to sing on Thursday nights at the Greyhound Track, the bar in Oakland that he frequented. At first, Nuala had actually claimed to like this cramped, cluttered space with windows that rattled when buses and trucks went by.

In the end, she told him, and then anyone else in the bar who would listen, that the reason she was returning to Mayo was the state of Paul's apartment – the awful sheets, the flat pillows, the pile of clothes on the old armchair, the smell of stale beer.

'That sort of thing is over,' she said. 'There isn't one fellow at home who's still living like that.'

Soon he would not be living like that, either. He would have to begin clearing out the apartment, put most of what he had in bags and take them somewhere. He liked the idea of travelling back with hardly any luggage, just the cash he had saved hidden in pockets and in socks.

'Hike bookd for Stday 18th' came from Sandra two days later. And then a text from Geraldine to say that he could collect her at nine, and they would meet Sandra and Stan in the parking lot.

All he needed now, he thought, was a text from Stan to say how much he was looking forward to meeting him.

They had to have realized, even if he had not spelled it out, that, having been in the United States for more than thirty years on a simple tourist visa, once he left he would not be allowed to return, probably not ever. He had made sure to have his passport renewed, but it was his Irish passport. He had asked a few friends if it would make a difference that he had a daughter in America, but everyone thought not.

Once, towards the end of the pandemic, when there was an Irish party in Daly City, he had joined others in asking the Irish consul if there was anything that could be done about their status. She was careful, he saw, not to give them room for hope.

Geraldine would have to come to Ireland if she wanted to see him. She could even get an Irish passport in addition to her American one.

He sometimes blamed Sandra for not including him in Geraldine's life when she was little, but, when he thought about it, he knew that that was his fault and only his fault. He should have offered Sandra support, including regular financial support, as soon as he knew she was pregnant – even after she'd made it clear that she didn't want to see him or have him around. He was drinking too much. But maybe that wasn't the problem.

Being undocumented at a time when no one bothered much about illegal Irish people had almost suited him. But he should have changed as soon as he learned that he was going to be a father. Sandra might even have considered marrying him.

The last night that he had seen Sandra, a month before she was to have the baby, he should have had one aim: to make her believe that he would help her. But, just before he set out to meet her at a restaurant, a job came up that he couldn't ignore, an old client living on her own. And, when he got to the restaurant late, he should not have taken another call from this woman.

In the end, Sandra would not even let him drive her home. She did not reply to texts or messages. He stopped sending them. He did not see her again for four years.

He looked around the apartment. In the bathroom, he would start by throwing out some useless razors and old bottles of shampoo. Maybe he would clean the tiles. Or maybe he wouldn't, he thought. It was fine. He could cross the bathroom off his list. With a black plastic rubbish bag in his hand, he began to empty the cupboards in the kitchen. Maybe some plates and cutlery could go to a thrift shop, and some furniture. But who would want any of this rubbish? He should have bought new stuff years before, and he should have had the posters framed, the ones that had not fallen down or faded. It was almost a relief, he felt as he looked around, not to have to make any more plans that he would not carry out. He would clean up what he could, pack the little he needed, and let the landlord know he was leaving when he was on his way to the airport. He would not stick around to get his deposit back. The landlord could probably charge the next tenant four times the rent that Paul had paid.

It could be worse, he whispered to himself, and then resolved that he must stop saying this, even though it was true. His parents, who were in good health, would welcome him back home, as would his sisters and their families. He would not stay here until he was helpless when they came to deport him, the oldest living illegal immigrant in America.

It could have been worse, too, had he gone on drinking or found some drug that would have spared him the trouble of sitting in bars. He could, indeed, have continued to pretend that

Geraldine didn't exist, even as she got older. He could have been the father living in the same city who had never once been in contact with his daughter. He could, as an old man, have passed her on the street.

All these things might have happened had he not been saved by Sean F. Sinnott.

He scoffed at the word 'saved', as did his friends who had also been rescued in some way by Sinnott.

Sinnott came from outside Wexford town and either owned the Greyhound Track or ran it as though he owned it.

Sinnott watched his customers in the same way that he watched his staff: 'I don't hire losers and I don't hire chancers and I don't hire anyone from Swanlinbar.'

If a customer had relatives visiting from Ireland, Sinnott made a fuss of them, with drinks on the house and the best table. If a group of people who weren't Irish came in, Sinnott danced attendance on them to emphasize that the Greyhound Track had no prejudices. If a man was drinking alone, Sinnott made sure that he was left in peace.

Paul was surprised one day when Sinnott came and sat beside him on a barstool.

'There's a young fellow from near Ballyshannon was found dead in a flat he had out near the airport in Oakland. He'd been there for a week or so.'

He showed Paul a photograph.

'Did you know him?'

'No.'

'I don't just want to raise money to send the body home. I can do that easily enough. I'd like to know if there are others here still living on their own like that. A lot of fellows went home or settled down. But some are still living on their own, working for themselves. I think we should make sure they're OK. Just check in on them.'

'Do you mean me?'

'I could mean you, yes.'

He took out a Biro and wrote six letters on a beer mat: 'SIMIBA.'

'Single Irish Men in Bay Area.'

'How do you know I'm single?'

'You look single.'

Paul stretched and yawned.

'I'd like to organize a meeting with you,' Sinnott said, showing him the photo again, 'and a few other fellows to make sure this sort of thing doesn't happen again so easily.'

Paul did not respond.

'I'm from Wexford myself,' Sinnott said, moving in close as though to say something confidential, 'as you probably know. Your mother is from there, isn't she?'

'She is. How did you—'

'Don't bother now,' Sinnott interrupted. 'Give me your number and I'll text you. And can you give me something towards this guy's funeral? As much as you can.'

Paul ignored the personal texts and group texts he received from Sinnott over the next month, until his phone pinged one night when he was close to the Greyhound Track. He texted Sinnott back and they met at the bar.

'I can't stay long,' Paul said.

'I'm the same, and that man there is the same, and his friend, too. None of us can stay long,' Sinnott replied.

'My mother,' Paul said, 'how do you know where she's from?'

'I was trying to get your attention. It was an inspired guess. I have no idea where she's from.'

'You made it up?'

'When the pressure's on, I have the power.'

Sinnott spread his arms out like someone in show business.

'I'm trying to gather together fellows who are here on their own.'

'Well, that's me summed up,' Paul said, before realizing that he should have said nothing.

'I need your help,' Sinnott said.

'You sound like a priest.'

'I was nearly a priest, but that's hardly an accusation. I was hit hard by that young fellow dying, that's all. I promise that's all.'

A week later, Paul went to a meeting in an upper room at the Greyhound Track to find Sinnott with four or five others, two of whom he vaguely recognized.

'I have to go in a second,' Paul said. 'I don't know what I'm doing here.'

'I thought there'd be more,' Sinnott said. 'I was expecting more.'

He began a speech to the group outlining his own feelings about home.

'Would you get to the point,' a man with a Kerry accent interrupted. 'If I want a sermon I'll go to mass.'

Over the next few months, more men came to this weekly meeting, where, despite Sinnott's inability to get to the point, they organized themselves into groups of four, like card players, as one of them said, and talked, about work and health insurance and the problems with ICE and the IRS. There were also a few who wanted to start a band, a mixture of country music and Irish traditional. There was even one who wanted to set up five-a-side football games. A few of them mentioned girlfriends, but no one spoke about inviting any women to these meetings.

Sinnott seemed to have won himself the right to move from one group to another, but he tended not to speak. No drinking was allowed. They stayed for two hours, and then they all appeared relieved to get away from one another. Two of them worked in tech and one was an accountant; two were part-time barmen, part-time singers and actors. The rest, it seemed, did anything that paid.

One evening, as the meeting was coming to a conclusion and Sinnott had quietly joined Paul's group, Paul told his companions that he had a daughter. None of them responded. If one of them had said even a word, or expressed surprise in any way, he was sure he would have said nothing more.

'At least I think I do. They told my girlfriend that she was going to have a girl.'

No one asked him a question. He would leave it at that, he thought. He hadn't even said Sandra's name. But he found himself needing to go on.

'I've never seen the girl. I often think about her. She must be four. She's probably in the Bay Area somewhere.'

Sinnott looked up at him and held his gaze. He wished Sinnott would tell him now, in front of the others, what he should do. But Sinnott didn't speak and, before long, the group broke up.

As soon as Paul got home, he went online to see if he could locate Sandra.

When he did find her, he was careful. He had his hair cut and tidied up the apartment even before he emailed her at the office where she worked. When he received no reply he called, and when he could not get through to her on the phone he waited. In his email, he had tried to make clear that he was not looking for anything from her. He gave her his phone number.

One evening, from a bar, he called Sinnott.

'You're drinking,' Sinnott said. 'Can we talk when you are not drinking?'

The next evening, when they met, Sinnott listened to the details.

'Write her a letter,' Sinnott said. 'Have it typed. Make sure the first paragraph has what you most want to say to her. You need to sound like someone who has his life in order.'

'And then?'

'Explain to her that your mother is from Wexford and there's no real harm in you.'

Paul laughed.

He heard nothing from Sandra for a month. But then a text came that said, 'Letter recvd.' He showed it to Sinnott, who advised Paul to do nothing hasty.

'You are halfway there,' he said.

At first, Sandra let Paul come to the rambling house she shared with some others in Bernal Heights. For a few hours on Saturdays, he could play with Geraldine and watch games on her screen with her. She was four and a half and seemed to enjoy calling him Dad and telling him what she wanted to do next. Just as she took his arrival as a normal part of her week, she made no fuss at his departure. She was able to take up the conversation, such as it was, or the game they had been playing, a week later, as though very little time had passed.

Sandra avoided him, often letting one of the others who lived in the house welcome him and see him out. Eventually, he began to take Geraldine to the park, and then he was given permission to take her on a trip in his car. He knew that he was being closely observed. If he had once turned up late or failed to bring her back on time, or if there was even a whiff of beer on his breath, Sandra would have intervened.

When she moved in with a man called Stan and married him, Paul found out by text, the tone brisk.

Soon, Stan became a figure in Geraldine's normal conversations.

Paul had a photograph of Geraldine on his mobile phone. He wished he could see more of her. But at least she was in the city, just twenty minutes' drive from him each Saturday. And at least she was happy and had everything she needed to make her comfortable.

Paul stopped going to the weekly meetings, but Sinnott kept in touch with him and spoke to him if he chanced to be at the Greyhound Track. They discussed Sinnott's search for love and his addiction to Grindr.

'I can't keep the app on in the bar, but one day I forgot to turn it off and when I looked – it was a Thursday at about seven – there were five guys in the Greyhound Track on Grindr. Can you imagine?'

'I had one of those apps for a while,' Paul said. 'The straight one. I didn't know what sort of photo to put up, so I put one of an Aer Lingus jet. But still I met a few girls. They were nice, some of them.'

'Five guys in an Irish sports bar! I looked at the photos, pretending I had some urgent texting to do behind the bar.'

'And then what did you do?'

'Two of them were on their own, one was working for me, one was with a loud group of fellows from Tipperary, and the other I never found.'

'The long-lost one.'

'Now you're talking. It's a hard city if you're looking for something,' Sinnott said.

'I think I know what you mean,' Paul replied.

Around the time that Paul was first given permission to take Geraldine out in his car, a new type of fitting for basins and sinks was installed in the bathrooms and kitchens of housing developments in the Bay Area. As those fittings began to leak, Paul's number circulated, especially once he sourced a good washer that could replace the dud. Four or five calls a day came, and then more. Every caller seemed to know the drill. They could expect him within an hour, and he would accept cheques but would also be happy if they paid in cash. Because he knew what tools and fittings he would most likely need, in the expectation that the leak came from the usual source, he would generally solve the problem in one visit. No one objected to paying him more than the going rate.

A few times, he was contacted by one of the large construction companies. The first occasion, they called him out on a job. It felt like standard work in an area he knew well. But, when he arrived, he saw a group of fellows waiting for him.

'Do you want to see the leak?' one of them asked, to general laughter. He could not tell where they were from.

He was lucky that he had not stepped too far from his car. He got away from them as quickly as he could.

Another time, he grew suspicious when a number came up that had a strange prefix. When he took the call, a woman gave him an address that made no sense. Nonetheless, he told her what he had told all of the others – he would, if she confirmed, be there in an hour and could accept cheque or cash. She did not call back, but for days urgent messages and texts came from that same number, requests to follow a link. When he clicked on the link the first time, he got a warning from the IRS saying that they were on his case. He was glad that he was using a cheap phone; he could not easily be traced.

When the pandemic came, Stan, who seemed to understand the technology, set up Zoom calls every week for Paul and Geraldine. Only once, half an hour into an hour-long Zoom, did Paul catch sight of Stan, who was crossing the room and shied out of the frame very quickly. He looked younger than Paul had expected him to be. He was wearing a suit and tie, like someone with a real job.

One morning, after Paul came back from some early calls, putting the cash he had earned inside a new pair of socks that he placed at the back of a drawer with other cash-filled socks, he decided to phone his mother in Dublin and tell her about Geraldine. It might have been wiser, he knew, to have informed one of his sisters first, but he didn't want advice or remonstrations from them.

'It's nice you had a girl,' his mother said almost distractedly. 'Now, when was she born?'

'She's nearly eight.'

'And she's American?'

'She lives with her mother, who's American.'

He heard his mother gathering her strength.

'I don't suppose you and the girl's mother are, by any chance, married?'

'No, we're not.'

'What is her name?'

'The mother or the girl?'

'Now I'm going to put your father on. He's in the other room and he still thinks that you have to wipe down every package that comes into the house. But I know otherwise. It's in the air, this thing. I'd be grateful if you could tell him that I am right and make him believe you.'

She made no further reference to his daughter.

In the final months of the pandemic, his mother and his father and he and Geraldine sometimes met on Zoom at ten in the morning California time. Geraldine and his mother took easily to the new medium, Geraldine showing new paintings she had made and his mother showing the pile of books she had read since the pandemic began.

'When all this is over,' his mother said to Geraldine, 'we might take a little trip across the Atlantic – sure it's no distance – and see you in the flesh.'

'"In the flesh" means "in person",' Paul said.

'She knows what it means,' his mother said.

'I'd have to ask Mom and Stan,' Geraldine said. 'But that would be great.'

The night after the election, Paul went to the Greyhound Track, where he found Sinnott, who joined him at the bar.

'They won't deport me,' Sinnott said. 'I got married to a nice local girl as soon as I arrived. I was always grateful to her. But what about you? If they saw you coming along the street, they'd deport you on the spot. You look illegal. There's nothing can be done about it. Why don't you get married? Why else do we have Americans, for God's sake? What else are they for? I could even find you a fellow who would marry you. For your rugged looks and all that.'

'I don't want to marry anyone.'

'How much money do you have?'

'That's what I wanted to ask you. Have you ever met anyone

who has a load of readies and needs to know what to do with them?'

'Wrapped in socks?'

'How did you know?'

He put out his arms, as though seeking applause.

'Stop talking shite,' Paul said. Sinnott sipped a coffee and looked around.

'How much in readies?' he asked.

'A lot for me.'

'Do you have a bank account?'

'Just about. I keep enough money in it to pay the bills. And I lodge the cheques I get. Otherwise, it's cash.'

'Your customers must resent you. That cash thing might work at home, but people don't like it here. It'll backfire, eventually. The people here prefer to be crooked while pretending to be holy. And if ICE or whoever finds you on a job, putting in one of your famous washers, they'll take you away. And they'll visit your apartment while you're being held, and you can say goodbye to your cash.'

'They would steal it?'

'No, not that. But while they were still counting it you would be on your way to the airport or whatever new way they might have of sending a fellow like you home.'

'You think it's funny?'

'I think you should take the law into your own hands and get out of here, cash in suitcase, before they put you out.'

'You think they're serious about it?'

'In the first month or so, yeah – they'll do it for show.'

'If I tried to leave the country, are you sure I wouldn't be detained on the way out?'

'You know the drill. They would let you out easy enough. But they'd never let you back in.'

'I came when I was eighteen.'

'You grew up here, so.'

'I have a daughter here. I told you.'

'Maybe some president in the future will soften up on the plight of Irish plumbers and their American daughters, but it will take a while.'

When Paul saw Stan accompanying Geraldine to his car on the morning of the planned hike, he was immediately aware of all the rusting tools and leftover pieces of piping on his back seat. He wished he had cleaned out the car. He opened the door and got out to greet them, shaking Stan's hand as soon as he and Geraldine approached.

'There's a place to park,' Stan said, 'but it's often full. If you get there first, try to see if you can hold a place for us, or call us if you can't find a spot.'

He made Paul feel as if he could not entirely be trusted on the matter of parking.

'We'll do what we can,' Paul said.

'I wanted to see your apartment before you go,' Geraldine said once they were on the road, 'but Mom says I can't.'

'It's pretty bare,' he said. 'I've thrown most things out.'

For a second, close to the turn-off for Marin, Paul, in the silence of the car, thought that he was out on a job and tried to remember the address. He had never been with Geraldine this early in the morning.

Just before the overlook for Muir Beach, they found a parking space and secured another spot not far away. Paul got his boots from the trunk and struggled as he changed into them.

'I don't think you've ever gone hiking before,' Geraldine said. 'Not a long hike.'

'You'll have to help me,' he said. 'Slow down, maybe, if you see me lagging behind.'

'When are you actually leaving?'

He turned away from her, not prepared for the question. He did not want to say that he was flying to Dublin on Monday. He had two more days in America. On Tuesday night, he would be sleeping in his old bedroom in the family house in Dublin. His apartment, where he had been living for more than twenty years, would be empty; his plan to leave it tidy had been fully abandoned. No one would ever guess why he had left behind so many pairs of socks that looked as though they had never been worn. He must be sure, he resolved, to check every last one in case there were stray banknotes still curled up inside.

It was strange, he thought, how often, even after all these years, he expected Americans to behave like Irish people. Thus, he presumed that Stan had been saving his comments on the state of Paul's car for now, when he and Sandra had arrived and parked. He expected Stan to approach the car, which Paul had already sold to Sinnott as a surprise for his new boyfriend, and peer in at its contents. Stan would then state how urgently this jalopy was in need of cleaning, and Sandra might remark dryly how men never change.

But Stan said nothing at all. He just smiled. And Sandra did not seem to notice his car.

He wondered if insulting each other's cars was something Irish people still did. Or had it ever been? Was it something he had imagined? He would ask Sinnott when he saw him tomorrow for his final non-drink in America.

They were going to climb using a trail through Muir Woods, Stan explained, even though it would take longer, because the incline was more gradual. All in all, he said, if they took it slowly but not too slowly and stopped only for one short picnic, they would be at the hostel before dark.

'It will be dark at five thirty,' he said. 'I checked that.'

'Oh, I forgot to tell you,' Geraldine said, 'that I have the Limonata you like in my knapsack. Two cans.'

'Gerry, you are the best,' Paul said. 'You—'

'Don't call her Gerry,' Sandra, who was just ahead, interjected. 'You know what her name is.'

Geraldine stopped dead. She turned and looked at Paul, raising her eyes to heaven.

'I have a lovely name,' Geraldine said, and then whispered, 'or I did, until just now.'

'You guys need to get going,' Stan shouted from a bluff above them.

Geraldine remained close to Paul as they set off up a steep winding path. Soon, Sandra and Stan were out of sight.

'I think the other way up is much easier,' Geraldine said when she saw Paul out of breath.

He decided not to ask her why, in that case, they had taken this route. As she strode ahead, he noted how strong she was, how long her legs were becoming, and how confidently she moved. He wished he had chosen a heavier jacket as the air became colder the higher they climbed.

'Are you a complete illegal in America?' Geraldine asked.

'Yes, I am. That is a good description of me.'

'Do you have health insurance?'

'Kind of.'

'What would you do if you got really sick?'

'I would go back to Ireland.'

'But that's not why you are going back now?'

'What an adult you are!'

'And you can't just go to Ireland now and then come back in the summer for a vacation?'

'That's right.'

She set out their lunch picnic in a flat area that had a view of the ocean below.

'I like coming here with Mom and Stan,' Geraldine said. 'But I prefer going to Point Reyes with you.'

Sinnott had advised him that when he got home he should move out of Dublin, away from his parents' house, as soon as he could.

'Going home is shell shock. Don't take it out on your mother and your father. Get out of Dublin. The midlands would be a good place. Plenty of leaks there, God knows. They need plumbers.'

'I'm not really a plumber,' Paul said.

'Why don't you train as one the minute you go home?'

'I'm nearly fifty.'

'Stan is good,' Geraldine said as she tidied up after their picnic. 'You mustn't worry about him.'

He wondered if Geraldine used this tone with Sandra and Stan, too, sounding middle-aged.

'He seems nice,' Paul said.

'He plays weird music sometimes. And it's all vinyl, so it takes up lots of space.'

'No one is perfect.'

'Do you really think that?'

It seemed to him that Geraldine wanted him to say something more about Stan. He would have to be careful.

'I think you and Stan and Sandra are good together.'

She looked dreamily down at the water.

'Problem is, if your mother ever came over from Ireland, I mean if she ever decided she should, I don't know where she would stay.'

'Well, maybe you'll come to Ireland first.'

'Would I need an Irish passport?'

'You could get one if you wanted. But an American passport would do.'

By the time Paul and Geraldine reached the hostel, Stan and Sandra had already opened a bottle of white wine and were sitting at the lookout spot.

'You want the good news or the bad news?' Stan asked.

'What's the bad news?' Geraldine asked.

'The good news is that this place is as beautiful as ever. I can't believe you didn't know it, Paul. We have our time in the kitchen reserved in an hour. And I remembered to bring everything we need for a drop-dead spaghetti with my own homemade pesto. I get the pine nuts—'

'They only booked two rooms for us,' Sandra interrupted. 'That is the bad news.'

'No way!' Geraldine said.

'One has a full bed,' Stan said, 'and the other has twin beds. That one has a balcony, but you can hardly sleep on a balcony in the middle of January.'

Stan sounded like a client listing what he wanted fixed. But what he was saying, Paul understood, was that there wasn't a room for Paul. He also knew that he could not let Geraldine down. He would have to stay somewhere.

They sat and watched the last rays of sunshine fold out on the calm, glassy ocean as the shadows deepened in the tall trees. When Paul went to look around, he noted a second vista that seemed to open towards the city. There was a haze over what might be the Golden Gate Bridge. It was hard to be sure. He was tempted to go back and get Geraldine so they could find a map on his phone with the bridges firmly identified and then work out if one of them, maybe even the Bay Bridge, might be visible from up here.

But he would leave the three of them alone. Stan or Sandra had made the booking. They could sort it out. He would not offer to find another place to sleep. It occurred to him that it might make sense for him and Stan to use the room with the twin beds. He hoped that Stan viewed the prospect with the same revulsion as he did.

When he returned, Stan was alone on the deck with his feet up on the wooden railing. He turned around and pointed to the wine and a spare glass.

Paul didn't bother telling him that he didn't touch the stuff. He stood and looked at the back of Stan's head. It was always the same, he thought, in every house whose call he answered. If he was greeted by a guy like Stan, then there would be some difficulty. The job he did would be criticized; the payment would not be ready. And there would be an undercurrent of how-much-better-off-I-am-than-you.

'It's paradise here,' Stan said.

'Yes, it's great, really nice.'

When Sandra and Geraldine reappeared, Sandra leaned against the railing, facing them.

'Geraldine says she wants to share a room with Paul,' Sandra said.

'Really?' Stan asked.

'This is my special outing,' Geraldine said. 'So I can decide. You and Mom are in one room, the room with one bed. And Dad and I are in the other, the room with two beds.'

Paul wondered if Sandra had ever heard Geraldine call him Dad before as confidently as this.

When it grew cold on the deck, they moved inside. Soon, Stan was busy boiling a large saucepan of water for the pasta. Sandra and Geraldine found a backgammon board and began to play. Paul tried to follow the game, but it was too fast.

Stan came to say that he needed help to chop the lettuce for the salad, but Paul ignored him. Eventually, Sandra, having won a game, went to the kitchen, leaving Geraldine to explain to Paul how to guess the odds in backgammon and when it was best not to take a chance.

They shared a table with another group. Once they had finished the pasta, Sandra stood up and said she would go and ask one more time if an extra room had become available, but she quickly came back to say that there was no change. Stan began to talk to the group beside him, finding that the daughter of one of the couples had gone to the same high school as he did.

'You go out for a walk,' he said, 'and you meet someone you know.'

'But you don't really know them,' Geraldine said.

'We do now,' Sandra interjected.

It was agreed that Paul and Geraldine would clean up the table and do the dishes. When that was done, having put their jackets on, they went out to join the others and take in the waxing moon over the ocean. Stan had his phone focused on the night sky and, with a man who had been at the table, was trying to identify certain stars.

'I'm cold and I'm tired,' Geraldine said to Paul in a low voice. 'Can we go in?'

He accompanied Sandra and Geraldine to the room with the

twin beds. Geraldine rummaged through her bag to find her toothbrush and toothpaste and went to the bathroom down the corridor. Now, for the first time in all the years, Paul found himself alone with Sandra, who made herself busy smoothing out the blanket on Geraldine's bed.

When she eventually stood and faced him, she smiled as though there had never been any problem between them.

'Geraldine normally goes to sleep fast,' she said. 'She's great like that.'

Paul hoped that Geraldine would hurry back.

'This is a nice place,' he said. 'I didn't know it existed.'

'We love coming here.'

He was happy to say nothing more. Neither of them, he saw, wanted to begin a big discussion. But the room was small and he felt awkward. He found himself smiling weakly and then scratching his head. Sandra sat down on Geraldine's bed.

Paul went out and stood on the balcony, sorry that he could not think of a way to make things less strained between them.

When Geraldine came back, Sandra kissed her, wished them good night, and left the room. Paul slipped out, too, so that Geraldine could change into her nightclothes, returning to the deck, which was now emptied of guests. Stan must have gone to bed.

He took in the scene below, the ocean all bright and glistening in the moonlight and then everything dark beyond, but, when he heard sounds, he worried that Stan or even Sandra might be about to join him. He edged down a corridor and into one of the bathrooms.

Geraldine appeared to be sleeping when he came into the room, and he closed the door as quietly as he could. Nonetheless, she turned when she heard him.

'Sorry if I woke you,' he whispered.

'I wanted to say good night, but I didn't know where you'd gone.'

'I wasn't far away.'

'Make sure you wake me in the morning as soon as you're awake,' she said.

Almost immediately, she was asleep again. Paul felt tired. When Geraldine made a soft, sighing sound in her sleep, he went to turn off the lamp in case it was disturbing her. He stood and looked at her. How perfect she was now, he thought, as he had when she had walked ahead of him on the trail.

He would probably never see her again in America; he would miss her life here. But she would visit him in Ireland – he was sure she would want to do that – and perhaps she would make visits in years to come when she had a real life of her own, her own children, a husband, even.

He removed his shoes and put his jacket back on and tiptoed to the balcony, closing the door tightly behind him. At first, since the balcony was facing away from the ocean, he could see nothing, but then a cloud cleared and he thought he could make out some stars, and even further down below some lights in the distance, but he had no idea what they were.

In the morning, they would be able to see one or two of the bridges, if not from here then from one of the other decks or balconies. They might have to wait until the fog cleared. He would show Geraldine from this vantage point some of the places where he had worked, tell her about the journeys in his car down leafy avenues to new condos or old bungalows or bigger suburban houses. And the people waiting for him, desperate to have a leaking tap fixed. He would describe some of these people to her. He knew she loved that.

More images of the world below came into his mind. He smiled at the thought of how many houses he had visited over thirty years, how many taps, how many washers. It hardly mattered, he supposed. Someone had to do it. He would not put a thought into it once he got home. And, if he could sleep for a while now, he would think about something else in the morning and make sure to wake Geraldine once he himself had woken up, as she had asked him to do.

Sleep

I wake before you do and I lie still. Sometimes I doze, but usually I am alert, with my eyes open. I don't move. I don't want to disturb you. I can hear your breathing and I like that. And then at a certain point you turn towards me without opening your eyes; your hand reaches over, and you touch my shoulder or my back. And then your whole body comes close to me. But it is as though you were still sleeping – there is no sound from you, just a need, almost urgent but unconscious, to be close to someone. This is how the day begins when you are with me.

It is strange how much unwitting effort it has taken to bring us here. The engineers and software designers could never have guessed, as they laid out their strategies and sought investment, that the thing they were making – the internet – would cause two strangers to meet and then, after a time, to lie in the half-light of morning, holding each other. Were it not for them, we would never have been together in this place.

One day you ask me if I hate the British, and I say that I do not. All that is over now. It is easy to be Irish these days. Easier maybe than being Jewish and knowing, as you do, that your great-aunts and -uncles perished at Hitler's hands. And that your grandparents, whom you love and visit sometimes on Long Island, lost their brothers and sisters; they live with that catastrophe day in, day out.

It is a pity that there is such great German music, you say, and I tell you that Germany comes in many guises, and you shrug and say, 'Not for us.'

We are in New York, on the Upper West Side, and when I open the blinds in the bedroom we can see the river and the George Washington Bridge. You don't know, because I will never tell you, how much it frightens me that the bridge is so close and in full view. You know more about music than I do, but I have read books that you have not read. I hope that you will never stumble on a copy of James Baldwin's *Another Country*; I hope that I will never come into the room and find you reading it, following Rufus through New York to his final journey up this way, on the train, to the bridge, the jump, the water.

There is a year missing in your stories of your life, and this makes everyone who loves you watch you with care. I have asked you about it a few times and seen your hunched shoulders and your vague, empty look, the nerdy look that you have when you are low. I know your parents dislike the fact that I am older than you, but the knowledge that I don't drink alcohol or take drugs almost makes up for that, or I like to think it does. You don't drink or take drugs, either, but you do go outside to smoke, and maybe I should take up smoking, too, so that I can watch over you casually when you are out there and not have to wait and then feel relief when I hear the doors of the lift opening and your key in the lock.

There is no year in my life that I cannot account for, but there are years that I do not think about now, years that went by slowly, in a sort of coiled pain. I have never bothered you with the details. You think I am strong because I am older, and maybe that is the way things should be.

I am old enough to remember when things were different. But no one cares now, in this apartment building or in the world outside, that we are men and we wake often in the same bed. No one cares that when we touch each other's face we find that we both need to shave. Or that when I touch your body I find a body like mine, though in better shape and twenty and more years younger. You are circumcised and I am not. That is a difference. We are cut and uncut, as they say in this country where we both live now, where you were born.

Germany, Ireland, the internet, gay rights, Judaism, Catholicism: they have all brought us here. To this room, to this bed in America. How easy it would have been for this never to have happened. How unlikely it would have seemed in the past.

I feel happy, rested, ready for the day as I return from the shower and find you lying on your back with your glasses on, your hands behind your head.

'You know that you were groaning in the night? Almost crying. Saying things.' Your voice is accusing; there is a quaver in it.

'I don't remember anything. That's funny. Was it loud?'

'It was loud. Not all the time, but just before the end it was loud, and you were waving your hands around. I moved over to you and whispered to you, and then you fell back asleep. You were all right then.'

'When you whispered to me, what did you say?'

'I said that it was all OK, that there was nothing wrong. Something like that.'

'I hope I didn't keep you awake.'

'It was no problem. I went back to sleep. I don't know what you were dreaming about, but it wasn't good.'

The fear comes on Saturdays, and it comes, too, if I am staying somewhere, in a hotel room, for example, and there is shouting in the street in the night. Shouting under my window. I keep it to myself, the fear, and by doing this sometimes I keep it away, at arm's length, elsewhere. But there are other times when it breaks through, something close to dread, as though what happened had not occurred yet but will occur, is about to do so, and there is nothing I can do to stop it. The fear can come from nowhere. I may be reading, as I often do on Saturdays while you are with your family. I am reading and then suddenly I look up, disturbed.

The fear enters the pit of my stomach and the base of my neck like pain, and it seems as if nothing could lift it. Eventually, as it came, it will go, though not easily. Sometimes a sigh, or a walk to the fridge, or making myself busy putting clothes or papers away, will rid me of it, but it is always hard to tell what will work. The fear could stay for a while, or come back as though it had forgotten something. It is not under my control.

I know where I was and what I was doing when my brother died. I was in Brighton, and I was in bed and I could not sleep, because there were drunken crowds shouting below my hotel window. Sometime between two and three in the morning he died, in his own house in Dublin. He was alone there that night. If I had been sleeping at the moment when it happened, I might have woken, or at least stirred in the night. But probably not. Probably I would just have gone on sleeping.

He died. That is the most important thing to say. My brother was in his own house in Dublin. He was alone. It was a Saturday night, Sunday morning. He called for an ambulance before two in the morning. When it arrived, he was dead, and the paramedics could not bring him back to life.

I have never told anyone that I was awake in that room in Brighton in those hours. It hardly matters. It matters only to me and only at times.

On one of those winter evenings when you are staying here, we go to bed early. Like a good American, you wear a T-shirt and boxers in bed. I am wearing pyjamas, like a good Irishman. Chet Baker is on low. We are both reading, but I know you are restless. Because you are young, I always suspect that you are horny when I am not, and that is a joke between us. But it is probably true; it would make sense. In any case, you move towards me. I have learned always to pay attention when this happens, never to seem distracted or tired or bored.

As we lie together, you whisper, 'I told my analyst about you.'

'What about me?'

'About your crying in the night and my coming home on Saturday to find you looking so frightened or sad or something that you could barely talk.'

'You didn't say anything about it on Saturday. Was it this Saturday?'

We lie there listening to Chet Baker singing 'Almost Blue', and I move to kiss you. You prop yourself up on your elbow and look at me.

'He says that you have to get help but it has to be Irish help, only an Irish analyst could get what is going on.'

'Do you pay him for this rubbish?'

'My dad pays him.'

'He sounds like a bundle of laughs, your shrink.'

'He told me not to listen to you. Just to make you do it. I said that you were OK most of the time. But I've told him that before. Hey, he likes the sound of you.'

'Fuck him!'

'He's good, he's nice, he's smart. And he's straight, so you don't have to worry about him.'

'That's true. I don't have to worry about him.'

Spring arrives, and something that I had forgotten about begins. Behind this apartment building is an alley, or an opening between two buildings, and if it is warm at night some students gather there, maybe the ones who smoke. Sometimes I hear them and the sound becomes part of the night, like the noise the radiators make, until it fades. It has never bothered me in all the time I have lived here, and I have no memory of your ever remarking on it. It is quiet here, quiet compared with downtown or the apartment you share in Williamsburg on the nights when you do not stay with me.

Nonetheless, I should have known that some night that noise would find me in my sleep. Maybe if I had got an Irish shrink, as your shrink suggested, he would have warned me about this, or I would have come to warn myself after many meetings with him.

I don't remember how it starts, but you do. I am whimpering in my sleep, or so you say, and then going quiet for a while. And then when there is more shouting in the alley behind the building I begin to shiver. You say that it is more like someone shuddering, recoiling in fright, but still I have no memory of this. When you try and fail to wake me, you are suddenly afraid. I know that everything you do, the way you manage your day, is driven by your need never to be afraid.

When I finally wake, you are on your mobile phone and you look frightened. You tell me what happened and then you reach for your shirt.

'I'm going.'

'What's wrong?'

'I'll talk to you in the morning. I'm going to get an Uber.'

I watch you dress. You are silent and deliberate. Suddenly, you seem much older. In the light from the lamp on your side of the bed I can see what you will look like in the future. You turn as you go out the door.

'I'll text.'

Within a minute you are gone. It is three forty-five when I look at the clock. When I text and say that I am sorry for waking you, you do not reply.

The next evening you come over. I can tell that you have something to say. You ignore me when I ask if you have eaten.

'Hey, I'm going to take my clothes and stuff.'

'I'm sorry about last night.'

'You scared me. There's something wrong with you. I don't know what it is, but it's too much for me.'

'You don't want to stay here again?'

'Hey, I never said that. That is not what I said.'

You sigh and sit down. I start to talk.

'Maybe we should—'

'No, no "maybe", and no "we should". You have to go and see someone. You can't do this on your own, and I can't help you, and I'm not staying here again until you've done that. It's not because I don't want to, but it's weird. It wasn't just once, just one bad dream. It's intense. You should hear it. I thought I should record it on my phone for you, so you would know.'

I imagine you holding the phone out in the dark with the record button on while I am having a bad dream I can't wake from.

'Why don't we talk during the week?'

'Sure.'

You go to the bedroom and after some minutes reappear with a bag.

'Are you certain you want to take your stuff?'

'Yeah.'

You have already taken the keys to this apartment off your key ring and you put them on the hall table. We hug and you leave with your head down. I stand with my back to the door and my eyes closed as I hear the lift arrive and open its doors for you.

There is always that sense of being released when the plane takes off from JFK to Dublin. Every Irish person who gets on that plane knows the feeling; some, like me, also know that it does not last for long. I read a bit and then sleep and then wake up and look around and go to the bathroom and notice that most of the other passengers are sleeping. But I don't think I will sleep again. I don't want to read. There are four hours still to go.

I doze and wake and then fall into the deepest sleep in the hour before we land, so that I have to be woken and told to put my seat in the upright position.

There is a hotel on St Stephen's Green, on the opposite side from the Shelbourne, and I have booked a room there for four nights. I have told no one that I am here, except the doctor, a psychiatrist, whom I met years ago, when he helped a friend of mine who was suffering from depression and could not sleep and could not handle anything. The doctor knew my friend's family. I remember the time he spent with my friend and how he came back again and again. His kindness, his patience, his watchfulness. I remember that I made him tea on a few of those nights, and we spoke about the Beethoven quartets and he told me which recordings he favoured, as my friend lay next door in a darkened room. I remember that he liked jazz and that he found it strange that I did not.

Until I met you, that is. I liked listening to jazz with you.

When I called him from New York, he remembered that time. He said that he would see me, but it would be best not to do it when I was jet-lagged. He told me to take a few days between landing in Dublin and the appointment. He was living alone now, he said, so he could see me at his house. He gave me the address, and we agreed on the time. When I asked about payment, he said we could work that out later.

In Dublin, I keep to the side streets on the first day. I go to the cinema in the afternoon and then up into Rathmines and find a few places to linger, where I think I will meet no one I know. The city seems low-key, calm.

There is a new cinema in Smithfield and I go there on the second day and see two films in a row. I find a place to eat nearby. I notice how crowded it becomes, and how loud the voices are, how much laughing and shouting there is. I think about the city I used to know, which was a place that specialized in the half-said thing, the shrug, a place where people looked at one another out of the corner of their eye. All that is over now, or at least in Smithfield it is.

I try not to sleep during the daytime on either of those days, although I want to. I go to Hodges Figgis and Books Upstairs and buy some books. In the evening, I watch the Irish news and some current-affairs programmes on the television in my hotel room.

And then on the third day, in the late afternoon, I go to Ranelagh to see the psychiatrist. I am unsure what we will say or do. I am scheduled to go back to New York the following day. Maybe there is a drug for what is wrong with me, but I doubt it. I need him to listen to me, or maybe I just need to be able to tell you when I come back that I have done this. Maybe, I think, he will refer me to someone in New York whom I can see in the same regular way that you see your analyst, as you call him.

There is a long room that was once two rooms, and it is beautifully furnished. We take our shoes off and sit opposite each other on armchairs towards the back of that room. I realize that he does not need me to talk; he listened carefully to what I said on the phone. He asks me if I have ever been hypnotized, and I say no. There was a guy, I remember, who used to do it on television and in the theatre. I can't recall his name – Paul something – but I have seen him on television once or twice. I think of hypnosis as a party game, or something that happens in black-and-white films. I did not expect the psychiatrist to suggest it as something he might do with me.

He is, he says, going to use hypnosis. We will both need to be quiet. It would be best if I closed my eyes, he says. I think for a second that I should ask him why he is doing this, or whether he does it all the time, or what it could achieve, but there is something about the calm way that he approaches the task, something deliberate, that makes me feel that it is better not to ask anything. I am still wary and I am sure he notices this, but it does not deter him. I close my eyes.

He leaves silence. I don't know for how long he leaves silence. And then in a new voice, a voice that is more than a whisper but still has an undertow of whispering, he tells me that he is going to count to ten, and at the word 'ten' I will be asleep. I nod and he begins.

His voice has a softness but also an authority. I wonder if he has trained in hypnosis or if he developed his method on his own with other patients. When he gets to 'ten', there is no great change. But I do not move or tell him that I am still awake. I keep my eyes closed, trying to guess how long it will be before he realizes that the spell has not worked, that I am not asleep, that I still know where I am.

'I want you to think about your brother.'

'I'm getting nothing.'

'I want you to take your time.'

I keep my mind empty and my eyes closed. Nothing is happening, but there is a density to the feelings I am having, although the feelings themselves are ordinary ones. I am oddly relaxed and also uneasy. It is like a moment from childhood, or even adulthood, in which I am able to stop worrying about a pressing matter for a moment in the full knowledge that the worry will come back. During this interlude I do not move or speak.

'I want you to think about your brother,' he says again.

I let out a small moan, a sort of cry, but there is no emotion behind it. It is as if I were just doing what he expects me to do.

'Nothing, nothing,' I whisper.

'Follow it now.'

'There's nothing.'

He leaves space for me to moan and tell him where I am going, but I am not sure where that is. It is nowhere in particular. But I am moving. I am also awake. He speaks several times more, his voice softer and more insistent. And then I stop him. I need silence now and he leaves silence again. I sigh. I am puzzled. I cannot tell where I am going. I know that I am sitting in an armchair in a house in Ranelagh and that I can open my eyes at any moment. I know that I am going back to New York tomorrow.

And then it comes, the hallway, and it is a precise hallway in a house I have known but never lived in. There is lino on the floor and a hall table and a door to a living room, the door slightly ajar. There are stairs at the end of the hallway.

And then there is no 'I'. I am a 'he'. I am not myself.

'Do you feel sad about your brother?' the psychiatrist asks.
'No. No.'

I am lying on the floor of that hallway. I have called an ambulance and left the front door on the latch.

The dying comes as lightness, a growing lightness, as though something were leaving me, and I am letting it leave, and then I am panicking, or almost panicking, and then feeling tired.

'Follow how you feel.'

I signal for him not to speak again. The idea that there is less of me now, and that this lessness will go on and there will be even less of me soon, that this diminishment will continue, is centred in my chest. Something is going down, going out, with a strange and persistent ease. There is no pain, more a mild pressure within me, or the me that I am now, in this hallway, this room. It is happening within the body as much as within the person that can think or remember. Something is reaching out to death, but it is not death; 'death' is too simple a word. It is closer to an emptying out of strain, until all that is left is nothing – not peace or anything like that, just nothing. This is coming gradually and inevitably. I, we, are smiling, or seem to be content and have no concerns. It is like pleasure, but not exactly pleasure, and not exactly the absence of pain, either. It is nothing, and the nothing comes with no force, just a desire or a need, which seems natural, to allow things to proceed, not to get in their way.

I think then that the experience is ending, and before it does I want to know if our mother is close now, but that comes as a question only. I see her face, but I do not feel her presence. I hold the thought and find myself longing for some completion of it, some further satisfying image, but nothing materializes. Instead, there is stillness, and then the sound of the door being pushed open and voices. I can hear their urgency, but it is like urgency in a film that I cannot fully see; it is not real. It is in the background as I am lifted, as my chest is pushed and pummelled, as more voices are raised, as I am moved.

Then there is nothing, really nothing – the nothing that I am and the nothing that is in this room now. Whatever has happened, it has ended. There is nowhere else to go.

I begin to moan again, and then I am quiet and stay quiet until the psychiatrist says softly that he will count to ten again, and when he says the word 'ten' I will come back from where I have been and I will be in the room with him.

'I don't know where you were, but I left you there.'

I do not reply.

'Maybe you got something you can work on.'

'I became him.'

'Did you feel sad?'

'I was him. I wasn't me.'

He looks at me calmly.

'Maybe the feelings will come now.'

'I became him.'

We do not speak for a while. When I look at my watch I think that I am misreading it. The watch says that two hours have passed. It is dark outside. He makes tea and puts on some music. When I find my shoes, I discover that I have trouble putting them on, as if my feet had swelled during the time that I was elsewhere. Eventually, I stand up and prepare to leave. He gives me a number I can call in a few weeks when I have absorbed what happened.

'What did happen?' I ask.

'I don't know. You are the one who has to do the work.'

He follows me in his stocking feet to the front door. We shake hands, and I leave. I walk through Dublin, from Ranelagh to St Stephen's Green, passing people on their way home from work.

It is winter in New York and I have not replied to your texts. They come more sporadically and get more and more clipped. It is down to 'Hey!' or 'Hi' and soon, I think, they will stop. When I go to Lincoln Center to see a film or hear music, it would not surprise me on one of those nights if I found you standing close by, looking at me.

I wake alone now. I wake early and lie thinking or dozing. In the morning, I carry the full burden of the night's sleep. It is as if I had been tiring myself out in the darkness, rather than resting. There is no one to tell me if I make a sound as I sleep. I don't know if I whimper, or cry out. I like to think that I am silent, but how can I tell?

The News from Dublin

After breakfast when the children went to get ready for school, Maurice and Nora had a few minutes alone.

'You woke at four,' Nora said. 'You know that.'

Maurice did not look up from the table.

'I fell back asleep.'

'And then I didn't want to wake you.'

'Forget about it,' he said. 'You don't have to worry about it.'

'You just can't go down there, that's all. I asked Dr Cudigan, and he says it's highly infectious. The others have probably become immune, but if you are not used to being in the house with him . . .'

Maurice glanced up at her. He needed to change the subject.

'All the teachers will have ashes on their foreheads and most of the boys.'

He put his hand over the cup when she offered him more tea. As the children came back into the room, he noticed her moving to the fireplace but did not think anything of it and so was looking away as she placed black soot from the chimney with her thumb on his forehead.

'Now, there,' she said. 'You have ashes. And nothing to worry about.'

He stood up as the children gazed at him in astonishment.

'You can't do that!'

'I just did.'

He went to the mirror. The black smudge on his forehead looked exactly as though he had received ashes at the altar rail in the cathedral. He laughed.

'No one will ever know the difference,' Nora said.

'If anyone found out—' Maurice began.

'You go to school,' Nora said.

A few times that morning in the staffroom and in various classrooms he had the impression that the ashes on his forehead were being studied carefully by colleagues or by students. But in the bathroom during a break when he looked at them himself again he could see no difference between the colour and texture of the soot on his forehead and the holy ashes which most of the others wore. The idea of it put him in good humour until later in the morning when he grew tired and felt desperately in need of sleep, having to suppress yawn after yawn in the classroom, and then he felt that what Nora had done was wrong and disrespectful. He was almost angry at the thought that she would not listen to him if he came home at lunchtime or at the end of the day and complained.

Later, as he sat in the staffroom during a period when he had no class, and Christian Brothers wearing ashes on their forehead came in and out of the room, he smiled to himself. How little they knew, these Brothers, he thought, about the secret life of the teachers, the things which married men had to tolerate! He had to concentrate hard on the copybooks he was correcting to stop himself laughing.

At the end of the day's teaching as he was walking from one of the classrooms which were in a building away from the main building, he saw his brother Tom waiting for him. Since it was Wednesday and the *Enniscorthy Echo* where Tom worked had gone to press, Tom would have time on his hands. But Maurice knew by the way he was standing that this was more than a social call, more than a casual way of meeting so they could go for a drink or two in Mylie Kehoe's before Maurice went home.

Maurice made a signal to Tom that he would be with him in a moment, and then he dropped some copybooks back in the staffroom. By the serious way Tom had nodded to him, he knew that this visit was about Stephen, their younger brother who had TB. Something must have happened. He lingered in the staffroom, arranging the copybooks and then rearranging them, and checking if there was anything else to do, because he dreaded going back out to the school yard and seeing Tom waiting in the shadows. When he went to the bathroom, he barely glanced in the mirror; suddenly the ashes and their origin had ceased to be of any interest.

'Is there something wrong?' he asked Tom when he found him outside.

'He's been bad over the last few days.'

He noticed the ashes on Tom's forehead and realized that Tom must have been at eight o'clock mass and must have looked for him there. He wished now that he did not have the smudge on his forehead; it would be hard to explain how it got there. They walked silently together over the railway bridge towards the bottom of Slaney Street.

'I can't go down. Nora is terrified about the children. She went and asked Dr Cudigan,' Maurice said.

'That's all right. They understand that. No one blames Nora for that. I had to call into Uncle George, King George, this morning after mass. Someone told me that he has a coffin at the back of the workshop and it has some flaw in it and that he said to someone that it would do for Stephen when the time came. He's one big ignorant gobshite.'

'What did you say to him?'

'I told him that there'd be no coffin for him when I was finished with him, but we'd sew him into a sack and send him wriggling down the river. I told him if he thought we had disbanded and gone all political, then he might be right, but we'd make an exception for him. And I'd know the boys to pick, and he'd be gone down the river and he'd be found washed up in Edermine.'

'Did you really say all that?'

'I did. Or most of it. He denied the whole thing and then he said that he wouldn't do it again. He is a big eejit.'

'Did Stephen hear about it?'

'No, none of them heard about it.'

They walked along Slaney Place.

'But Stephen heard about something else and so did Mammy. There's a drug, it's been discovered, and it does the trick. I have the name of it written down.'

'A cure?'

'I suppose.'

'Who told him?'

'It was in *The Irish Times*. Freddie Sutton brought it to the door. And it's on Stephen's mind now that this drug can be got.'

'Where?'

'It's not available to everyone yet, but it will be, or it might be. I don't know when. But some people can get it. They're trying it out on some people and it's working.'

'What's it called?'

'I have it written down.'

Once they were sitting at the bar in Mylie Kehoe's and had

ordered two pints of ale, Tom showed him a slip of paper with the word 'streptomycin' on it.

'Sounds like something you would use for cattle,' Maurice said.

When their drinks came, they sat at the bar for a while without saying anything.

'So?' Maurice asked eventually.

Tom sighed.

'So Daddy was in Frongoch with Jim Ryan, and you introduced him on the platform in the Market Square, and you must have met him a few times. I know he's only a month or so as Minister but he must have all the information on this drug. It'd have to be a priority.'

'There were hundreds in Frongoch.'

'Daddy says they took Irish lessons together and they were in a punishment cell together. Or maybe it was the same thing.'

'Don't insult Irish lessons. I have just spent most of the day giving precisely such lessons.'

'Don't insult punishment cells, you mean,' Tom said. 'The one thing I could never do was learn the first national. It's hard enough to talk English.'

'Was that the time in Frongoch when Daddy shouted, "Is liomsa é!" when the guard asked whose bed it was, and the guard said, "Lumps or no lumps, you get into it, mate,"' Maurice asked.

'Yes,' Tom said, 'it was that time all right. And Jim Ryan was there too, and now he's Minister for Health.'

'You see, I just introduced him once, and I met him another time, but we've never actually talked,' Maurice said.

'They want you to go up to Dublin and ask him.'

'When?'

'Soon.'

'But I said I don't know him.'

'Daddy is going to contact Sean Flood, and he will decide what would be the best day. He's going to do the introductions.'

'But he's just a backbencher.'

'They're in the same constituency, and they talk. Anyway, we're waiting to hear back from Sean. Can you get a day off?'

Maurice nodded in assent.

'A day off for good behaviour,' Tom said. 'Speaking of which, I didn't see you at mass this morning.'

'I slipped off as soon as it was over.'

'Where were you sitting?'

'I was at the back.'

'Funny now,' Tom said, 'I didn't see you going up to get the ashes.'

Maurice sipped his drink.

'And you slipped off before it was over?' Tom continued. 'That's a bad example for a teacher to be giving.'

'That's not what I said. I didn't slip off before it was over,' Maurice said and smiled. 'I waited until it was over, and then I slipped off. Journalists should listen.'

Tom looked at the ashes on Maurice's forehead.

'You slipped off anyway. I'll say that for you.'

When Maurice arrived home, Nora was in the kitchen. She turned when she saw him.

'Ash Wednesday, that's a nice day to go drinking,' she said in mock anger.

'How did you know I went drinking?'

'They can smell you in Ballon.'

She laughed and moved towards him.

'I don't know what this house is coming to,' she said. 'No religion and falling home from the pub at closing time.'

'It's not closing time. It's only six o'clock.'

She laughed again and put her arms around him.

'And your ashes are a work of art. Did anyone admire them?'

'The whole town,' he said.

Later, he told her what Tom had asked him to do.

'I saw the article in *The Irish Times* too,' she said. 'Vera Irwin showed it to me. But the drug won't be available for a year or more.'

'Yes, but it must exist.'

'That's what Fianna Fáil is for,' she said.

'It's for more than that.'

'Well, you're in the party. If you weren't in it, it would be different.'

'I have never asked them for anything before.'

'Well, this is important. What could be more important? It's worth trying. I mean, you can't even go in the door of the house where you were born.'

He glanced away from her.

'You didn't go down, did you?' she asked.

'No.'

'You don't even have to touch the person, that's what Cudigan said. You don't even have to touch them. It's in the air. It's the most frightening thing.'

That Friday during a break between classes he found Brother O'Hara in the staffroom and asked him if he could take the following Wednesday off.

'Of course you can,' Brother O'Hara said. 'As long as you're back on Thursday.'

'Just one day,' he said.

'That's fine, so,' the Brother said. 'I might take a few of your classes myself on Wednesday. I might learn something.'

* * *

THE NEWS FROM DUBLIN

The following Wednesday he got out of the train at Westland Row and walked to Kildare Street where he asked at the porter's desk, as he had been told to do by Tom, for Sean Flood.

'He's expecting me,' he said.

'Are you another yellow belly?' the porter asked.

'I am,' Maurice replied. 'I'm from Enniscorthy.'

'Oh Enniscorthy's in flames,' the porter replied as he dialled a number, 'and old Wexford is won and the Barrow tomorrow we cross.'

There was, it seemed, no reply from the number he had dialled. He checked through a book of numbers and tried another.

'He doesn't appear to be there,' the porter said. 'Would you like to leave a message?'

'He's expecting me.'

'Well, there might be a vote soon, so if you take a seat I'll try again in a while.'

He had visited the Dáil before as part of a delegation from the town. He remembered how nervous the others were as they waited to be taken beyond the porter's box and how strange it was to see figures, ministers and prominent opposition politicians, whom they knew only from photographs and whom they read about regularly in the newspapers, walking the corridors. He remembered being led in to see the Minister for Local Government and the sense of occasion as each of them was introduced. They were taken by Sean Flood afterwards to the public bar where other TDs were buying drinks for constituents.

He did not know what Sean Flood had arranged, whether he would meet the minister in his private office, or in the bar or the restaurant. Now that news had been published about the drug, he wondered if others had come asking as well. Surely, he thought, Sean Flood would have advised him not to make the journey if he had believed that his request was likely to be dismissed or handled brusquely. It struck him for a moment that maybe he would actually have to say very little to the minister, that he might be told that the drug was available, given the name of a doctor or dispensary to contact, and there would be nothing else to discuss. But he knew also that Stephen was bad, that the drug would have to come soon, or maybe it might even be too late. He resolved that he would make clear to the minister that it was urgent. It might be better, he thought then, not to say too much about his own work for Fianna Fáil in case the minister thought that he was involved in the party only for what it might give him in return. Instead, he should emphasize his father's time in Frongoch after the Rising, maybe even Tom's time in the Curragh, although it might be best not to dwell too much on the Civil War.

When he caught the porter's eye, the porter made a gesture indicating that he had not forgotten about him, and then he checked a list of numbers and dialled again. This time there was a reply, and he spoke for a moment before putting the phone down.

'He'll be right with you,' he said. 'He didn't even want to know your name. He's expecting you.'

As soon as Sean Flood appeared and shook his hand, Maurice regretted the many jokes which he and Tom had made about him over the years, about how long and repetitive his speeches to the local cumann were but how in the Dáil he had only ever spoken to ask them to open the window a bit to let in some air. Or how he was the only GAA official who didn't know the difference between a hurley stick and a shovel. He was all friendly now as he explained that it was one of those days when there could be a vote at any time, when most of the ministers were in the house, but it would be impossible to pin any one of them down about a precise time for a meeting. He was going to leave Maurice in the visitors' gallery, and he would signal to him from the Dáil chamber itself if he should come back down, if they could get the minister's full attention in between votes, or if it seemed that a debate or an extended question time was going to hold business up. The opposition had grown long-winded, Sean said, they smelled an election, especially the Labour Party, and it was always hard to know what they would do.

Maurice had presumed that an appointment had been made with the minister, or at least he had been told why Maurice wanted to see him, but it seemed now, as Sean Flood ushered him into the visitors' gallery and disappeared, that nothing had been arranged in advance and that it was maybe not even certain that he would meet the minister face to face.

The debate was about agriculture, and someone on the opposition benches whom he did not recognize was speaking passionately against the export of live cattle. The two men sitting close to the speaker seemed busy with paperwork. The Minister for Agriculture was on the government front bench with another minister. There were four or five deputies scattered in the seats behind them. There was no sign of Sean Flood or Jim Ryan.

He studied the speaker, supposing him to be from Fine Gael, and then he looked over at the government benches. The Fine Gael people were different, he thought, they wore better suits and seemed more prosperous. The Fianna Fáil backbenchers, on the other hand, had a look that he recognized and liked, less arrogant than the Fine Gael deputies – they were softer in some way, like men who would be easier to approach, men who would send their sons to the local Christian Brothers school and be satisfied with that and whose sons would respect the teachers and the Brothers and do their best.

Maurice turned to watch as the men who had been following

the debate on agriculture beside him in the gallery stood up to leave. He noticed two or three people coming to sit in their places. When he looked back down into the Dáil chamber there were a number of figures who had recently sat down in the front row of the government benches. Among them was the Minister for Health, Jim Ryan, who was whispering to the minister beside him.

Suddenly, Maurice saw that a way was being cleared on one of the central stairways as the figure of Éamon de Valera was being helped down the steps. De Valera was as tall as he remembered him when he had seen him speaking in Enniscorthy, but he seemed even more dignified now, almost solemn, as he moved slowly down towards his seat.

One of the visitors who had arrived at the gallery a while earlier tapped him on the shoulder and pointed down into the Dáil chamber where Sean Flood was gesticulating to him. Maurice had been so wrapped up in watching de Valera that he had not noticed Sean. Once Sean Flood saw that he had Maurice's attention, he indicated to him that he should leave the visitors' gallery and come out into the corridor that led to the chamber. When he checked to see where the minister was, he saw that he was still in his seat on the front bench, busily talking to a colleague.

'I told him I have a constituent who wants a few minutes with him,' Sean Flood said when they met. 'So what we do is we wait here, and we'll either go to the bar or to his office when he comes in. It's a busy day but he knows we are here.'

Maurice was about to ask if the minister knew why he had come but he understood from what Sean Flood had said that the minister did not. In the way Sean Flood had said 'constituent' he realized that he would have to tell the minister from scratch who he was and who his father was before telling him why he wanted to see him. He hoped that he would not have to do this with other people competing for the minister's attention.

As they waited, deputies from all the parties began to spill out from the chamber into the corridors. Maurice knew how much Tom and his father would be interested in them, and was surprised at how friendly they were with each other, no matter what party they belonged to. Most of them greeted Sean Flood pleasantly. He wished that he were just here on a visit with no purpose and would have loved coming home with the account of how he saw de Valera, and which ministers he had seen, and how men his father and Tom hated seemed friendly and ordinary as they came into the corridor and stopped for a second to speak to Sean Flood.

When the minister appeared he was joined by a man whom Maurice later learned was his private secretary. It took Sean Flood a minute to move towards him, having signalled to Maurice to stay where he was. He spoke quietly to the minister as the private secretary stood by impatiently. Maurice noticed the minister's shoes, which were of soft black leather, and his grey suit, white shirt and dark red tie. As he listened to Sean, the minister's face remained impassive, his expression thoughtful; he was concentrating. Eventually, he nodded but did not speak as Sean turned and gestured to Maurice to approach.

The minister shook his hand. And then, Maurice saw, he looked around him, the look on his face suddenly severe and distant. He was, it seemed to Maurice, alert to his own dignity and wanted to see who was watching him and wanted to be sure that it was apparent that he stood apart from Sean Flood and his private secretary and Maurice. As he led them down a number of corridors, he did not speak. He walked slowly, deliberately, like a man with much on his mind.

When they reached the bar the minister's private secretary found them a corner table and placed himself opposite the minister and Maurice, with his back to the door. He had a file in his hands which he opened and studied while Sean Flood went to the bar, having been told by the minister and Maurice that they each wanted tea.

'My father,' Maurice said to the minister, 'isn't well at the moment, and he asked me to come. He is Patrick Webster, and he sends you all his best regards. He says that you might remember him from Frongoch.'

'Frongoch,' the minister repeated, smiling faintly as though it was a place of which he had fond memories.

'And I am the secretary of the local cumann, Sean might have told you. I introduced you when you came to Enniscorthy, the time you spoke in the Market Square.'

'That's right,' the minister said vaguely.

'Sean might have mentioned that my brother is sick,' Maurice said.

'He did,' the minister replied and, glancing around, moved close to Maurice so that Maurice would not have to raise his voice.

'At home they saw a report in the paper that there was a new drug for TB—' he began.

'Is your brother in the sanatorium?' the minister interrupted.

'No, he's at home.'

'He might be better in the sanatorium.'

He examined Maurice sharply.

'There are coffins coming out of there every day,' Maurice said. 'And they are not letting visitors into the wards themselves. You have to shout things out from the door for everyone to hear.'

The minister knitted his brow and did not reply. Maurice

was worried in case his seemed like a criticism of the health service.

'Well, it's infectious, you know,' the minister said.

Sean Flood came back with a tray and put it down on the table and sat opposite them.

'We read about the new drug,' Maurice said, addressing the minister only, 'and we were wondering when it might be available.'

The minister nodded his head and moved forward and began to pour tea for himself and Maurice, putting milk and sugar into his own cup and then taking the cup and saucer in his hand.

'It'll be a while,' he said.

'Do you mean a few months?'

'It might be longer. It's still being tested.'

'We read that some people are getting it as part of a trial.'

The minister sipped his tea.

'They are all being done in England and on the Continent. I wish *The Irish Times* hadn't reported it. It's irresponsible of them.'

'So there's nothing here?'

'He would be better in the sanatorium. If anything comes in, it will be through the sanatorium.'

'And will they have the drug?'

'In the course of time, I hope.'

Maurice put milk into his tea and lifted the cup and took a sip.

'We thought that because of my father . . . I mean that you might have some way of helping us.'

'It's a bad business, TB,' the minister said.

'They asked me at home to come up and see you anyway.'

'We're doing the best we can,' the minister said.

'Oh, I know that.'

'Sean says that you are a teacher?'

'That's right.'

'Secondary or primary?'

'Secondary. I'm with the Christian Brothers.'

They were silent for a while. The minister looked around him as Sean Flood sat quietly opposite them and the private secretary continued reading the file.

'There's not much we can do at the moment,' the minister said eventually. 'But they have to worry about infection. If you need any help to get him into the sanatorium, let me know.'

'Ah no, it's all right.'

The minister smiled. He was almost friendly.

'I hope I see you the next time I'm in Enniscorthy.'

He stood up.

'Did you say your father isn't well?'

'He has a bad heart.'

'Will you give him my best wishes? From one Frongoch veteran to another.'

'I'll do that,' Maurice said.

As Sean Flood saw him out to the front gate of the Dáil Maurice made no effort to break the silence. Even as they parted, he said nothing, merely walked away curtly. He would see Sean Flood in Enniscorthy, but he hoped it would not be for a while.

He had missed the train that left Westland Row in the early afternoon and would have to wait, he realized, until six o'clock for the last train. It was hard to think what to do. For a second, he began to imagine that he was a student again and he could walk from Kildare Street to Earlsfort Terrace, and he quickly realized that he would have given anything to be back in Dublin then with only exams to face, with long days to himself, with the welcoming smiles of his landlady Mrs Ruth and her sister when he came home every evening in Terenure, how they had soda bread or currant bread and butter and jam waiting for him, the table set as though for someone important. At the beginning, when he went home to teach in Enniscorthy, he had sent them Christmas cards each year and then one year had forgotten and had lost touch with them. Mrs Ruth must have been seventy when he last saw her, he thought, and her sister older, and he calculated then that that was fourteen years ago, so maybe they were dead now, or too old to have lodgers.

In Dawson Street he walked into Hodges Figgis, smiling to himself when he saw the same sales assistant at the cash register, the one he had always remembered. She had not changed. Once she would have known him by sight, but she must have forgotten him now. Years ago, she was on the lookout for students like him who would spend hours in the shop reading a book and taking notes as though the place was a library. She would come over and stand silently behind him, he remembered, blocking his light, glowering at him and then accompanying him to the door with an expression of grim satisfaction on her face.

He perused the section on history and saw a few books that he might have bought had this been a different day. He would buy nothing now, nor even look at any volume for too long. He had to keep his mind busy, force himself to think of anything except how he was going to face them at home, what he might say to them. They would, he knew, expect him to walk over from the train station to their house before he went to his own house, if there were any sort of news. He could imagine Stephen sitting by the fire, with a book maybe in his hand, or playing chess with his father, his cheeks red from the heat of the flames. He could imagine his mother moving in and out of the room. They would expect him to knock the door and then walk back along the path to the gate before it was answered. His mother, he knew, might blame Nora for his not coming into the house, but Tom would understand. And it would probably be Tom who would answer the door and step out towards the gate to hear the news.

He had nothing to tell them. He knew that they would, once the train whistle had been heard, wait in silence for his arrival at the door. He wondered now, as he went to look at the shelves of books in Irish, if it would be worse to visit in person with the news, which was no news, or if it would be better to leave it, go home to Nora. And let them realize as time passed that he had not come to them because he had no reason to come. The clock over the mantelpiece would tick and then chime gently on the hour. By nine, they would know he was late; by ten, they would be certain that he was not going to appear.

Out on Dawson Street again he could not think what to do. Perhaps go to Bewley's on Grafton Street and have soup and brown bread, or maybe a sandwich. He bought an evening newspaper in Duke Street. He liked the crowds in the streets as he walked along and began to wonder if he should have looked for a job in Dublin once he got married, if Nora and he would be happier in a house, say, in Terenure or Stillorgan, where they would know only some of their neighbours, where they could go to the shops, or into the city centre, without meeting anyone they knew at all and not have to stop and talk to anyone.

It struck him as he reached Grafton Street that he had just fooled himself into thinking that if he lived in Dublin none of this would be happening. He sighed at the thought that everyone would, in fact, be just the same, the scene in the house where he was brought up, the house where his younger brother was now in slow decline, would be just as tense and watchful and would later be just as forlorn as each of them went to bed knowing that there was no news from Dublin and that there was nothing that could be done.

It was when he came to Bewley's that he noticed the lane which led to Clarendon Street church. He decided to walk down towards the church. He would not pray, he thought; he would not ask for anything which would not be granted. There had been enough prayers said, and they had made no difference. He was not sure, despite what others believed, that God interfered in small matters. But this was not a small matter for Stephen, he thought; it was only a small matter for those who did not know him. No one on this street knew anything about him. They were all themselves, living in their own minds, just as Stephen now was living in his and dreading its own extinction, the great change beyond imagining, which nobody knew about for sure, no matter how strong their faith was, no matter how hard they prayed.

He sat at the back of the church and let the minutes go by. There was a time, even when he was a student, that he would come into this church for mass, or on Saturday evening for confession. He had no knowledge then what a desolate place this church would be at a time in the future that was now. He could not think of anywhere more desolate. He stood up and genuflected and quietly left, realizing that he was tracing steps in the city which he would never be able to retrace without remembering this, the day when he had been to the Dáil and seen the minister.

He knew that Tom would be waiting for him after school the next day, and as he walked up Grafton Street towards the Green, he pictured Tom's face when Tom understood that Maurice's not coming the previous evening had been deliberate, that he had nothing to tell them except that his journey to Dublin had been in vain. They would walk over the railway bridge together, past the bottom of Slaney Street, and they would walk past the Cotton Tree and into Slaney Place past Kelly's pharmacy and then up Castle Hill. They would stop and face each other at the door of Mylie Kehoe's, and Maurice would shake his head, and then Tom would nod to him blankly, and they would turn away from one another in silence. They would not go into the pub. Tom would go home. And Maurice would walk on his own along Friary Place and then up Friary Hill to Court Street and John Street, feeling with each step he took that he was leaving a ghost trailing behind him, hovering in the darkening air, a solitary figure asking him if there was any news, if there was any hope.

Barton Springs

We had time left – a week, maybe more – and you thought that our two days in Marfa had been enough and we should move on. As you were looking at the map of Texas spread out on the bed, it was obvious, at least to me, where we would go next; it was almost as though it had been planned.

'Austin is about ten hours,' you said. 'We might do it in a day if we left early and we shared the driving.'

'I used to live there,' I replied.

You were too busy studying the route and the names of places in between to notice the tone. But maybe there was no tone, or not enough for you to notice.

I used to live there.

My brother had been dead for seven months when I came to Austin that last time. In the first months after his death I had kept myself busy and moved around. Now, I was in one spot; there was to be no more moving for a while.

I wonder if I am alone in feeling that Texas is a place for grieving. But grieving is too strong a word. I do not know what the word is. Maybe there is not a single word, not a stable word. But in the softness of these streets, in the leafy laziness of that late September, it came, whatever it is called, and it lurked in the background, and it stalled, all considerate and watchful, the way drivers do in Austin at a crossroads sometimes, and then it inched forward, confident and brave, having checked that it could.

And then it hit hard as though there would not be a better time. As though it had been waiting for this.

My brother was dead and in his grave. There was nothing could be done for him. There would come a time when no one would know who he had been, what he had been. He, or what was left of his body, was edging towards the end of something.

Each evening, using my GPS for guidance, I made my way to Barton Springs. It did not close until ten o'clock, but by the last hour, when the lifeguards had finished, most people had already left.

It had then a strange, unearthly aura. The spring water, the bright lights which cast long shadows, the muffled city sounds, the old-fashioned dressing rooms up the steps, they all appeared to take me close to another world. I wallowed in the water. There was no one on the diving board; there was no shouting or splashing. People leaving in ones and twos, and then just a few of us there, the stragglers. I swam until I was tired and sat on the steps, and then I lowered myself into the water again.

If someone had told me on one of those nights that this is what it will be like when death comes for us, I would have understood. There will be water, and there will be distant sounds, and people will fade into the shadows one by one as the time comes.

On one of those nights at closing time I took a shower in the men's dressing room and then as I sat on the concrete bench drying myself, a young man came to the bench opposite me where he had left his things. Nonchalantly, he removed his tight swimming trunks and then walked naked to the shower. I had noticed him in the dressing room earlier, noticed how fit and lithe he was, and ready for exercise in the water; how white his skin, how perfect he was.

Now in the dim light and the silence, I watched him soaping himself and then rinsing his body. I studied the strength of his legs, the muscled whiteness of his buttocks, his broad back. As he came from the shower and stood close to me, there was something both distant and exquisite about his presence. He seemed focused on the task in hand, not for a second conscious that I was watching him, and not conscious either of his own beauty. When he turned, I saw his dick and his balls and the pubic hair that seemed manicured, and then the full hairless torso, every muscle toned, the nipples perfect like nipples from a marble statue.

As he put one foot on the bench, it was hard to imagine that his body, so cared for, had the oddly shaped, strangely coloured, primitive and ungainly organs we all have inside – the kidneys, the bowels, the liver, the spleen, the pancreas, the intestines, the stomach, the heart, the lungs. He looked as though he would never be in need of those things, that his skin and the muscle inside the shining surface would do the work of keeping him alive.

Somewhere out there in the night there was another person who would come to know his body, or there was another person who knew it already. Someone who would put a hand on his buttocks and feel his dick hardening; feel his hands seeking and caressing the parts of the body we associate with pleasure; feel his lips and tongue searching for a mouth to kiss; feel his breathing becoming heavier; feel his needs more intense. He would no longer then be apart from things, apart from my eyes as I looked at him, or apart from the shadowy silent space of the dressing room itself. He would seek a tenderness that was alien to him here in the dressing room, beyond him as he rummaged in his bag for some clean underwear, a clean shirt, fresh socks. He would be as a figure in a painting who is depicted as the one imploring, his ease erased and replaced by dark urgency, by want, by something that he could not name.

I am driving across Texas towards Austin and you are in the passenger seat smoking with the window wide open so the smoke can escape. There is soft music playing. I do not mention Barton Springs, but as soon as we arrive in Austin it is where I want us to go.

As I drive, I dream about you in the dressing room just as it is ready to close. Everyone else has gone. You are walking naked towards the shower. I watch you. And when you return I pretend to be busy drying myself, dressing myself, but I am still watching you. If I were someone else I would notice how invulnerable you seem now, almost absent from yourself, preoccupied, casual. The whiteness of your body stands out against the shadows.

But I know what you are like when you are asleep. I know the way your hands move towards me in the bed when you half-wake and then how you relax as you begin to doze again. I know the need you have to be touched and held, to have all distance taken away, the casual made deliberate and private, the body filled with itself, the beating heart, the breath coming fast, the wet tongue filled with desire seeking comfort and pleasure, and then something more than comfort or pleasure.

It is hard to know who we are. The dead have gone from us; that much is true. That body I watched those years ago in Barton Springs must be different now. Only the memory is pure, the image. You are dressed, drying your hair with a towel. Other things matter, but I do not know what they are. Our car is waiting outside. We will be the last to leave.

A Sum of Money

In the days before Christmas Dan's mother had lost the small key that opened the lock on the box where she kept her savings. On the morning when they were due to go to Enniscorthy to finish the Christmas shopping, she was desperate. She emptied out her handbag one more time, checked every pocket, pulled out drawers and rummaged through their contents.

'Don't tell your father,' she said just as his father appeared in the doorway.

'The key,' she said, 'the key to the cash-box. I put it somewhere and now it isn't there.'

His father, still in his farm clothes, crossed the room and studied the small lock on the box.

'I could open that in one second. Any fool could open that.'

He returned some moments later with a few pieces of thin wire.

'One of these will do the trick.'

He inserted a piece of wire carefully, but when it became clear that this would not work, he selected one of the other pieces.

'It's important not to try too hard. You have to be patient. It has its own rules.'

Dan saw the lock spring open, almost of its own accord.

'There you go,' his father said.

After Christmas, before he went back to boarding school, when Dan began to practise opening small locks with pieces of wire, he learned not to be too deliberate. If he didn't think about it too much, then it could happen. If he lost patience, however, it would fail.

He was uncertain how he would actually get back to school. His father's car was neither taxed nor insured. His father was wary of taking it anywhere beyond the outskirts of Bunclody or Carnew. Also, there was something wrong with the clutch so that, as they made their way down the long lane to the main road, Dan had to run ahead to open the gates so that his father would not have to stop and change gear.

When it came to the time for him to return to St Peter's after the Christmas holidays, his father still had done nothing about the car.

'We'll get you as far as Enniscorthy,' his father said, 'and you can get the bus to Wexford, or maybe the train.'

He imagined himself walking through the town of Wexford in the January rain and trying to sneak in through the back gate of the school so that no one would realize that his parents were too poor to have a proper car.

He had asked them a few times why he was being sent to a diocesan boarding school, with fees to be paid twice a year, when he could easily have gone to the local vocational school. He knew that the money came from his Uncle Lar in Liverpool but he did not understand why those funds could not be put to better use, such as taxing and insuring the car.

'We have high hopes for you, so it is worth every penny,' his father said sarcastically. 'When you strike oil you can pay it back. Or maybe when you get a decent job.'

As he was preparing for his return to school, he realized that there was no chance of getting any pocket money. Even the pittance handed to him before would not be available now. This would mean that when others were travelling on a Sunday to an away match, he would not be able to go. Nor would he be able to buy cigarettes or even sweets. It would hardly be worth his while to go downtown on the half-day when he was given permission.

When he opened the lock on his mother's cash-box, he found two ten-shilling notes and some loose change. If he took one of the notes, he was certain that his mother would miss it. But he had no choice. She might blame his father, accuse him of opening the lock, but it might not occur to her that Dan, her only child, was the one who took the money.

One of the day-boys, Frank Kirwan from Wexford town, had become a boarder. Frank's mother, someone said, had died and there was no one to look after him.

'She drowned near Rosslare, but it wasn't an accident,' Matt Whelan said. 'Or that's what they say. It wasn't a day when you would go swimming.'

'And what about his father?'

'He's a nervous wreck. He can't even go out on the street.'

Frank Kirwan was nervous himself, Dan knew, and brainy. He had been useful for buying cigarettes in the town when he was a day-boy and selling them in ones and twos to the boarders without charging too much. Now, as a boarder, he would be looking, in turn, for a day-boy to get him cigarettes.

In the Attic dormitory, there were twenty cubicles on each

side of a narrow corridor. Each cubicle had a bed, a sink, a mirror and a locker.

By the end of January, Dan was familiar with many of the locks. A few of them were too strong, too silvery and shiny, but most were basic. He managed to open them more quickly and effortlessly as time went by.

Not many people knew that the sliding door to the Attic dormitory was opened by one of the maintenance staff at about six o'clock each evening and not locked again. The important thing was not to go there too often. He needed to select quiet nights and get there just after tea. Soon, he was doing it once a week, able to unpick three or four locks in a few minutes.

Some kept their cash in their blazer pockets, the blazer that was worn only on special days. Others hid their money well enough so that he could not easily find it. But most were careless. Often, he took just a single note or a few coins in the hope that they would not be missed. Once he took money from a cubicle, he did not tend to return to it. But there were a few who had a pile of notes and it was hard to resist the temptation.

It was Frank Kirwan who caught him. He had not known that Frank was sick and told to stay in bed by Sister Dominic. Dan was working on John Hardy's locker, presuming that the Attic was as empty as it was silent. But when he turned, having fastened the lock, he saw that Frank Kirwan had got out of bed and was now standing in his pyjamas watching him. Since there had been talk on the dormitory about money missing, Frank could be in no doubt about what he was witnessing.

Dan responded to Frank's gaze blankly, as though he was not really standing there, as though he had never ascended these stairs, as though he was to be found at this very moment walking around the sports field with two or three fellows, sharing a cigarette with one of them.

For the next few days, he kept an eye on Frank Kirwan. When study was over, Frank drifted towards the door or hung around, not joining any group. He seemed to fit in. But he did not appear to have a special friend, someone in whom he might confide.

He must be aware of what he had seen. Perhaps he was waiting to tell one of the priests, but surely, if that was his intention, he would have done so by now. He would not be thanked for delaying.

Dan's worry was that Frank would make some casual remark that might seem inconsequential to one of their fellow students about seeing Dan in the dormitory, and somebody might draw a conclusion from this.

He had already hidden the cash he had accumulated in a small gap in the wainscotting beneath the mirror that hung over the sink in his cubicle. He would have to be careful. A few days ago, no one knew; now one person knew. Perhaps it was a sign. He should stop, make do with what money he had. It would keep him going until Easter.

He wished he knew what Frank was thinking. It struck him that the best way might be to start talking to him. He would not refer directly to the episode in the dormitory, but he would try to discover how afraid he should be.

There was a place, a kind of balcony, above the squash courts where the more senior students gathered after tea. Dan found Frank there when there was still time to go for a walk around the playing fields. He was at the edge of a group who were laughing about something. Dan should not make his approach too deliberate. He would have asked for a drag of Kirwan's cigarette except that Kirwan wasn't smoking. He might have asked him for the loan of a cigarette except he didn't want to be refused. For Dan to offer Frank a cigarette out of the blue might be too forward and too direct.

He stood close to Frank, his hands in his pockets. He worried that it might be too cold for them to take a walk around the field.

'I saw you that day on the dorm,' Dan said in a kind of undertone. 'I didn't expect you to be there.'

Frank glanced at him sharply. Then he almost smiled. He kept his voice low.

'I saw you all right. But I mind my own business. That's what I do.'

Anyone else in the school, he thought, would not be able to keep this to themselves, they would tell someone. He had hit on one of the few who might take another approach. Frank would tell no one. Dan wondered if it was something you learned in the town where so much was known, so much observed. Or maybe it was Frank himself. He seemed friendly.

No one could leave the college grounds without express permission from Father Murray, the dean of discipline. When parents visited, they had to park in front of the college and, as long as their son was in the car, they could not drive out of the grounds. On Saturdays and Sundays the front drive was packed with cars. Students who were expecting visits watched from windows. When it was time for rosary, they walked back into the school with their laundry and some supplies from home. They also came in with fresh pocket money.

In the first weeks of term, Dan's parents did not appear. Since he had never received a letter from them in all his time in the school, he saw no point in writing to them.

There was still not a word from them as February gave way to March. He put his clothes into the school laundry, unsure how laundry was paid for. He supposed it would be sent to his parents as a bill. He could imagine his father's face if such a bill were to arrive by post.

Two weeks before the Easter holidays he was approached by Matt Whelan, whose father owned the butcher's shop in Bunclody and a farm on the other side of the village.

'You haven't had a call-out since Christmas, have you?'

'What do you mean?'

'Your old man's car is banjaxed.'

'When it gets going, it's fine.'

'Well, it's in Bunclody these last few weeks. It's an eyesore. It collapsed. Rats are living in it. And your mother was spotted riding a bicycle. Even that is a jalopy. Or so I hear.'

'You're great the way you hear things.'

'I'd say you'll be looking for a lift home when it comes to the holidays.'

Matt left him with the impression that such a lift would not be on offer, at least not from him.

Since there was to be a match in New Ross the following Sunday, it struck Dan that he should, if it were possible, try St Aidan's, the senior dorm, to see if he could find the locker belonging to Larry Howlin who, as a prefect, was collecting the bus fares. Dan himself had paid Larry the previous day. He would have to find the right moment, as he would have no excuse for visiting a dorm that was not his.

Just before tea ended, he slipped out of the refectory and made his way along the corridor that led to the stairs to St Aidan's. He knew that the prefect on a dorm had a larger cubicle than the others. Larry Howlin's was easy to identify, right inside the door.

Once he had opened the lock, he spotted a wad of banknotes and a plastic bag full of coins on the middle shelf of Larry

A SUM OF MONEY

Howlin's cubicle. Since the notes were wrapped in a piece of paper with a list of names, he presumed that they had been carefully counted. Anything he took would be missed.

He would not get a chance again to take as much as this. Why could he not take the whole thing, all the change as well? That would be the equal of twenty other lockers. Having thought for one more moment, he made the decision. He filled his pockets with the silver and put the notes in his back pocket. He locked the cubicle. He walked with a slow, casual air down the stairs, meeting no one. And he saw no one on the shadowy corridor. He went straight to the Attic where he deposited the money in the hiding place under the mirror. And then he went to the balcony above the squash courts where he found some fellow students who were smoking. He joined them for a while, taking a drag from a cigarette that was offered to him. He was glad when the bell for study rang. No one could guess where he had been.

After rosary on the following evening, Father Murray came into the church and stood solemnly at the lectern. Even when there was complete silence he waited, staring ominously around the church as though daring one of them to cough or shuffle or make the smallest sound.

'Gentlemen,' he began, 'there is a thief among you.'

He stopped so that what he had said could sink in. A few times he made as though to continue, but he waited. And then he spoke as if he were confiding in each one of his listeners.

'We have known this for some time. Whoever the thief is, he has operated, so far, with care. Gentlemen, he is cunning. But so are we. We are cunning too. We will soon know who he is. We will find him out and unmask him.'

He lowered his voice even more.

'What we know for certain is that he is here among you. I want him to listen to me. I am appealing to him not only in the name of common decency, but I am appealing to him in the name of God. Until yesterday, the thief pilfered on a small scale, but yesterday he stole a sum of money that places him outside the pale. It was a considerable sum of money and it was stolen from a fellow student. Gentlemen, I want you to look left and look right. Yes, do that now. One of you, no, two of you, have looked into the eyes of a thief. He might seem ordinary, he might seem friendly. But after yesterday, because of the sum of money involved, he is in a state of mortal sin. His soul is in great danger. I call on him now to approach one of the priests of the college and confess his sin. He must remember the sacred secrecy of the confessional. No priest will ever reveal what has been said in the confessional. God is merciful. But time is short. None of us knows the day nor the hour.'

Father Murray cleared his throat and raised his voice.

'I repeat: one among you is a thief. Let him desist from his thieving or he will be expelled forthwith from this college, never to return.'

And then he bowed his head and whispered, 'And let us pray in silence to thank the Lord for his infinite mercy and let us call on the thief to repent with a firm purpose of amendment so that his soul does not suffer eternal damnation.'

After tea, Dan heard that the sum of money had been stolen from Larry Howlin's locker. It was the money that had been collected for the bus. News was spread that Father Murray had decided that anyone who had paid for the bus would still be travelling, even if the money was missing.

On Sunday morning after mass the dormitory was busy with those going to the match in New Ross fetching what they needed for the day. Dan usually carried a small amount of pocket money with him but he had spent it all. He regretted that he had not withdrawn what he needed for New Ross from the hiding place during the night when there were no fellow students walking past. Now, he would have to wait for a moment when there was no one looking.

He lay on his bed as if he were resting; he was waiting for Liam Golden, who was standing at the entrance to his own cubicle, to step away. But Liam did not budge. After a while Liam was joined by Matt Whelan so that both of them had a full view into Dan's cubicle.

They spoke of the match and had a bantering conversation with a fellow from Enniscorthy, Donal Webster, whose cubicle was close by, who boasted that he would not be caught dead at a hurling match and insisted that St Peter's, anyway, was bound to lose. Dan could not think why they were idling here for so long. The time for the bus's departure was getting close. Soon, they would all have to gather at the front gates of the school where the buses were waiting.

What was strange, he thought, was that even though they were fully aware of his presence, Golden and Whelan did not address a single remark to him. As it became pressingly urgent for him to get the money, he had the impression that he was being watched. They couldn't just be standing there for no reason. If he didn't manage to get money, he would be in New Ross for a few hours without a penny as the others went to shops and cafes.

He opened his locker and moved things around as noisily as he could. Maybe he should just not go, pretend that he had got word at the last minute that someone from home was planning to visit that very afternoon. He changed his shoes and put on his school blazer. He did not look to check if they were watching him. They were still talking in low tones. He took a facecloth from his locker and made as though to wipe a stain from the mirror. And, as he did so, he reached into the space where the money was hidden and took out the plastic bag where the notes were kept. He took what he would need.

When he looked, he saw that Golden and Whelan had disappeared. He would have to follow them quickly to make the bus.

It was more than a year since he had gone to a match on one of the school buses. He had forgotten how enjoyable it was, the hum of mild expectation on the journey out, the freedom of being away from the school. A few of the priests would drive to the match in their own cars but they would not come near the students. After the game, when they would have two hours or more to wander in the town, they would not go into any pubs. It had become a matter of legend that a number of seniors had got drunk after a match in Carlow years before. It was believed that the owner of the pub had sent word to the school. Ten of the students had been sent home for the rest of the term. Two others had been expelled.

It would be enough, Dan thought, to walk the streets of New Ross freely, especially if St Peter's had just won the match, but even if they hadn't. And what was strange, he remembered, was how nice it was then to return to the school, walk its corridors once more as though it had become a warmer place because he had been away. This was a feeling that he did not have after holidays where the refectory and the dormitories could promise little, where excitement lay in the memory of the last few days at home. But coming back after a match carried with it a sort of lift that could last into the week that followed.

Liam Golden and Matt Whelan were travelling on one of the other buses. He determined that once they arrived in New Ross he would seek them out and walk with them to the grounds and talk to them. This was what he had done with Frank Kirwan. He reminded himself that he should make sure to see Frank when they came back to the college. He should go on spending time with him.

In New Ross, he walked from the bus to the pitch with Golden and Whelan and another boy called Cogley who was hoping that his father and older brother would be at the match.

'I might get to go home for about an hour after it's over. I hope they parked the car somewhere handy.'

When he tried to engage Golden in conversation, Golden nodded but he would not look directly at Dan. It was best to wait for a while, he surmised, wait until Golden said something to him and then let things flow from there. But Golden did not seem interested in conversation. Whelan and Cogley were assessing the chances of St Peter's team.

'The thing about New Ross,' Cogley said, 'is that it's nearly Kilkenny. They get a lot of training from Kilkenny players.'

'Kilkenny had a great team last year,' Whelan said. 'I mean the senior team.'

'The minors were nearly better,' Cogley said. 'I heard someone say that.'

'I heard that too,' Dan interjected. 'But there's a big difference between minor and senior. It's another level.'

Neither Whelan nor Cogley paid any attention to what he had said. He felt as if his effort to join the discussion had closed it down completely. All four moved silently towards the pitch. Dan did not know whether he should try to stick with Golden and Whelan for the duration of the match.

* * *

The New Ross team concentrated on scoring points. They made it look easy. It was evident that three or four of their players had been trained just to do this – to get the ball and turn as though the space in front of them had been suddenly cleared and then swing the hurl with accuracy and confidence. Beside him, Golden and Whelan lost themselves in the game, shouting and yelling, cajoling their team to stop tackling so awkwardly and pointlessly. They also began to believe that the referee was on the side of New Ross.

'That ref needs to cop himself on,' Golden said.

'Ref or no ref,' Whelan said, 'I'll tell you one thing, our fellows will get some talking-to at half-time. They have no discipline at all.'

Dan followed each pass of the ball, each tackle. No matter what St Peter's did, New Ross could produce a star player who would effortlessly put the ball over the bar. By the end of the first half, they had scored eleven points to St Peter's two.

Early in the second half a player from St Peter's called Quigley caused one of the New Ross team to require medical attention.

'That fellow asked for it,' Golden said.

'I know who he is,' Cogley said. 'He's a Rochford. He's a dirty player and his brother Mick before him was a dirty player. It's time someone gave him a dig.'

'A few stitches will set him right,' Whelan added.

'Look at the ref,' Dan said.

The referee was hopping up and down in front of Quigley, lecturing him before sending him off. He gave a free to New Ross from within the twenty-one-yard line. With this, they scored what would be the only goal of the match.

Cogley went and stood on the sideline, shouting abuse at a player called Roche who had scored the goal.

'You're a fucking eejit, Roche. You need a kick up your hole, you right eejit.'

'Cogley doesn't like Roche,' Whelan said.

'I don't like Roche either,' Golden replied.

Once the match was over, Dan lost Golden and Whelan in the crowd and spent time walking through the streets looking for them. He passed groups of students from St Peter's but saw no one from his own class and none of the seniors. Some of them might have gone to the dressing rooms, though after such a defeat it was unlikely. But Golden and Whelan must be somewhere.

He imagined them going to one of the priests and telling them that they thought they knew who the thief was. Or they could have met Larry Howlin and informed him that Dan was the one who had raided his locker.

Or maybe he was worrying too much. They might be in some cafe or pub that he had not located yet.

But what if they did point to him? What would happen next? Would he be taken off the bus? Would they try to contact his father? How could he be sent home when his father had no car?

He went over the time he had spent with Golden and Whelan in the past. He had surely walked around the playing field with them and he must have sat beside them in the chapel and talked with them late at night in the dormitory. But they had never been special friends so it might be normal for them to keep to themselves on a day like today. He was probably making too much of how they had responded to him.

He found himself circling the same few streets of New Ross, coming back to the river each time, feeling an icy wind. He went to a cafe where some of the students from St Peter's were finishing up. He ordered a plate of chips with sausages and peas.

When he went to find the buses, the first two were already full. He got onto the third where half the seats were empty. It was almost dark by the time the buses departed.

As they walked up the drive to the school after descending from the buses, Dan realized that the team would have already arrived and the news would have spread that they had lost the game badly. There would be a gloom over the school.

He had slept on the bus and felt sleepy still. It was a relief to be able to go straight to the dormitory.

In his absence, he saw as soon as he reached his cubicle, somebody had moved the mirror over the sink so that it was not hanging straight any more. And a piece of plasterwork beneath it had come away. Someone had found where he kept the bag with the money. He checked that no one was looking before he searched the small space. He could not be mistaken. There was no bag there.

It had to have been Golden and Whelan. He had gone from the school to the bus that day with just a few minutes to spare. Could they have waited behind and then sneaked into his cubicle and taken the bag? If so, they must have been fast. Or, as they had been on an earlier bus on the way back, they might have taken the money on their return. Where was it now? Or had they told a priest who then had driven back to the school in his car and discovered the stash?

It struck him that he could hardly wait here until others arrived and then get into his pyjamas and slip into bed as though it were an ordinary night. What would Golden and Whelan do when they saw him? How would he sleep?

Maybe someone was going to appear soon to accuse him. Maybe once the lights were out, he would hear a sound and turn and have a torch shone in his face. It would be Father Murray himself, his voice grave as he told Dan to get dressed and gather his belongings and be prepared to leave St Peter's this very night.

He lay with his hands behind his head. Some boys came onto the dormitory. He could hear talk of the match. Soon, he could hear Golden's imitation of Cogley shouting, 'You're a fucking eejit, Roche.'

'But it was Roche who scored the goal,' Golden went on, 'so he wasn't such an eejit after all.'

'I'd say the ref wasn't on your side,' Donal Webster interjected. 'I think the lousy team should blame the ref.'

'That's enough out of you, Webster, you're only a gom,' Golden said.

A week went by. Dan was being watched, or he presumed he was. He knew not to raid any further lockers. But he also had lost any taste for taking money. At any moment, he believed, he would be approached and told to get his things. He continued to have a smoke some evenings after tea with Frank Kirwan and he even considered telling Frank his worries. But their relationship depended on a tacit agreement that he and Frank would not discuss what Frank had witnessed. So he could not easily raise the subject with him. Also, there was nothing Frank could advise him to do.

He wondered who would inform his parents. He supposed that he could deny it and tell them that he was taking the blame for some fellow whose uncle was a priest or who was destined for Maynooth. But that would hardly matter. He was in disgrace.

The only one who didn't judge him, and who wouldn't judge him, was Frank Kirwan, who kept the conversation general as they walked around the playing field. Just as they did not mention what Frank had seen, there was never talk of Frank's mother's death or how his father was.

When the Easter holidays were a few days away and Dan guessed that he would not be returning to the school once the break was over, he was tempted to ask Frank if they could keep in touch, maybe he could write to him, or come to Wexford town in the summer if Frank were there. But he wasn't sure how Frank would react.

On the night before the holidays, on the corridor leading from the refectory to the study hall, he saw Father Murray walking towards him.

'Oh listen, Dan,' he said, 'will you go up now to the nuns' office, Sister Dominic is looking for you.'

'Should I go now?' Dan asked.

'Oh yes, I think you should go now.'

The nuns' office was the small room where medicine was kept and where Sister Dominic was available in the mornings for anyone who was sick.

The nun was at the door of the office. As he approached, she pointed towards the hallway on her right. Standing there, facing them, was Father Fenlon, the parish priest of Bunclody. Dan had never seen him in St Peter's before. He noticed that the priest was smoking a cigarette. He was well known for his chain-smoking. He realized that Father Fenlon was here to drive him home.

'Father Fenlon is going to take you,' Sister Dominic said, 'and we have put all your belongings in the boot of his car.'

'Why am I going?'

'Oh here now,' she said and pursed her lips. 'Oh here now. You just do what you are told. I don't want any guff from you.'

She led him towards Father Fenlon.

The priest drew hard on his cigarette before he turned to open the front door.

'We'd better get going then,' he said to the nun, ignoring Dan. 'I hope the rain lifts a bit.'

'Safe journey now, Father,' Sister Dominic said. 'And say a prayer for us all.'

'Right you be,' Father Fenlon said.

Dan wanted to ask if they had packed all his clothes and if they had remembered to include the contents of his desk or if they might have forgotten his coat. When he hesitated as though he might turn back, Sister Dominic intervened.

'Don't even consider keeping the good father waiting after all the trouble he took coming down here.'

It seemed strange walking out towards the car in this weather with no coat, no suitcase.

Outside, Father Fenlon had left the headlights on in his Ford Anglia. He took one last pull on the cigarette before throwing it, half-smoked, to the side. He opened a large black umbrella and accompanied Dan to the car. Dan saw that his father was sitting in the front passenger seat. His father, without greeting him, got out and folded the front seat to let Dan into the back of the car.

'It's a wicked night,' Father Fenlon said as he settled into the driver's seat, handing Dan his wet umbrella. He lit another cigarette as he turned the car and directed it down the drive. Dan's father also lit a cigarette that he took from his own packet.

As they drove towards Ferrycarrig, Dan understood why Father Murray had sounded casual, almost friendly when he had told him to go to the nuns' office. There would be no shouting or blaming. He had been removed from the school quietly, without fuss.

Dan waited for his father or the priest to say something.

'Did you ever try the Rothmans?' his father asked Father Fenlon once they had crossed the bridge and were on the way to Oylgate.

'I'll tell you something,' the priest said, 'they are not for me. I got a present of a carton of them for Christmas. Oh I smoked them, mind you. But they weren't for me.'

'And Benson & Hedges?' his father asked. 'Have you tried them?'

'I don't know those boys at all.'

The rain came down harder. Father Fenlon leaned forward in the driving seat, peering through the windscreen.

'Once we've weather like this,' he said, 'my policy is to go slow. I have no time at all for fast cars. We don't have the roads for them. It's as simple as that.'

'You couldn't be more right,' Dan's father said.

'Are you stuck with the Player's?' the priest asked.

'When I went to England before the war,' his father said, 'I was a young fellow and we all smoked Afton, Sweet Afton, and you bought them in ones, at least in Bolton you did, in one of the corner shops.'

'I'd say they were very satisfying.'

'The American soldiers had Lucky Strikes. But I never tried them. Some people liked them.'

Dan wondered what was going to happen. Father Fenlon must have been told everything. He supposed that Father Murray must have phoned him. At some point, his father and the priest must have discussed why they were driving to St Peter's to collect Dan and why they were taking him home.

They spoke as though he was not there. Even the silence that lingered in the car as they approached Enniscorthy seemed to exclude him. There was no chance, he thought, that either of them was going to offer him a cigarette or ask him what his favourite brand was.

When they arrived home, his mother would be waiting for them, but he could not picture her response to him when he appeared in the doorway. At least the rain would be some sort of distraction. It would be easier if the journey did not end soon, he thought, if Father Fenlon took a wrong turn, if they could drive and drive.

At Bunclody, they veered right towards Carnew, as sheets of rain slapped against the windscreen of the car.

'It's a dirty night,' his father said. 'That's what it is.'

'I thought it might ease off,' the priest said. 'But that's the way it is.'

Father Fenlon was going slowly so he would not miss the turn into the long lane that led to the farmhouse. On the way, his father, he realized, would have to get out of the car to open the three different gates on the lane.

'I'm going to end up in Carnew village,' Father Fenlon said, 'if you don't tell me when I am close to the turn.'

He sounded irritated as he opened the window and threw out the lighting stub of a cigarette, the fourth he had smoked on the journey.

When they turned into the lane and came to the first gate, Dan's father opened the passenger door and got out of the car, and then pulled back the seat so that Dan could get out.

'You can open the gate,' he said, 'and make yourself useful by closing it behind you as well.'

The headlights of the car seemed to be focused directly on him as he levered the gate open. He stood back to let the car get by. And then, when it had inched past and he went to shut the gate, the car drew away from him up the lane, leaving him behind.

The rain was dripping from his hair down the back of his neck. His shoes were quickly soaked. He presumed at the beginning that the priest had let the car go forward so that the wheels might not get stuck in the mud. But soon he saw the tail-lights fade.

He would have to walk the mile or so to the house.

He thought for a second that he might turn around, go down to the road and hitch a lift to Bunclody. But he had no idea what he would do once he was there.

Even in good weather, the dip in the rutted lane after the first bend could be mucky and slippery. He could not avoid the puddles and the potholes. The squelching muck was now in his shoes. When he took a step, the shoes went in even deeper, and it was an effort to wrestle them from the mud.

It was hard to see how this had happened, if the priest had driven forward on his own initiative, without saying anything to his father, or if his father, once Dan was out of the car, had made some sharp remark to suggest that Dan should be let walk the rest of the way, he deserved nothing less. Or maybe on the journey here from St Peter's they had not really been ignoring him but silently planning what to do with him. Maybe, in fact, they had agreed on leaving him behind without having to speak or consult each other at all.

It was dark and the rain still came down hard. When he put his hand out in front of him, he could see nothing. If he could keep to the grassy centre of the lane, it would be easier, but soon he found that he had almost walked blind into the ditch. All he could do was imagine a direction. There were two more gates. On a normal day, this would take him half an hour. It hardly mattered how long it would take him now.

At some point, surely, the priest would pass him in his car, driving away. Dan would pretend not to see him. Or maybe he should stand in front of the car, demanding that the priest turn around and drive him home. But there was no sign of the priest. He must have gone into the house. They must be talking.

As he trudged on, he let himself dream of a plate with a slice of ham and a tomato and a piece of buttered bread. And then a pot of tea. But it had been set out on the table by his mother for Father Fenlon. She was surely telling him that they could never thank him enough for what he had done for them.

He hoped he was moving in the right direction. There were a few gates from the lane into fields and he would have to be careful not to mistake those gates for the gates on the lane. But he couldn't see any gates.

He hit up against the second gate with a shock. Swinging in the wind, it felt like something alive. Still, he was relieved to find it there. If he closed it, having passed, then Father Fenlon would have to get out of his car to open it. The rain would douse his cigarette, Dan thought with some satisfaction.

Sunday, he imagined as he pushed forward, would be a big night at the dancehall in Carnew. He thought of what it would be like there. Would they all have found out about him? He could see Matt Whelan watching him and maybe coming up to him with others by his side to tell him that he had no place here, he should get out of here right now or he'd be sorry. And he wasn't to show his face anywhere around here again.

His shoes had got so heavy that he wondered if he might take them off and carry them in his hand and stop dreaming about Sunday and start thinking about what would really happen when he got home.

* * *

The priest and his father were at the door when Dan reached the house. The rain was still coming in sheets. One of the gutters was broken and rain was pouring down from the opening above one of the windows to the cement ground.

'Here he is,' his father said.

His mother appeared. She had her arms folded.

Dan slipped past the priest and then edged past his father. He followed his mother into the kitchen where he sat on a chair and took his shoes off. He heard the front door closing.

'Look at him, he's drenched,' his mother said.

'You took your time,' his father said. 'Did you close the gates behind you?'

'I did,' Dan said.

'That's good news anyway. I hope the priest thinks of closing them too. But he'll have to get out and open them first. The very thought of it cheers me up.'

'You'd better change into dry clothes,' his mother said. 'I got such a fright when I saw the priest earlier on. I couldn't think what it was. And then he told us.'

Dan was imagining the Attic. The others would see his bed empty and they would guess. On nights like this, nights before a holiday, it would take a long time for the dormitory to become quiet. Even when most of them fell asleep, there would always be a few who would keep the conversation going.

Frank Kirwan would be too shy and too careful to join the talk. He would listen, however, to see if any of them mentioned Dan, if they spoke about why Dan was not here, if any of them knew how Dan had managed to open the locks.

He remembered Frank standing in his cubicle watching him. Maybe he would try and get in touch with Frank. It would be time enough to do that in the summer.

He glanced up and saw that his father and mother were watching him. He was waiting for his father to blurt out some accusation or for his mother to press him to explain exactly what had transpired. But then he saw what was happening – his father and his mother did not know what to say. They were almost embarrassed.

If he relaxed now, he felt, if he did not speak, if he stood up quietly and casually, as though it were natural, and went to his own room across the hall to see if he could find dry clothes, then no one might follow him.

He would leave the door open for the moment, certain or almost certain that they would not come into his room or stand in the doorway. He would close the door only when he was sure they had gone to bed.

A Free Man

With his left hand he tilted his credit card towards the window so that he could see the numbers more clearly. He keyed them in with care, adding the date of expiry plus the three digits on the back. He checked once more that he had spelled his own address correctly. Since Barcelona city council did not want tourists to have instant access to the city bikes, permits could be sent only to a home address.

It was early June, the days warm and windless. What he liked was the freshness in the air in the morning. Later, traffic sounds competed with street noises to rise like heat into the apartment. He left the balcony doors open in the main room and also in the bedroom. In the kitchen, the window looked onto the shadowy well in the centre of the building. At mealtimes he could hear a woman talking Catalan to her husband in the apartment whose kitchen faced his, and the husband's gruff replies. He could smell frying food.

The previous day, as he tried for the first time to fill in the online form, the door from the hallway into the main room suddenly banged shut and the door to the balcony had also banged. For a second, the apartment felt almost chilly. The unexpected sound had unsettled him. When he went to the balcony, he reassured himself that it was nothing, just a gust of wind. But by the time he came back to the laptop, the form had timed out and he did not think he would be able to concentrate on filling it in again.

He waited a day. And he slowly, painstakingly, completed the thing. He had clicked on the box that said 'pay' and, in due course, an acknowledgement arrived. Within seven working days, he would have the card that would allow him to use the city bicycles.

He stood up and stretched and walked out onto the balcony and stood in the golden light.

Although he liked getting a taxi to the beach and returning on foot through the side streets, and he enjoyed walking to the Ramblas to buy a newspaper, he was always worried that someone from home, some tourist, would notice him on the street and point at him, even follow him. On a bicycle, he would get away quickly.

In the top left-hand drawer of his desk was the letter he had received towards the end of his time in prison. He took it out and read it again before resolving to destroy it or at least edge it into the pile of documents at the very bottom of the drawer. The letter had been printed out so that it looked more formal; he was sure it had been composed by his sister Marian. It had her tone, and that of her husband Shane, the Monaghan solicitor. It addressed Joe directly, using his full first name Joseph, a name they had never called him. It read:

> We, the undersigned, your brothers and sisters, hereby sever all ties with you and wish to make clear to you that, because of the disgrace you have brought on us, we demand that you refrain from contacting any of us at any time in the future, and that you do not use any of our names as next of kin or

people to contact in an emergency. We also demand that you make arrangements now for your own funeral and burial, and also that you make plans to be buried in a graveyard far away from Ferbane. We are thankful that our beloved mother and father went to their reward before what you did came to light. Kindly do not reply to this letter.

It was signed by all eight of his siblings, beginning with Teresa and ending with Maisie, her signature childlike and spindly. He could imagine Marian standing over her in the sheltered accommodation where middle-aged women with Down's syndrome were looked after by social workers.

In the middle of the list were the signatures of his two brothers. He wondered if the letter had been sent to Declan in Vancouver or if it had been signed by him on one of his visits home.

The signature that hurt him most was Seamus's. Seamus, the closest to him in age, had been in the courtroom when the charges against Joe were first read out and also, later, for the victim statements. He had been there too when the sentence was passed, and he had moved towards Joe and tried to embrace him before Joe was taken away. In the first two years he had visited and sent parcels and presents but in the years that followed Joe had heard nothing from him. He had written to him five or six times but received no reply. The others, he thought, must have put pressure on Seamus to sever contact, as they must also have put pressure on Seamus to sign the letter.

Since his arrival in Barcelona, Joe had thought a few times of letting his brother know where he was, and he might still do so, putting nothing else in the letter except an address and a line to say that he was well, or was still alive. But maybe it would be better to do nothing.

The only regular visitor to his apartment was Juan López Martillo, the policeman who oversaw the conditions of his release. When he went each week to the police station, he had to ask for López Martillo and wait until he appeared. A few times, the policeman had come to the apartment without warning, as was his right, perhaps even his duty, and he had made Joe turn on the laptop in the corner. He checked 'history', examining recent sites visited. But he found nothing that interested him. When he went into the bedroom, he looked as if he were sniffing the air.

The other person Joe knew in the city was Denis Doran who had been in the same year as him in Maynooth and had left in the same week. Denis co-owned the Shamrock Shore, one of the Irish bars near the Ramblas.

Joe remembered the afternoon forty years earlier when he had decided to announce to the director of vocations in Maynooth that he was thinking of leaving the seminary. He did not believe that he was cut out to be a priest, he had told Father Barrett. Even as he spoke, he realized how lame this sounded. Father Barrett left him alone for what must have been an hour. When he returned, they had a conversation that seemed to Joe remarkably casual and slack. He wondered if they were waiting for someone more important, or a person trained in convincing seminarians to leave their doubts aside for the moment and listen closely to the voice of God.

When a knock came to the door, Father Barrett took in a plastic bag with clothes in it. Handing Joe the bag, he told him he might change into civvies there and then.

Father Barrett, at his desk, seemed to be reading his breviary as Joe disrobed and put on the grey suit and check shirt that he had left hanging in the wardrobe of his room, not having used them since the Christmas holidays. When he was ready, Father Barrett stood up and handed him a five-pound note.

'I would like to say goodbye to a few of the lads,' Joe said.

'No, you won't be doing that. You won't be disturbing them in their vocations. You'd better be off.'

Joe did not know the priest who drove him to Dublin. As he sat in the front passenger seat, the priest asked him which railway station he wanted to go to and when he said Heuston the priest nodded. They did not speak again.

The story of the speed with which he had been dispatched from Maynooth caused much indignation at home. His mother insisted that every student priest, including the most holy and dedicated, had doubts until the very second of their consecration. She was so indignant at Father Barrett that Joe was glad he had not told her of the priest's slow and deliberate stare as Joe was removing his soutane and his clerical trousers to change into the clothes he was wearing now. It was something, he thought, that his mother would not understand.

A few days later, Denis Doran rang.

'I heard about your departure,' Denis said. 'I nearly had to pay Mabel in golden ducats for him to tell me.'

'Who's Mabel?'

'She's the priest who drove you to the station.'

'Are you phoning from . . .?'

Joe imagined the single public phone in the lower corridor of the seminary.

'No, I jumped. Or, to be truthful, Mabel gave me a lift as far as O'Connell Bridge. If one more seminarian departs, you'll have started a stampede. Listen, I need to see you.'

'My mother is watching me,' Joe whispered. 'I am meant to be contemplating my future.'

'Tell her that you must go and see your old friend Denis Doran to discuss your vocation. And you'll be back soon. I'm going to Mullingar now. I have wheels. What if I collect you at nine in front of the courthouse?'

'And then?'

'We'll drive mad through the countryside and ask God's forgiveness.'

Joe liked to think it lasted a week, his spree with Denis Doran. It began in Cork. Was it really possible, he wondered, that there was a gay bar in Cork in that year? A bar that Denis seemed to know and enjoy? And then, on the Naas dual carriageway driving towards Dublin when he had said that in all his time in Maynooth he had never guessed about Denis, Denis replied, 'That gay stuff, Joe. You're on your own with that. There's plenty of fellows out there, queer or gay or whatever you want to call them, but Denis Doran is not one of them.'

In the briskness of his tone, the dry certainty, Denis left no room for Joe to remind him of what had transpired the night before in their shared room in a bed and breakfast on Magazine Road. Denis had come to his bed and made his position passionately plain both then and as soon as they woke in the morning, the landlady banging on the door to say that it was well past checking-out time.

Finally, on a Monday afternoon, Joe had, once more, taken the train from Heuston to home. That September he went to UCG and began an arts degree and then did a teaching diploma. He got a job in a school in Rathfarnham and settled down there. He never saw Denis Doran again nor did he ever meet anyone who had news of his friend.

But as the time of his release was approaching, when his name was in the papers regularly, he got a letter from Denis Doran from an address in Barcelona suggesting that the city might be a good place for him to visit when he was free, adding, 'It would be an even better place for you to spend your retirement.'

It was unclear if this was an invitation or a friendly note during a period when only abusive letters were coming his way.

As his release grew imminent, he asked Scully his solicitor to contact Denis Doran.

'He's the sort of fellow who means what he says, or at least he used to be.'

Joe did not mention that he had not been in touch with Denis Doran for years. But he could not, he knew, stay in Ireland once he was freed, and he had no other options. Scully also agreed that he would find out what would happen if a man just out of jail on probation and on the sex offenders register were to take up residence in another EU country.

One Christmas years before, something strange had happened. Joe, as was his custom, had called by the house of the family of an ex-student. He usually had a few drinks with the parents on one of the days between Christmas and the New Year. He did not have to wait for an invitation. He knew these people well. But he did detect a coldness and a hesitancy in the way he had been ushered into the front sitting room by one of the daughters. The door had been closed behind him.

He waited in the sitting room that had been decorated for the festive season, with Christmas cards lined up on a long piece of string attached to the wall. There was not a sound. He stood up and looked at some photographs on a sideboard and sat down on another armchair. They must have forgotten he was here. He was sure he had seen the family car parked outside. It was the late afternoon. He listened; there was silence. Eventually, he went into the hall and called out. And then he went into the kitchen. There was no one in any of the downstairs rooms, even though some of the lights were on. He called out again before returning to the sitting room, leaving the door ajar. Surely someone would come! Most of the family was usually home for the Christmas holiday but, in any case, it was a house that was normally full of life.

He waited for another fifteen minutes, and then decided he would stay for five more. He would time himself. And, if no one appeared, he would go.

For a second as he looked at his watch it struck him why this might be happening, why some of the family, the ones who were in the house, might be upstairs, huddled in a room, hoping that he would get the hint and let himself out of their house without their having to meet him or even see him.

One afternoon a few weeks later he noticed a Garda car outside his house. The two Guards looked at him closely as he stood in his driveway. Soon afterwards, two Gardaí visited to say they wished to interview him on a most serious matter.

When he had been buying his house in Templeogue, his solicitor had mentioned in passing a colleague who did criminal cases and favoured the most difficult ones.

'He'd get Genghis Khan out on bail, that fellow would,' the solicitor had said. 'I don't touch the criminal stuff myself.'

Joe remembered that description of the solicitor whose name was Scully.

Even when he was charged, he was sure that nothing could be proved. It would be his word against theirs. And some of it, he believed, might be covered by a statute of limitations.

It was well into the spring before he had his first full meeting in Scully's office with Scully and a barrister called Geary who was a famous figure in the Law Library.

'He is the best for a case like this,' Scully said. 'There isn't anyone to match him.'

Joe felt that if Scully was using the best barrister available, then this was hopeful, it meant that something might be done.

As the meeting began, Joe felt reassured. It was obvious that Geary had gone through the evidence very carefully. His manner was businesslike. And then he spoke.

'My suggestion is that we put in a guilty plea,' he said.

'Put in?' Joe asked.

'Yes. You plead guilty to all the charges.'

Joe said nothing. Geary did not seem to notice his shock. Scully was looking only at Geary.

'And we can get letters saying how marvellous you are, as a teacher, as a friend, et cetera. But we keep these to a minimum.'

'And then?' Joe asked.

'Nothing. You will be sentenced.'

'And then?'

Geary studied the ceiling for a moment as though something there had briefly amused him.

'Then you will serve your sentence.'

'Is this a defence? May I enquire what your strategy is?' Joe asked.

'Indeed you may. In the future, when you are being considered for release, we want nothing that happened in the trial to become an impediment to any remission of the sentence.'

'What type of remission?'

'If you are sentenced to fifteen years, we would like you out in ten.'

Joe set about counting the seconds as if his sentence had already begun.

'What we really want is none of this material I have here to be read out in court and we want the victim statements to be not especially memorable. It is important for example that the parents don't feel compelled to speak.'

Geary found a couple of sheets of paper in the file and read them quietly to himself.

'I don't think the judge would take kindly to the idea of you going on holidays with the whole family and calling in on them at Christmas like a close friend. I think the son will speak, and I hope that's enough.'

'I didn't . . .' Joe began.

'We don't need to hear what you did or didn't do. It's all here. You found a young man who needed help with his maths. And you called to the house. You did that a number of times in a number of houses. It's a pattern. It's all here.'

'Some of them . . .'

'Joe,' Scully said, 'Mr Geary says it's better for you not to deny anything. There's no point in arguing.'

'I mean, it would turn your stomach,' Geary said, having stood up.

When he had gone, Joe turned to Scully.

'There has to be another way of doing this. And I forgot to ask him about the statute of limitations.'

'In cases like this,' Scully said, 'the statute of limitations has been abolished. It wouldn't matter if it was fifty years ago.'

'Was he exaggerating when he said fifteen years?'

'He knows how the courts work. He would not have said that if it were not true.'

'Do you agree with him?'

'It would be foolish not to. That is my experience.'

'How could he be the best if he's not going to do anything?'

'Listen to what he said. Saying nothing, doing nothing will help down the road. It could get a year off the time you serve.'

'I am definitely serving time?'

Scully nodded. Joe decided not to ask him why he, Scully, had been recommended as a solicitor since he seemed so ready to do so little.

Before the trial, Scully advised him to seek early retirement from his teaching job, to suggest to his union representative that he was suffering from a serious nervous ailment and would take a lower pension if he could retire as soon as possible. When Joe was offered a full pension, Scully studied the small print to make sure that the pension could never be taken from him, no matter what sort of sentence was handed down to him. It was this deal that subsequently caused great indignation among the public. 'THE PEDO & HIS PENSION,' the *Sunday World* headline ran.

Scully ensured that, at the beginning, he was not named as the defendant in the case. And Scully found him a safe house when his name was finally published in the *Sunday World* with news that he was still teaching. The authorities had neglected to notify the school even after he was charged.

And it was Scully, having consulted Geary, who advised him not to appeal when it was clear that the judge's remarks before sentencing were less than judicious.

'Stay close to any probation officer they send into you,' Scully said. 'Don't use words like "remorse". Just show remorse. And take your time with them. We are looking at the long perspective.'

With power of attorney, Scully sold Joe's house, having paid someone to clear out its contents. Scully put the money into a bank account. He saw Joe once or twice a year on small legal matters over the ten years he served in Arbour Hill Prison.

* * *

'No matter what we do,' Scully told him before he was freed, 'the press will be outside when you are released. Even if the authorities keep it secret, the prison guards will leak it.'

'Where will I go?' Joe asked.

'That's up to you. Besides some restrictions, you are completely free.'

'To leave the country on the day I get out?'

'As long as you sign on every week at a specific police station that will be agreed on once you are settled somewhere. They will have their own way of doing things. And this Denis Doran, whom I have spoken to twice, said that he could be useful to you if you decided to come to Barcelona.'

'In what way?'

'I didn't ask him. He says he has a bar in the city and he says the address he gave you is the address of the bar.'

Scully must presume, Joe saw, that Denis Doran was an ex-lover or a partner, or even a partner in crime.

'And my passport's OK? I can simply go to the airport?'

'That's fine, and I got you a debit card, but I've had trouble getting you a credit card. New rules in the bank. They need an address for you.'

'I have an address.'

'They won't send it to a jail. And they won't send it to my office.'

Joe was going to ask why it might not be sent to Scully's own home address, but he saw that this would not be on offer.

'There's no one?' Scully asked. 'No family? No—'

'No one.'

'I have a small bag for you,' Scully said. 'It will have your passport and your bank book and your old address book and some papers you need to keep. And some letters. It will be given to you just before you walk out the door. The prison will also give you some money, not much, in cash.'

Joe thought for a second. And then he understood that Scully was letting him know that he himself would not be present when Joe was released from Arbour Hill.

'So, I'll say goodbye then,' Scully said. 'You have the office number if something arises.'

He gathered some papers and put them in his briefcase. He stood up and turned, leaving Joe to go back to the prison workshop.

Joe asked the prison social worker who came to see him some days before his release if she could have a taxi waiting for him outside and book him a room in the most anonymous hotel in Dublin she could think of.

'Maybe your family would know—?' she began.

'I don't have a family.'

It was difficult to get through the crowd of journalists and photographers that had gathered outside the prison gates. And, once the taxi driver discovered who he was, he shouted an abusive remark and drove away. Another taxi had to be called as Joe waited in the reception area. Joe wondered if any hotel would take him since images of him leaving the prison were about to appear everywhere. In the end, the prison governor decided to keep him in a visitors' room for a few hours and then deposit him anywhere he cared to nominate using a prison van. Joe asked the social worker to tell the governor that he should be dropped at any city centre branch of the Bank of Ireland.

In the bank, using his passport to identify himself, he withdrew most of the money in his account in the form of a bank draft.

He then hailed a taxi on the street and made his way to the

airport where, using his debit card, he found a seat on a direct flight to Barcelona that would leave in two hours' time.

No one in the airport recognized him and no one on the plane and no one in Barcelona airport paid him any undue attention.

He caught a bus going to the centre. Since it was June, he could feel the heat as he began to sweat in his stale clothes.

Whatever hotel he chose, he decided, should not give onto a main street, but it should be nondescript, a place where Irish tourists would be unlikely to lodge. He was aware that he might appear strange to a hotel receptionist with no reservation and carrying a single small bag. In a bathroom mirror in the airport, when he had caught a glimpse of himself, it struck him that he did not look unlike a man who had just served a lengthy prison sentence for molesting teenage boys who were under his care as a teacher of mathematics.

Years earlier, he had prided himself as he travelled each year to Italy or southern Spain or Greece on being able to seek out, without using a guidebook or a recommendation, a perfect small hotel, a good cafe, a family-run restaurant. But, as it grew dark in Barcelona, his old talents failed him. He walked along what seemed like a main street and ventured into a narrower street. The few hotels he passed looked precisely like places where Irish tourists would gather. He imagined an entire breakfast room of his fellow countrymen sporting fresh sunburn. It would not be long before one of them called out his name and the others began to hurl insults at him.

It would be better to walk on. As he found himself back in the main street, he made another turn into a more promising-looking narrower street. He passed two small hotels and still could make no decision. And then he realized why he was procrastinating. In prison, he had dreamed of this night without ever putting a name on the city of his first freedom where he would be sleeping in a room with a proper bed and mattress, with lights that he could turn on and off and doors he could open or leave shut.

Now that he was close to having his dream fulfilled, however, he was almost afraid. He could imagine the luxury of a long shower, but the prospect of the hotel room itself, the silence, the softness of things, made him wonder if he would not lie there through the night, sleepless, listening out for every sound, missing the security of his cell.

When he became exhausted, he decided on a hotel he had already passed. Once he was installed, he would not want to move again for at least three or four days.

The hotel had a vacancy. The old man at reception barely bothered to look at him. He checked the passport and swiped the debit card, he handed Joe a form to fill in and then he gave him his key.

He supposed he should ask himself if he were dreaming. Last night he had been locked in a cell. Now he was alone and free in a teeming city. Yesterday he had been watched and guarded. Now no one in the world knew where he was.

He woke and slept and woke again. The room was stuffy; there was a faint smell of mould. And then, as he lay still in the small hours, he caught a whiff of his own shoes and socks, his own sweat-infested clothes. In the morning, he promised himself he would buy new shoes and socks, a new shirt, new underwear.

The following day was a Saturday. He went to a pharmacy where he bought a shaving kit and a toothbrush and toothpaste. He felt drained, unsure if he had actually slept and desperate to return to his room. Even though he was hungry, he refrained from stopping at a cafe on the corner.

* * *

All morning, he found himself going over his years in jail as though this was a story he would need to put a shape on. He remembered that once he had been sentenced and was slowly getting used to conditions at Arbour Hill Prison, Scully came to see him and warned him about probation officers and psychologists.

'One bad report from one of them could take a year off a possible remission. Good behaviour matters, but these reports matter more.'

His fellow inmates were all sex offenders, mostly men of a certain age, with, among them, a good few Christian Brothers in their seventies, doddery old fellows, bewildered-looking. There were some priests, including men who had not been forbidden by the Vatican from saying mass and carrying out their priestly duties. So they said mass quietly, using a tiny amount of wine that had been smuggled in.

The majority of the prisoners, however, were laymen – fathers and husbands, and bachelors like himself. During the day, they went to the workshops or the library; they had classes and training sessions; they gathered in the dining room or they worked in the kitchen; they sat in the reception room or, during recreation, they worked out in the gym or walked in the yard.

And then at night each went alone into a cell. They carried what secrets they had with them, as many would, Joe thought, to the grave. It might be believed that during the night they went over their crimes and considered their victims and felt shame and guilt, but as far as Joe could see, they each had a great distracting topic or obsession – as banal, say, as the excessive noise that came from the prison heating system, or the failure to provide a proper breakfast some days, or a farm they believed they had the deeds to, or the antics of a rogue solicitor, or the denial of day release at Christmas – and that was what preoccupied them most.

No prison psychologist ever stayed long in the job. Joe supposed it was work anyone would dread, listening to these captured men trying to avoid dealing with why they were here. But the meetings had some effect. Joe soon observed how oddly disturbed some of the men were when they came back from an hour with one of the therapists or psychologists, who were usually young women.

'It's bad enough being here without a near-teenager with a social science degree asking me about shame,' one of the priests said.

At the first meeting, Joe saw that the young woman assigned to him had a transcript in front of her of a victim statement.

'Now, Joe,' she said, 'what you're going to do is to see the world not from your own point of view, but from the point of view of one other person and then of two such people and then more. Do you know who I'm referring to?'

Joe glanced at the prison guard who was sitting on a chair by the door looking bored.

'I do,' Joe said.

On the Saturday evening, having spent the day in his hotel room, Joe went to a nearby burger joint, sat with his back to the window with a cheeseburger and fries and a Diet Coke. It was foolish, he knew, not even to have got new socks and underwear, but in the afternoon he had fallen into a sleep so deep and satisfying that he wished to return to it now. It was dreamless and all-embracing, helped on by the heavy air in the room. If he could have that even some nights in the future, he would not want much more, he thought – an intense night's sleep and then the day recovering from it.

But he hardly slept when night came and on Sunday morning when he saw how full the cafes were, he felt frightened. He looked out of place; he knew that. It wasn't just his shoes and his clothes, it was his haircut, his skin, his eyes, everything about him.

In prison, he often wished for an entire day to pass, just be nothing, be over. He did not ever imagine that he could feel this on release. Surely it would be the opposite. However, he felt it now. He went back to his room and lay on his bed. He was wide awake.

On the notepad beside the bed he wrote a list of what was most urgently needed. A laptop computer. A mobile phone. New shoes and clothes. A haircut. A Kindle.

And then he wrote: 'To make contact with Denis Doran.'

If he set out walking with a map, he thought, he might find the bar whose address Denis Doran had sent and also locate a street that might have shops that opened on a Sunday.

Once he crossed a square, he saw that he was in Carrer de la Princesa and that the Shamrock Shore had to be close by. He passed an Irish pub whose large-screen TV was showing a Gaelic football match. If his face had been all over the newspapers and the television screens on Friday, then Irish people who travelled to Barcelona the next day might now be sitting in this very pub.

Just as he contemplated turning back, he saw that he was directly in front of the Shamrock Shore and when he peered inside he saw that Denis Doran was sitting at the bar with his back to a partition, facing outwards. He seemed to be nursing a large cup of tea or coffee. He had changed, of course, but he could not be mistaken for anyone else. Then Joe realized that all

Denis had to do was look up and he would catch sight of his old friend as a most dishevelled fellow. He moved out of Denis's line of vision.

The following evening Joe, having had a haircut and bought new clothes, came back to find Denis in exactly the same position, once more nursing a large white cup. Denis stood up when he saw him and invited him to join him at the bar.

They talked at first about nothing much. Every so often Joe noticed Denis studying him, staring at him openly.

'So, how long are you staying here?' Denis asked.

It struck Joe that Denis Doran presumed he had somewhere to go, that he had no inkling that the only friendly letter he had received was from Denis himself and that Joe had understood the letter to be a kind of invitation.

'I don't have many options,' Joe said.

Denis took him in calmly. Clearly, he had no idea how much Joe, in his mind, had come to depend on him. It would not do to blurt out that he had, in fact, nowhere to go. He was here without a word of the language. Today, when he had attempted to open a bank account, he had been met with puzzlement. The bank draft he had was for eight hundred thousand euro. In the bank, as it was passed around by the staff, each one looked at it doubtfully.

'I tried to set up a bank account today,' Joe said. 'But before I do anything I have to have an address.'

'You're not going home to Ireland, so,' Denis said. 'No, I don't suppose you are.'

If he did not speak now, Joe knew, he would regret it.

'I need an address in Barcelona to open a bank account. I can't do anything without an address. They won't accept a hotel address.'

He knew he was sounding too desperate and asking for too much. He hadn't even finished the glass of sparkling water he had ordered. When Denis ordered another cup of tea, Joe watched him judiciously squeeze the quartered lemon into the hot water, with the string of the tea bag dangling down the side of the cup. Joe noticed he was wearing a wedding ring.

If this had been years before, Joe thought, and if Denis had sought to open a bank account in Ireland, Joe would have offered him all the help he could. He observed Denis considering what he might do. Obviously, he was not going to offer Joe his home address.

'Let me think about the bank,' Denis said. 'Can I call you or text you?'

'I don't have a phone yet. I have to get one.'

He felt an urge to go back to the hotel and curl up on the floor with a blanket over his head. But he knew that if he were seen to behave erratically, Denis Doran would judge him to be a potential nuisance.

'I have to get a phone, a laptop and a bank account,' Joe said. He sounded, he hoped, businesslike. He was determined that he would not discuss his plight any further with Denis.

It might be more fruitful if they started to reminisce about Maynooth. He asked Denis if he had ever regretted leaving.

'I always thought I'd like to say mass,' Denis said. 'You know, have the power. But it wasn't to be. It is a long road that knows no turn.'

Before he left, Joe gave Denis the name of his hotel and his room number in case he had any ideas about the bank. He was tempted to tell him how much the bank draft was for.

In the morning, when he returned from searching for a shop that sold laptops, there was a note at reception from Denis

Doran giving him the address of a bank and the name of an official who would look after him. This man, Denis wrote, had all the details.

It was strange to meet a man who was openly and casually friendly. As the official accompanied him to an inner office, Joe was unsure how long it had been since someone had spoken to him in this way. Even if prison guards were on occasions friendly, they maintained a distance. The atmosphere could easily darken. A few times when he grew close to a fellow inmate, the friendship had all too quickly become fraught and would end in recrimination, once even in violence.

He handed over the bank draft to be told that it could take two weeks or more to go through. When he did a quick calculation, he saw that the money in his debit account would be used up in a week, even when he factored in the pension payment that came in every fortnight. He was lucky he had not bought a laptop or he would have nothing left. He should think about moving to a smaller and cheaper hotel. But even then he might not have enough money.

He had become so exercised with adding up sums of money that he did not hear the official trying to get his attention.

'Are you all right?' he asked.

'I presumed that the money in the bank draft would come through immediately.'

'It depends on your bank, how soon they release the money.'

'It has already left my account. It is not a personal cheque.'

'Yes, but the money has to arrive here. As soon as it does, I'll let you know.'

When Joe explained that he might change hotel, the man expressed surprise that he was in a hotel.

'I thought you were actually living in Barcelona?'

'I am,' Joe said. 'But I might need to move into a hotel for meetings, you know.'

The official nodded but Joe could see that he did not believe him.

Denis Doran sat in the Shamrock Shore like the captain of a ship. Soon, Joe came to understand that he was not always in need of company. If Joe was passing by and saw him at the bar, facing the door, he would look in, but Denis would often, by raising a hand as though to push him away, emphasize that now was not the time.

Often, he was busy dealing with the staff or on the phone to suppliers. He had an office but he preferred, he said, to run things from his perch at the bar.

Sometimes he could be all talk and useful advice.

'There are a few Australians running real estate agencies here. They are the best ones for you to deal with.'

Joe had managed to stay in the hotel until the bank draft came through by avoiding the manager and not replying to messages about his overdue bill. If the money had arrived one or two days later, he would have already been out on the street.

Although Denis remained friendly, he let Joe know that there were barriers. He referred only once to his 'missus' and his kids and a house they had in the Empordà; he never mentioned them again and he left no opening for Joe to ask about them. He did not encourage the conversation to be personal. He followed Irish politics and Spanish politics closely. He seemed to know a great deal about the Vatican and spoke of some of the Irish bishops like old friends.

'The ones that trained in Rome of course are the best, not in the Irish college, mind you, but in the other colleges. If I had been sent to the German college, I probably would have stayed.

I'd be an archbishop now. Would you have stayed if they had promised to send you to Rome?'

'I don't think so,' Joe replied.

'Were there many diocesan clergy in with you?'

'In where?'

'Where do you think?'

'A few, yes, a few.'

On subsequent visits, Denis quizzed Joe about the priests and brothers who had served time in Arbour Hill. Were there any Franciscans? What about Blackrock? Any priests from Blackrock?

Slowly, as they got to know each other, Joe saw how much detail Denis wanted him to go into. He began to understand that Denis's curiosity on the subject was insatiable; he wondered if this was why Denis had got in touch with him in the first place. Each time they met, his friend would guide their talk back towards life for the imprisoned clergy in Arbour Hill. Often, he would start by discussing something else and then nudge the conversation to the prison.

'Sunday is a long day. I often find it long. Do you find it long?'

Joe agreed that it could be long.

'I'd say it was long inside.'

Or he would mention the Christian Brothers, if a vocation to be a Brother was a real vocation.

'Did you know any of them well?' he would enquire.

When Joe went first to the police station with the relevant papers and his passport to sign the register of sex offenders, the young policeman at the main desk shrugged when Joe asked him if he spoke English and shrugged once more as he perused the documents. The policeman seemed not to understand. Finally, he looked at Joe straight in the face and grinned.

'No speekee,' he said in a mocking tone.

As Joe tried to explain his plight to Denis, he realized that Denis was becoming uncomfortable. While he wanted to hear as much as possible about defrocked priests and disgraced Christian Brothers, he did not want to hear about Joe's problems with the police in the city here and now.

Nonetheless, Denis opened his phone and scrolled down some numbers.

'I can call a man, a solicitor, and he'll do it. He'll go with you to the station. But I need to ask one thing. Is there anything I don't know about this business? I don't want any surprises.'

'It's exactly what I said it is.'

'Well, that's bad enough.'

Joe, using an Australian recommended by Denis, eventually located the apartment he wanted: on a top floor, with one bedroom and a living room with a balcony looking out onto the street.

'Hardly any of the locals live on their own,' Denis had said. 'At least not by choice. It's only foreigners who will queue for one-bedroom apartments. It helps that you don't need a mortgage. You can pay the last hundred thousand in actual cash.'

'That will not be a problem.'

As Christmas approached, Joe found himself asking Denis, as a way of breaking the silence one day, if Barcelona city closed up completely on Christmas Day, if it was like Ireland. Once he had spoken, however, he realized that his motive for posing the question was being misconstrued. Denis, it was clear, believed that Joe was fishing for an invitation to his home for Christmas. There was a blank expression on his face as he gazed towards the street. There was nothing Joe could say that would save the moment.

'I don't think so, young Joseph, I don't think so. The missus wouldn't have it. It's as simple as that.'

They left silence for a while. Denis ordered more tea. He took his time squeezing the lemon into the hot water.

'But it's a nice time of the year in Barcelona. The market around the cathedral is nice. Yes, the city is nice then.'

Joe was surprised at how early spring came to the city, how quickly the chill eased in the air and how soon the strawberries appeared in the market. At about four o'clock in the afternoon the front part of his living room filled with sunlight. He could open the balcony door, move the armchair and sit in the mild heat reading a book on his Kindle.

He got such satisfaction from buying even the smallest item for the apartment that he had to ration purchases. He wrote out lists of what he might need. He had money left over from buying the apartment and he planned to use some of that for acquiring a good music system and a large-screen TV. His regular bills he paid from his debit card, using the pension that still came in every two weeks into his bank account in Dublin.

He wanted his life to be orderly. In general, restaurants did not welcome lone diners, especially at the weekend. At first, he had tried to cook, boiling vegetables and frying pieces of meat. But he could not get it right. He thought back to the time when he lived alone in his own house and had his own kitchen but his efforts to recall his life there, his habits, caused him a sudden sharp anguish.

Deciding not to bother cooking made him feel better. He found a shop that sold fresh pasta and take-away salad dishes. If he was hungry, there was always bread and cheese and salami. He did not touch alcohol.

Often, he went to the cinema. The English-language films

were not dubbed into Spanish. The screenings allowed him to forget everything else. He could not be spotted since he was in the dark. He could become nobody. But it was difficult to face the city afterwards. He became afraid as he made his way back home, worrying about crossing the street even if the lights were red, becoming easily irritated if someone was standing in his path.

A few blocks away from the apartment, there was a street that had traditional small family restaurants. The one he liked, run by a husband and wife, opened at eight for dinner but did not have its first clients until close to nine, especially on weeknights. He realized that they wouldn't mind him coming on his own so long as he was gone by nine and did not appear at the weekend. He sat with his back to the door and did not order anything too expensive. Slowly, the couple and the young waiter came to appreciate his tastes and habits.

Denis, he learned, lived in his moods, often growing bored or increasingly combative. If the waiter was from Andalusia, he might begin an argument about how inferior life in southern Spain was. Or he would needle a Catalan customer about the Catalan character. Or he would inform an Irish tourist that Gaelic football was a game best played by savages and Kerrymen. Or he might have a newspaper spread out in front of him and be immune to interruption.

'From what I can see, there is a world war coming that will outlast us all. What do you think?'

Or he would stare glumly into the distance.

'Let's not talk today. But sit here. Don't go away. Keep me company.'

Joe would take the newspaper and try to decipher the front

page. On his laptop each morning he took a Spanish lesson, but it was hard to see any resemblance between what he was learning and what he heard on the street and it did not help him to understand a headline in the newspaper.

Often, as expected, the conversation with Denis returned to Arbour Hill.

'It still amazes me,' Denis said. 'Preaching to the faithful one minute. In handcuffs the next. The Penal Laws indeed!'

Joe told him about the arrival of a Jesuit in the prison and his joining with a theologian to set up a study group called 'Philosophy versus Theology'.

'We got all the books and I was reading away. We did two seminars, but the governor put a stop to it, just like that. I never learned why.'

'Ah, it's a well-known thing,' Denis said. 'Prison governors don't like open enquiry.'

'What do you mean?'

'Imagine even the possibility that some things are relative. What would happen to the absolute – to the key, to the lock, to the cell, to the heavy sentence? In Maynooth, I was writing a thesis on moral relativism, showing its flaws, when I saw the light and got the hell out of there.'

'I only got as far as the paradox of faith,' Joe said.

'I grew to hate some words,' Denis said. '"Paradox" was one and "dichotomy" was another. One of the great things about this bar is that you never hear those words, or not when people are sober.'

Joe asked himself if Denis remembered the room in that bed and breakfast in Cork and the doorway in Dublin all those years before. Denis had not been shy or timid. Joe wondered if he went home to his missus and his kids directly from here each evening.

There must be times when other things came into his mind and there were, it was obvious, plenty of opportunities in these streets.

'Do you ever feel sorry for what you did?' Denis asked.

Joe had the impression that Denis was playing with him. This was just another way for him to while away the afternoon.

'I mean really sorry,' Denis added, 'for your victims.'

'I am sorry I was found out,' Joe said.

It was like a flash of temper, a moment when his guard was down. For years, he had watched every word. He had made sure to control himself. When the money from his bank draft was delayed and he had to go to the bank in Barcelona day after day, he felt a rage that was new to him. But he knew not to say a word. Only once, in a phone call to the bank in Dublin, did his temper emerge.

What he had said now, in response to Denis's question, was not uttered in temper. Rather, it had sprung out, unconsidered. He could hardly take it back or soften it. He could not suggest that he was joking.

'It's refreshing when someone speaks the truth,' Denis said. 'You don't often hear it.'

Halfway through his sentence, some things changed in the prison. He was alerted to this by the Jesuit.

'There's a new one on the beat here. She's a type of psychologist. She's not to be trifled with. She smiles and she looks nice. Watch her. That's all I have to say. Watch her.'

Joe only recalled this when he was sitting at a table opposite this woman for the first time.

'I've been looking through your file,' the woman said. 'I have the victim statements and your statement. It must be all fresh in your mind?'

She waited for a reply.

'It's a good few years ago,' Joe said. 'But, yes, it's fresh. Yes, it is.'

'I have one of the victim statements here,' she said. 'And I wonder if you could read it for me, just so we're clear about things.'

She handed Joe two sheets of paper.

'Out loud, please.'

'Out loud?'

'If you don't mind.'

Once he began, Joe was determined that he would not falter, and then he worried that he might be sounding too matter-of-fact. He had not forgotten the young man's statement. He thought that it had been given off the cuff but now it sounded more formal, like evidence. The man had, in one part of the statement, gone into detail and, as he read, Joe taught himself to feel that these were merely words, they were like other words, even if their import was excruciating, even if it seemed preposterous that anything like this had happened at all, let alone that it had been done by him, by Joe, in a real day to the person who had remembered it vividly and recounted it with such clarity.

'How do you feel when you read this?' the woman asked him when he had finished.

'I feel what I feel every day. I feel . . .'

He stopped and looked down at his hands.

She left silence, flicking through pages in the file. Then she glanced up and smiled.

'It's plain from the file that you were a great teacher. I see this: "He could get anyone through pass maths in the Leaving." That is what one of your character witnesses says. "He was dedicated." That must make you feel proud.'

'It was nice to hear at the time.'

'I suppose what I want you to think about, if you would, is whether you are the much-loved dedicated teacher who happened to abuse some of his students, the ones to whom he was giving maths grinds free of charge, or whether you are the abuser, dedicated also, who happened to be a brilliant teacher. Is the abuse – and some of the victims' statements are really shocking – who you are, or is it something you did?'

'That's too much like a philosophical question. My days—'

'It's a simple question.'

The Jesuit said it was like being a mouse in a room with a cat.

It lasted for a year, this monthly interrogation.

Joe thought for a while that it was worse than sitting in court to hear the victims read their statements and later coming back for sentencing, but he was wrong. It wasn't worse. It was in a private room and he could follow her line of thought and decide, as he wished, not to resist her. She wanted him, as the Jesuit said, 'to inhabit his guilt'. Her report on him could keep him in Arbour Hill for longer, or have him released with full remission.

While some of her colleagues had made use of a prearranged, formulaic process, this young woman, slight in build and almost delicate, did not. She could come up with the most unsettling questions. Joe asked the Jesuit if this was the system they had used in the Inquisition.

'It was indeed,' the Jesuit said. 'But they would burn you and pull you asunder in between.'

One day the young woman asked him if he were to sum up his life, how would it be.

He spoke slowly, trying out a tone of considered certainty.

'I am a man who in an intimate and invasive way ruined the lives of some young men. I did what I did for pleasure without any consideration for my victims. That is who I am. I did other things too, but these pale into insignificance against the fact of what I did as an abuser.'

None of this was new; these words and phrases had already been used in their conversations. But he had never spoken like this before in full, declarative sentences. He guessed that it was precisely what she wanted to hear and he should have been relieved.

But his words, so finely tuned, had, in the days immediately following, as he allowed his saying of them to sink in, given him no relief.

In the silence of his cell, he wanted to put the episode out of his mind, hoping that it might merely serve to help his case for release.

It was only now, after his conversation with Denis, that the feeling came back of the unending gap between what others saw in him, in all its solidity, and what he believed about himself, in all its confusion. His reply to Denis's question had been too glib. It had served no purpose. He should not speak like that or think in that way, even if what he said in the second when he had lost all caution was as close to a clear statement of the case as he would ever have the courage to make.

The encounter with Denis and the memories it evoked aged him, he thought, or maybe the humidity in the city as May gave way to June forced him to walk more slowly or made him tired more easily.

So when the pass for the city bikes came, he determined he would use the bike to free-wheel towards the beach; he would not pedal back uphill until he felt more energetic.

At first, he was nervous about taking a swim. If someone stole his clothes, he would be helpless. No one else had a key to his apartment. He saw, however, that if he kept his belongings near the shore and did not turn his back on them for too long, then he could go into the water.

And then afterwards he could lie in the sun, trying to keep all thoughts away, concentrating on the heat, the ease. And then the journey home by metro, relieved at the knowledge that, as a year had passed since his arrival, Irish tourists might be less likely to recognize him.

The restaurant where he went each weekday evening decided to redecorate, so his usual table had been taken away. They asked him very politely if he would mind, just for a week or two, sitting towards the front at a small table with just one chair that looked out onto the street. Even now, any small act of kindness or use of a considerate tone could lift his spirits and make him feel grateful.

He did wonder, however, why they had not shut the restaurant completely while the work was going on or why they had not waited until August when many similar restaurants closed.

One evening, when the air was heavy, he arrived as the decoration work was ending. He could smell the dust lingering in the air. He sat at the new table they had assigned to him and, after a long wait, the wife came and took his order, putting his usual bottle of sparkling water on the table.

In the sea that day, there had been a steep ridge of sand just where the waves broke. It had surprised him, made him lose his footing. He had retreated to his towel and his belongings afraid to return to the water until he saw others falling at the same precise point. He was relieved that it was something that had not happened only to him.

As he was thinking about this, he noticed a woman passing on the street outside and then coming back and peering into the restaurant. She had blonde hair and was wearing bright clothes.

Her skin was red with mild sunburn. She moved forward and called to someone and then turned and gazed directly at him. Soon, she was joined by two others.

He looked down and, glancing up again, put on his glasses. They were talking animatedly among themselves, the three of them — the sunburned woman, another woman of around the same age, and a man whose accent when his voice rose was unmistakably Irish.

'Oh that's him,' the man said. 'That's him, that's him.'

The sunburned woman was scrolling down on her phone while the other woman fixed her eyes on him.

Just then, as the waiter came with his main course, Joe spoke to him in what he hoped sounded like fluent Spanish. He concentrated on his food. Once, when he lifted his head, he saw that the three of them were still there. They were deciding what to do. He was trying, on the other hand, to become invisible.

They could shout if they wanted. He would not move or pretend he understood a word. He was safe so long as he remained in the restaurant. When he ventured into the street, however, they could attack him and insult him with impunity. Perhaps they were already texting others or getting ready to take photographs.

If he worried about them too much or worked out too detailed a strategy, he believed that he might begin to appear vulnerable. So he thought about the beach and the ridge of sand where the waves broke. He imagined the warm sun on his body and then he dreamed of his apartment. The sun would have faded now, but he could stand at the balcony when he got home, as many of his neighbours did at this time, and take in the street below, see the swifts threading frantically through the air and know that this was merely the start of the summer, there would be many such evenings.

When the waiter asked him if he wanted the bill, he nodded. He would pay and leave. He would pass by these three strangers, still outside the door of the restaurant, as if he were someone else entirely. Nothing they would say or do could matter. He would make his way slowly home. They could follow him if they wanted; he would not look behind.

The Catalan Girls

The security door was strong and made of metal bars. Now, for the second time, someone had put glue into the lock. Before, she had managed to scoop out the hardened glue with a pair of scissors, but this time nothing worked. It was a hot Saturday in February. Montse phoned the two locksmiths in Chivilcoy but there was no answer from either of them. When she called the police station, a man's voice asked her what exactly she wanted them to do.

'I told you,' she said, 'I am locked inside my own house.'

'Is it an emergency? Do you need to go to hospital, for example?'

She put down the receiver, without replying. Until now, she had felt safe living in this cul-de-sac and was content when her neighbour on the left, Fonso Garay, who was nosy, had moved to an old people's home, leaving his house empty. On the other side was Manu Fontana, who growled in low Italian each time he saw her approach. She had used his bin to deposit much of her rubbish. It had taken him a year to catch her in the act. She had promised never to do it again, but he must realize that she had never had any intention of keeping her word.

If she saw him passing and called out to him, he would not help her. He did not like her; he would be happy to see her, as she was now, behind bars.

She had no choice but to wait until Monday morning and then call the locksmiths again. There was enough food for two days. She should relax, she thought, not worry, and the time would go by quickly.

Saturday, however, passed slowly. She could not stop herself trying the scissors several times more. Having failed to open the gate, she stood behind it like a trapped animal gazing solemnly at the high, blank walls on the other side of the street.

On Sunday afternoon, she was tempted to call her sister Núria in Buenos Aires. She knew that Núria usually went to the cinema at around six o'clock each Sunday. Perhaps she should phone before then and see what Núria had to say.

Now that her husband was dead, Núria's son Alejandro looked after the family business with a mixture of flair and prudence, as Núria told Montse the last time they had spoken. That was when the roof of her house was leaking and Montse had asked Núria for a loan of money that had been refused at first and then sent as a cheque in an envelope with no note inside.

But what could Núria know about locks that Montse did not know? The news that her sister was stranded would only confirm how superior Núria was, how all the intelligence and charm had come to her rather than her two unfortunate sisters. She would contact Núria, Montse thought, only if she needed money. That was not what she needed now.

As Sunday night descended and the smell of cooking from Manu Fontana's wafted into her house, Montse thought about what she would do if a fire broke out. She saw herself desperately calling into the empty street, the smoke growing denser and the fire becoming more menacing. She imagined herself down on her knees screaming for help, her hands clinging to the bars of the guard door.

She must calm down. Why would a fire break out? Nothing would happen. She was locked into her own house, that was all. She decided she would feel safer if she remained in the living room until morning. She sat in her usual armchair with only the small lamp near the television turned on. She closed her eyes and convinced herself that if she slept for a while, she would be in better condition to deal with the locksmith once the morning came.

Most evenings when she came back here, Montse imagined what life would be like if she were her sister Núria. She sat in the armchair as Núria might sit and asked, in Núria's voice, one of the servant girls for tea, or reached for the telephone so she could speak to her son at his office.

She often walked home from work as though she were Núria on her way home from the cinema. She imagined a mirror in the hallway and checked her hair as she made her way into the house. She must really try that new lipstick she had seen the advertisement for! And, when she had taken her shoes off, she sat down in the armchair in the dingy room. She closed her eyes. It was time to relax. Núria's shopping sprees often exhausted her. Montse dozed for a while, trying to dream what Núria might dream.

It occurred to her how different her life would be now if, fifty years earlier, her widowed mother had not made an abrupt decision to take her three daughters – Núria, aged fifteen, Conxita, aged twelve, and Montse, aged ten – to Argentina.

While her mother had cousins in Argentina, they were in the

interior somewhere. Once contacted, they offered hospitality, but were sure that the prospects outside Buenos Aires for a middle-aged woman with few skills were limited.

The person who helped them settle in Argentina was not a relative but a Sacred Heart nun who came from a village in the Pyrenees near Burg, the place where Montse's mother had been born. Their aunt Julia had got an address for this nun, Sister Teresa, from her relatives. She wrote to her. Within a few weeks, a reply came saying that the nun would be pleased to help the widow and her three daughters in any way she could.

By the time they arrived in Argentina, Núria had grown tall and developed a poise that impressed anyone who met her. Montse noticed her watching the Pan Am air hostesses, observing how elegantly they moved, and how perfectly their hair was tied in a bun at the back, imitating how they smiled in a way that was warm but also dignified and distant.

'They are like dancers,' Núria whispered to her mother.

'I would love to be an air hostess,' Montse said.

'In future, there is a ban on you listening to our conversation,' Núria said. 'You would love to be nothing.'

Montse appealed to their mother for support, but their mother was, once more, rummaging in her handbag, sure she had forgotten something.

Throughout the aeroplane journey from Lisbon to the stopover in Brazil, Conxita went from one of the tiny bathrooms to the other, coming back to marvel at the liquid soap and the free perfume.

'I would like to fly on this plane back and forth, back and forth,' she said.

'I'm sure Pan Am would get tired of you very quickly. They probably have a policy against people like you,' Núria said.

'What kind of policy?'

'One that is well considered.'

The plane landed with a great shudder at the stopover in Brazil. As they were herded off, forced to take all their belongings with them, and then herded back on again, Montse wished she had been left behind in Barcelona or handed over to her aunt in the Pyrenees for safe keeping like a package.

And then, on the last leg of the journey, it seemed more satisfying to dream that she was there – in their old apartment or her old school or in one of the houses in Burg that her aunt often visited. She would love to be asked by one of her aunt's neighbours which of the sisters she was, and to be told that she had grown since last year's visit. Soon she would be as tall as Conxita.

In Buenos Aires, the first hotel room they stayed in had only two beds. Her mother and Conxita shared one. In the other, Núria forced her to curl up at the bottom, avoiding Núria's feet. She cried when Núria kicked her.

'She is a liability,' Núria said.

'Soon we'll have plenty of beds,' their mother said. 'And there will be no need for crying.'

'Could she be sent to those relatives we are meant to have?' Núria asked.

'I have other things to worry about,' their mother said. 'We have to see this nun. I don't suppose there is anything she can do for us, but she is our last chance.'

'Can we not just go home?' Conxita asked.

'Who will pay for the tickets?' their mother replied.

Later, Montse was unsure if Núria had actually interjected to ask them to leave her here if they were planning to go home, or if she had guessed what was in her sister's mind.

In her first meeting with their mother, Sister Teresa told her that the school she taught in was, sadly, fully booked up, being one of the hardest to enrol in. But when her mother brought Núria to the next meeting, the nun seemed to change her mind.

'I don't know what Núria did,' their mother reported, 'because she appeared to do nothing. And it wasn't anything she said, because she just said hello and thanked the nun for seeing us. I suppose she said nothing wrong. Maybe that is what she did.'

'I thought she was a formidable individual,' Núria said, 'and I made sure that she understood how much I appreciated her.'

Conxita did a brief imitation of a cross-eyed person as a way of mocking her sister.

'Darling, I told you not to do that,' her mother said. 'If the wind were to change, you would stay like that. And I can tell you one thing: antics like that will not be appreciated by Sister Teresa. She is, as your sister says . . .'

'A most formidable individual,' Núria said.

When it was agreed that their mother could visit the school with all three girls, she instructed the two younger ones to follow their sister's example in every way.

'Look at the nun directly when she speaks to you,' she said.

Sister Teresa, having shown them around the building, took them to a private room for refreshments.

'I gave my life to God,' she said, 'and I have never regretted it. But I miss hearing the Catalan language spoken, and so it will be a comfort to me to have the girls here in the school. I will slip them in. If anyone asks you how you managed it, refer them to me.'

'We will be very tactful,' Núria said.

They moved to another cheap hotel. The room this time had

four beds and Núria took the one nearest the window. One day, when their mother came back from a further meeting with the nun, she told them that Sister Teresa had been under the illusion that they had money and had come into the room with a bill for the fees written out in a neat hand.

'Seemingly, Núria gave the impression we were rich.'

'I didn't give any impression,' Núria replied.

'Maybe that was how you impressed her. In any case, I told her I was a poor widow. She seemed a bit surprised, to say the least. I think she uttered the Lord's name under her breath. And she asked me why I didn't stay at home where at least I had relatives and friends. And when I told her that I thought we would have a better life in Buenos Aires, that I had heard great things about Argentina, and I was hoping to get a job soon, she looked at me like I was mad.'

'But what did she say?' Núria asked.

'Nothing at all. She left me in the room on my own for more than an hour. She said she went to the chapel to pray. I suppose she got inspiration for a long speech she made.'

'But what did she say?' Núria asked again.

'That only in the rarest cases do they ever let a girl into the school without paying fees. But by good fortune, or because of God's will, the sister who controls admissions is on retreat with the Reverend Mother, which was why you could be quietly admitted in the first place. For the moment, she said, no one would notice that you have not paid fees, and she would not eject you, having agreed to take you. But she doesn't know for how long. She kept saying what a shock it was. She thought we had money. I told her we had none at all.'

'Did she say anything else?' Núria asked.

'Once she started talking, she couldn't be stopped. And she has the sort of accent you don't hear any more, even in the most far-flung village in the high Pyrenees. She sounds like one of those farmers' wives, the ones who haggle about prices at the market. And she doesn't know how she will explain to the other nuns why she enrolled three poor girls. She could hardly tell them it was because you speak Catalan. She now thinks that was mad and is quite happy to speak in Spanish and forget about Catalan completely. I didn't know where I was with her. But you are still going to the school. We have to get the uniform for all three of you before we run out of money completely.'

'Did the nun really think we were rich?' Montse asked.

'I don't know what she thought,' her mother replied. 'She is confused. Maybe it is that time of life for her. But she is letting you into the school.'

The following day, when a message came to the hotel requesting her mother to call the convent, the sisters were sure that the offer to take them as pupils was about to be revoked. Instead, Sister Teresa told her mother that, having made many enquiries, she had found a place that might employ her. It was a depot for spare parts for cars that needed someone to look after invoicing and to answer the phone and pass on messages. 'You will be dealing with a lot of desperate people in garages all over the province,' Sister Teresa said, 'looking for spare parts to be delivered urgently. And don't ask me how I know all this. What I can say is that we have a gardener and if anything moves in the entire Distrito Federal, then he knows about it. He is the one who found out that this job is available. People like doing favours for nuns so they have agreed to hold the job. I told him you were very polite but were afraid of no one. I hope that is true.'

'Does this gardener think you are some kind of mechanic?' Núria asked.

'I should have told her that you would be better for the job,' their mother said. 'You are very polite and afraid of no one.'

'Who is very polite?' Conxita asked.

'You are the essence of rudeness,' Núria said.

That evening, Montse studied her sister closely to see if she could create the same impression as Núria. She noticed that her sister did not smile even when something funny was said.

Their mother went to the hairdresser's before she went to see her prospective employers. She made sure she looked as elegant as her limited wardrobe allowed. The salary offered was low, but it would enable them, she said, to manage for the moment.

Before the girls started school, their mother found an apartment in a single-storey house in Retiro that had been divided into three. At first, she was so happy to be out of the cramped hotel room that Montse did not mind that there was only one bedroom, to be shared between the three sisters, with their mother making a bed for herself each evening on a mattress on the floor in the corner of the living room.

At school, the three girls learned not to tell anyone where they lived. Since their schoolmates spoke of tennis clubs and swimming clubs and skiing holidays, they gave accounts of their lives in Barcelona and their holidays in the Pyrenees. Because Sister Teresa was respected and feared, and the three new girls were favoured by her, they were included as much as possible in the life of the school.

They were known from the beginning as the Catalan girls. Among themselves and to Sister Teresa, they spoke in Catalan, but with others they used a Spanish that even the teachers had trouble understanding.

When girls sought to place her socially, asking her what her father did for a living, Montse replied that her father would be joining them before long. Soon, there were other questions – about clothes and holidays and why their mother seemed to have no car. Later, she saw that it was better to avoid conversations with her fellow pupils.

Quickly, Núria separated herself from her sisters, walking from the bus to the school by a different route, trying to speak Spanish with an Argentine accent, finding friends of her own age and getting herself invited to their houses.

Their mother's employer agreed to pay for a phone line to be connected in the apartment so they could locate her if there was an emergency in the evening or a weekend. Soon, Núria's new friends began to call, boys as well as girls. At the weekend, Núria had a rich social life but Montse saw how precarious her sister's position was. If anyone learned the truth about them, she believed, no one would invite Núria anywhere.

Núria developed a new way of ignoring not only her sisters but her surroundings. She behaved as if she were elsewhere. If she were to speak to her sisters, Montse knew that she would emphasize that she did not want to hear them or see them and that her progress in the new country would be fatally impeded by any association with them. They were no one; she was everyone. If they did not realize that, then they were even more foolish than Núria had ever guessed.

They waited for Sister Teresa to tell them that they would have to leave the school once the term had ended. Montse knew that Núria must have a plan for this eventuality. She would do anything to stay. Montse prayed that the nuns would take pity on Núria. Herself and Conxita could go to any school, but not her older sister.

Although Núria was meant to be afraid of nothing, Montse knew that she dreaded this news. But it never came. Sister Teresa never got in touch with her mother about the fees. They went to school each day as though it were the most normal thing to do. Montse wondered if Núria had done anything or said anything, but she did not think so. Nothing had happened to cause them to be asked to leave. Maybe Sister Teresa had strange powers or else, Montse thought, she remained confused.

One day, as Montse was leaving the school building, she found herself almost in step with a girl in Núria's class. Since the girl was older, they walked together without saying much. Montse was ready to lag behind if she felt that the older girl didn't want to be seen with her.

'You are so lucky,' the girl said. 'My father says that owning land is the only thing.'

Montse did not know where this was leading.

'And my father also thinks that there is a great future in Mendoza wine. But you have to have the expertise. So your father is in the right place. When will you be joining him?'

Núria must have been making things up about the family.

'Soon,' Montse said. 'Soon.'

Núria's absences and her refusal to deal with her sisters, even putting up a curtain around her own bed, meant that Montse and Conxita were often alone with each other. They sought each other out at breaks in school and walked home together. They did not try to make friends among their classmates. When they spoke Spanish, neither made any effort to change her accent. Conxita even made fun of the Argentine accent. They were, for the moment, quite content to be different.

But this did not continue beyond their second year in the new country when they broke off contact with each other in public. In school, Conxita avoided Montse if she could. On the street, if she came across Montse, she would turn away. Conxita, like Núria, attempted to fit in. When Montse tried to follow her example, she became nervous and awkward and soon gave up. She had no real friends. It was not that girls didn't like her; rather, it was that they didn't notice her. She wasn't there. She found lessons difficult and never seemed to have the right books or be on the same page as everyone else.

Núria told them nothing, but she shared her hopes for social advancement with her mother. She left school after two years and trained as a typist and secretary. With the help of Sister Teresa, whose admiration for her had only increased, she got a job in an import-export firm whose offices were in a modern building in the city centre. While she handed over a part of her salary to her mother, most of what Núria earned was spent on clothes and accessories. After a while, shoes filled the entire bottom of a wardrobe, and a special drawer had to be set aside for her underwear. She had three pairs of sunglasses.

Beside the phone, Núria placed a list of those to whom she wished to speak. If anyone else called, they were to be told that she was not available.

'And I don't mind if they don't believe you, whoever they are.'

Núria's evenings were taken up with dinner or visits to the cinema in the company of a single admirer or with a group whom she favoured at that time. Soon, some of her weekends were spent in country clubs. She excelled at swimming and even played some tennis.

By the time Núria was twenty she could talk with ease about the smartest beaches and the best restaurants at Villa Gesell and Mar del Plata, even though she had never enjoyed a holiday in either place. She informed her mother that she had to pretend to her new social circle that she had suffered an injury while skiing in the Pyrenees and that explained why she could not ski.

When her mother recounted this to Conxita and Montse, Conxita responded, 'Does she not worry that her new friends will find out?'

'Find out what?' their mother asked.

'That she is not who she says she is.'

'But she is who she says she is,' their mother replied. 'Have you seen her as she goes out to meet her friends? She just changes a few details. She is the real Núria. Who else could she be?'

One day, alone in the apartment, Montse answered the phone and was immediately mistaken for Núria. Before she could explain who she was, the caller, a woman, began to talk of some outing from which both she and Núria had been excluded.

'Someone has been talking about us,' the woman said. 'I don't know who. But they wonder why we never invite them to our houses. I have a good reason. Everyone knows how we lost all our money. But we did have money, I think that is the difference. Our parents all knew each other. But you are from a different world. So I know I can maybe get an invite for myself but I can't get one for you. That's why I am calling. But I'm sure you have plenty of other things to do on Saturday.'

'In fact, I was about to contact you to say I'm not available,' Montse said. 'You see, my aunt is coming down from Miami and the whole weekend will be a family affair. These things are sent to try us, but I do love my aunt. Love her to bits. Maybe we can arrange something while she is here. So I'll call you if I get a chance.'

She then hung up gently and calmly.

* * *

Montse woke with a start. She had been dreaming that she was locked in that small apartment in Buenos Aires not because the door was jammed but because there was no door at all. She was moving from room to room in search of an exit but there was none.

It was almost nine thirty on Monday morning. By now, the locksmiths would be working. To her relief, the first call she made was answered and it was arranged that a man would come as soon as possible.

When she phoned the garage, she hoped that the call would be answered by one of the young mechanics, but instead Facundo, the boss, picked up the phone. It would not be a good idea, she thought, to tell him what had actually happened. So, she simply told Facundo that she was sick, too sick to come to work.

'Thank you for letting us know,' Facundo said.

When she did not reply, he left silence for a moment before adding, 'And this is the very day we need you.'

'Well, maybe I can come in the afternoon,' she said. 'Or I hope I can.'

'Hope does not mend a puncture,' he said. 'Hope does not fix a gearbox.'

A while later, the locksmith came and, using a thin screwdriver, cleared glue from the lock, but not enough for the key to turn and open the security gate. He told her that he could work to rid the lock of all the glue, but it would be easy to put more glue into it, if anyone wanted.

'This could be a daily occurrence,' he said.

'I need the security gate,' she replied. 'Otherwise I won't feel safe.'

The locksmith told her that he could replace the lock with a panel of numbers. She could select four numbers as her code and that would be her way of opening the door, instead of using a key.

When he told her how much this would cost, she looked at him coldly.

'What can I do?' she asked.

It was agreed that he would come back at the end of the day and install the new system.

Since she had noticed leaves and bits of paper that had accumulated in the small tiled space between the main door and the security door, Montse decided to spend the morning cleaning it. She fetched a black plastic bag and began to fill it with rubbish. As she did so, she discovered a few envelopes, post that must have fallen to the side on delivery.

The first envelope was from the bank, letting her know the new rate of interest. The second one offered her a subscription to a women's monthly magazine. The third was addressed to Montserrat Capdevila i Grau, her full name. No one knew her by that name, she thought. The envelope was larger than the others; her name and address were neatly typed. The stamp was Spanish. She put the other two envelopes in the plastic bag but this one, the one addressed to her, she slipped into the pocket of her apron. Once she had cleared out all of the rubbish, she would go into the house and read it.

As she turned to enter the house, another moment in the dream from the long night before came to her, something she had not remembered when she woke up. The reason she was desperate to find the door of the apartment was that her mother and Núria and Conxita were going back to Spain. They were waiting for her at the port, they were the last ones to embark. Men were shouting at them that soon the gangplank would be rolled back. They answered that they were waiting for Montse. But even if she found an exit now, Montse knew, and even if she got a taxi directly, it would be too late. They would go without her.

She sat at the kitchen table and forgot about the dream as she opened the envelope. It was a typed letter from Oriol Mas, a solicitor in Sort, a town she knew from her childhood summers spent in the Pyrenees. The letter stated in formal language that the company was searching for her and her sisters Núria and Conxita who were, with her, the beneficiaries of the estate of their aunt, Julia Grau, being her closest living relatives. The letter asked her to respond as soon as possible.

Her aunt Julia, her mother's younger sister, had lived all her life in the family house in Burg in the Pallars in the High Pyrenees. Montse, once they left for Argentina, had written to Julia a few times each year and had always received a reply until about a year before this. Even though she had written twice more, Montse had still heard nothing. She had thought of writing to one of the neighbours whom Julia had mentioned in her letters, but she had not done so. She had presumed that she would hear something about Julia from someone.

And, now, here it was, a typed letter making clear that Julia was dead.

What she remembered most vividly was Julia's kindness and tolerance when they had stayed with her. The girls were required to turn up on time for meals, and help in the house, making sure that everything was clean. But otherwise they could do as they pleased. If Conxita wanted to have a nap after lunch, she was left in peace to do so. If Montse wanted to stay inside with her aunt in the kitchen, then Julia did not send her out to play. And if Núria wanted to venture down to other villages, Julia did not object.

Years later, she was shocked when she heard Núria and her mother deploring conditions in Julia's house. Montse had no memory at all of the absence of electricity that Núria mentioned. She was sure that there were always electric lights, at least in her time. Then her sister complained that hens came into the kitchen and were often to be found in the rooms above.

When Núria said that she could not bring any of her friends to the house, Montse did not know what she was talking about. Everyone in those mountain villages, as far as she remembered, lived as Julia lived. But she did not argue with Núria or her mother, who also expressed her aversion to the house where she herself was brought up. Montse realized that they would hardly want to hear, even if it were true, that her time at Aunt Julia's in Burg was the happiest in her life.

In her sporadic communication with her two sisters, when she had asked them if they knew anything about Julia, they both had replied that they had not been in touch with their aunt for a very long time, Núria expressing surprise that Montse had been maintaining contact.

'I live in the present,' Núria had said on the phone. 'And I look forward to the future. But I think about the past only when it's pleasant. And that aunt of ours and that village and all those hens and the terrible neighbours! I couldn't wait to get away. Why do you try to remind me of the most unpleasant things?'

Montse wondered now what time of year the death might have occurred. She hoped it was in summer when there would have been visitors in Burg and the funeral would not have been too lonely. She hoped, too, that Julia had died in a hospital with plenty of people looking after her, and not alone in the house. She wished she had known that Julia was sick. Not that she could have done anything to help, and not that her sisters would have felt much sympathy, but it would have taken some of the sadness out of hearing the news now.

Even though the sisters and their mother had left fifty years ago, there must be some people still alive in Burg and the villages around who remembered the three girls from Barcelona who came to stay with Julia each summer. But there must be many more, people born since then, who would have no idea who they were. The three sisters would now be like a field returned to forest.

The solicitor would have found Montse's address on one of the letters she had written to Julia. She wondered if there was a time limit on inheritance and if they needed to respond quickly to the letter. If they had inherited Julia's estate, then it would include, she presumed, Julia's house in Burg, the house where they had spent their childhood summers.

Alejandro, Núria's eldest son, would, she was sure, know what to do. He could even telephone Spain if he thought it was urgent. Montse had met Alejandro a few times and found him courteous and trusted that Núria would let him deal with this.

She decided to fold the letter, put it in an envelope and post it to Núria that very afternoon.

When her mother died, the three sisters had gathered for her funeral in Buenos Aires. This was the first time they had been in the same room since Núria's wedding more than twenty years earlier.

Before she met Vicente and agreed to marry him, Núria had done everything she could to flourish in tennis clubs and country clubs. She was always a guest, never a member, but she learned to behave as though she were a member. Montse watched her carefully, wondering if she was as welcome in these clubs as she suggested.

'I have a policy with men,' she told her mother, with Montse listening in the other room, 'to pay close attention to everything they say. I ask intelligent questions and I attend to the answers. And, once I began to apply this system to women as well, I have become very popular. Also, I have let it be known that I will have nothing to do with married men.'

'You are so right,' her mother said.

'Everyone watches a woman like me. And they know in their deepest hearts that I have no money. And I come from nowhere. Nobody is fooled. So why wouldn't I take advantage of a married man who is tired of his wife? And there are young women who would indeed do this – in fact they do nothing else – and good luck to them, that is what I say. But not me. You won't find me cavorting. Keep mixed doubles to the tennis court. I like a single man.'

'Oh yes,' her mother said. 'A single man is a golden treasure.'

'That is how I have triumphed,' Núria said. 'I have always had a single man who wanted me in the club, at the party, in the group. As long as I had him, I had everyone. And I always picked the nice one. And that is how I got where I am today.'

Soon, the name Vicente Rojas appeared at the top of the list of those from whom Núria wanted to receive phone calls. His family was involved in business, Núria told her mother, including real estate and import-export.

'They have a finger in many pies,' she said. 'And Vicente is a trained accountant. He plans to expand the business. He is most charming.'

Because Núria made sure that he never came in person to the apartment, Montse did not meet Vicente until she and Conxita were invited to his family's large apartment near Recoleta Cemetery.

Vicente was like a man from an advertisement, Montse saw; he was young and handsome, exceedingly polite, with an easy smile and very white teeth. The apartment had three large sitting rooms opening onto each other. There were landscape paintings on the walls and rich, colourful rugs on the floor.

Núria had warned her sisters not to ask to go to the bathroom.

'You can do all that before you come to the house. We don't want you snooping. And it is also unseemly for a young woman even to mention the bathroom.'

Since Núria had also warned Montse and Conxita not to speak if they could avoid it, they sat demurely on soft armchairs as a servant carried in a tray with tea and cake. Núria and Vicente spoke about the wedding, Núria making remarks about many of those who were invited.

Each time Núria said anything, Montse glanced at Vicente's mother, wondering if the older woman would display the slightest disapproval of her future daughter-in-law, if she would smile knowingly if Núria spoke too boastfully about the arrangements. But old Señora Rojas smiled in full agreement with everything Núria said.

The older woman spoke only once.

'It is so lovely, so lovely. You remind me so much of myself when I was a bride, Núria. I mean not entirely. Of course I came from money. In fact, I had more money than all the Rojases put together. But I was a girl from the countryside, unspoiled. And just like you, it was all new to me.'

'But I think you have grown into it,' Núria said. 'After all this time it must seem almost natural. I hope I will learn from you.'

Montse could see how at home Núria was here. This was her world even before she came to live in it.

She was surprised at how poised Conxita was. Conxita said nothing, but followed the conversation as though mildly amused.

She was wearing a black-and-white skirt with a cream blouse, which her mother had selected for her.

Of the three sisters, Conxita was the most beautiful. When Montse looked from Núria to Conxita, it was like seeing two versions of the same person. They were both tall and thin-faced, with dark eyes and black hair. But Conxita wore her beauty more lightly. It struck Montse that day that, if Conxita were to spend time in the company of Núria and Vicente and their circle, she would soon have a large number of admirers.

Montse was so busy thinking about Conxita that she found herself standing up and asking where the bathroom was before she remembered that such a request had been forbidden.

Núria rose to accompany her, taking her down a long corridor.

'I have a good mind to pinch you very hard,' she said. 'This is the maid's bathroom and she is very particular so be careful to leave the room the way you found it.'

Montse took her time returning. She looked into a number of bedrooms that were so elaborately tidy that they must, she thought, never be used. Perhaps they were just for display. As they were leaving, Núria followed her into the lift and, with Conxita as witness, pinched her hard on one arm and then on the other.

The wedding party was in one of the best-known country clubs. Some friends of Vicente, Montse thought, surely must have noticed that the bride was represented only by her mother and her two sisters. They appeared to have no friends.

Their mother had been carefully groomed by Núria. Montse wondered if Núria had also given her a tranquilliser since her mother was unusually calm and unresponsive. While some other women were ostentatiously dressed, their mother, in pale pink, looked effortlessly elegant. She could easily have passed for a rich woman.

It seemed strange to Montse that no one asked Conxita to dance when the music began. Conxita sat alone, staring into the distance, appearing content with things, but also remote. She lived in her own world that evening. Once, when a cousin of Vicente's was dancing with Montse, she pointed to her sister and noticed her dance partner's look of admiration, enough for Montse to believe that the cousin would soon ask her sister to dance, but he did not.

Now, instead of imagining life in the best restaurants and most fashionable beaches in Villa Gesell and Mar del Plata, Núria was about to experience both. And an apartment had been found for them close to Vicente's parents in a building where his sister and her husband already lived. The building had a service lift and bedrooms on the top floor for servants. Vicente's grandmother had furniture in storage that she was offering to give them. But Núria was determined that some of the rooms would have modern furniture and be decorated in bright colours.

She also told her mother that, since Vicente worked nearby, he often came home at lunchtime feeling not only hungry but amorous. Núria worried that the two servant girls might have heard them on one of the days when their coupling was more vigorous than usual.

'I suppose it's normal, and maybe I should be grateful that he is so interested. But just after lunch! The servants must talk about us.'

Montse's mother told her two younger daughters all of this in a whisper.

'In the middle of the day?' Conxita asked.

'I never heard of that before,' their mother said. 'But if Núria is doing it, then it is the height of fashion.'

Montse presumed that she and Conxita would soon be asked to one of the dinners that Núria and Vicente gave. She was sure that Conxita, if she could shed her diffidence, would shine at one of these events. But no invitation was forthcoming. Even when she answered the phone to Núria, her sister's tone was brusque. She wanted to speak solely to her mother.

Conxita's completion of her formal education coincided with the birth of Núria's first child, Alejandro. Though neither sister was invited to view the child or attend the christening, they learned a great deal about the baby and were shown many photographs by their mother.

It became clear to Montse through stray remarks that Núria wanted their mother to give up her job and spend more time with her. Núria had even spoken, it seemed, to her mother about the possibility of finding her a small apartment near where she and Vicente lived. Her mother had a way of talking breathlessly about Núria and her life and was difficult to pin down on any detail. While she mentioned the possibility that she might indeed give up her job, she did not return to the subject. She must have realized, Montse thought, how ominous this sounded to her two younger daughters.

'If she gives up her job,' Conxita asked Montse, 'how will we live? And where? I'm sure Núria isn't going to pay for us too.'

Montse liked the new locking system on her security door and felt comforted by the whirring sound when she put in the fourth number and the lock snapped open. She went to bed early and woke only once in the night when she thought again about the letter from the solicitor. She should have had a copy made, she realized, and then emailed her two sisters about it from the garage computer. But of course Conxita didn't have email! Maybe she might have found an email address for Alejandro.

Then it occurred to her that she really should have dealt with it all herself. No matter what, she should not have sent the only copy of the letter she had to her sister.

Now, the letter could easily be lost in the post, or Núria, so high-handed, might manage things on her own and not share the outcome with anyone. If only she had had a proper night's sleep, Montse was sure that she would never have sent that letter to Núria.

In the morning when she arrived at the garage, Facundo was waiting for her in the office. As she settled herself at her desk, he moved towards her.

'You were meant to be sick yesterday,' he said.

'I was sick.'

'Well, I heard differently. I heard there is a new policy in the area that puts glue into locks to encourage *locas* to stay at home. And I believe that the efforts to prevent you from leaving your house have made the committee proud.'

'What committee?'

'The committee against *locas*. They want all madwomen to stay indoors.'

'I am not mad.'

'I am sure we lose plenty of business because of you. Toti Diaz's garage has a lovely young blonde looking after business. And we have you. Look at you!'

He left the office and began to shout at the mechanics. He was just putting on a show, but she was disturbed that news of the gate had spread so quickly.

Over the next two months, despite regular attempts, she failed to make contact with Núria. Having telephoned a few times and been informed by the maid that La Señora was not available, she wrote her two letters and sent several emails, but received no reply. She also phoned Alejandro in his office, who told her that he knew nothing about any letter, but would ask his mother. When Montse called again, determined to get a mobile number for Núria, having been put on hold for some time, she was informed that Alejandro was not in the office. She left her work number and her home landline number and her mobile number, but he did not return her call.

At the garage one day, when Facundo was not there, she googled 'solicitor in Sort' and recognized the name Oriol Mas as the writer of the letter, finding an email address for him. She wrote to say that she had mislaid his letter but would like to have further details of what her aunt Julia's legacy entailed. Within a day, a reply came asking her to call the office as Oriol wished to speak to her personally on the phone. Without waiting to consider what to do, she called Spain on Facundo's landline and found herself speaking Catalan to a pleasant secretary who connected her immediately to Oriol Mas.

'We despaired of ever locating you,' he said. 'Your aunt left a will, leaving her estate to her three nieces, but the only address we could find was yours. It was on a letter you wrote to your aunt that arrived just after her death.'

'When did she die?'

'Just over a year ago.'

'Was she sick?'

'No, her death was unexpected. I think everyone was shocked by it.'

Montse looked through the glass partition to the workshop to make sure that Facundo was not around.

'You and your sisters,' Oriol went on, 'have inherited the house in Burg. And there is a small amount of money.'

'Did she not own fields?'

'She sold them a few years ago and had the house redone from top to bottom. She was a great lady. My mother used to see her on Tuesdays when she came down to the market.'

'What has to happen next?'

'Are you in touch with your sisters?'

'Yes.'

'Well, the three of you will have to fill out forms and sign them. The only problem has been that we couldn't find you.'

'Can you send me the forms? To my address?'

Montse expected him to say that he would require the home addresses of her two sisters as well, but he agreed that all three forms could be sent to her by email and also to her home address.

Montse wrote to Conxita when the forms arrived. Conxita usually contacted her a few times a year. Her letters, in clear handwriting, were funny and often fanciful. Montse tried to reply each time in a tone that was witty as well. Now, she began her letter with an account of the pervasive smell of axle grease and of her constant fear that Facundo or one of the mechanics was going to paw her and leave a mark that no amount of washing would erase.

She then told Conxita about the death of Julia and the legacy. She did not include the form. Conxita would have to ask her for it. When she read the letter over, she realized that her account of conditions at the garage did not sit well with the news of Julia's death. It seemed disrespectful. She took out another sheet of paper and wrote a new letter to Conxita, telling her plainly about the death of their aunt and adding, almost as an afterthought, news of the legacy.

Conxita wrote letters, often laced with whimsical descriptions of a cat's efforts to entice a bird into its orbit, or the antics of the temperamental cook, or some new purchase made by Maria Luisa Bustamante, for whom she worked as companion or live-in confidante. She had worked first for Señora Bustamante, Maria Luisa's mother, but the old lady had died the previous year, leaving her fortune to her daughter and a legacy to Conxita for her long years of service. The news of the legacy had animated Núria enough for her to invite Montse to stay with her for a weekend to discuss it.

No matter how many different ways Núria had approached the subject with Conxita, however, she could not discover how much the legacy was.

'No one leaves much to a maid,' Núria said.

'She was never a maid,' Montse replied.

'What else was she?'

'She was close to the old woman.'

'I did not like that old woman,' Núria said. 'No one liked her.'

'Conxita did.'

'She was paid to like her.'

Conxita responded promptly to Montse's letter. She invited her sister to come and stay for a night in the small cottage she had in the grounds of the house in San Isidro inhabited by Maria Luisa Bustamante, with the French furniture and the collection of early Argentine painting that was, Conxita boasted, better than the holdings of any museum.

Neither her mother nor Núria, not even Montse herself, ever discovered how Conxita had made contact with the Bustamantes. Since the job Conxita landed was not the sort of position that might be advertised in a newspaper, it must have come through word of mouth. But none of them could think who might have told Conxita that the Bustamante family wanted a young woman from a good family to be a companion to mother and daughter, look after their wardrobes and their general welfare. Conxita would not be required to wear a uniform, but she would not eat with the family. She would share a guesthouse in the garden with the housekeeper and, if requested, assist the housekeeper. But most of the time, she would be required to devote her attention to the mother, who was capricious, and to Maria Luisa, an only child of delicate health and high intelligence, who was two years Conxita's junior and had just returned from England where she had been attending school.

Conxita told her mother about the job one evening when her mother was about to go to Núria's. Montse remained in the bedroom while Conxita and her mother remonstrated with each other, Conxita blaming her mother for paying too much attention to Núria, their mother, in return, blaming Conxita for not consulting those who knew better than she did about her job prospects.

'No one knows about my job prospects better than I do,' Conxita said.

'I know better! Núria knows better! Vicente knows better!' their mother shouted.

'You can shout all you like, but tomorrow you will have only Montse to shout at.'

'Who fed you all your life? Who bought clothes for you?'

'Do you want the clothes back? Will I take them off now?'

'Don't be ridiculous. I will ask Núria what to do.'

Núria said that she and Vicente knew the Bustamantes and often attended parties in their house in San Isidro.

'Núria wants to know,' their mother said, 'if her sister Conxita is really to be a servant in a house that Núria often visits, then how should they greet each other? She also wants to know if Conxita would be offended were Núria to pretend that she did not know her?'

'I don't care what she does,' Conxita said. 'If she speaks to me, I will reply. If she ignores me, I will ignore her too.'

'She wants you to put the entire idea out of your mind. And so do I.'

When Conxita had departed to work for the Bustamantes, her mother raised the possibility of enrolling Montse in a commercial course.

'We can tell them that you are older,' she said.

Montse did not want to leave school early. She decided to appeal to Sister Teresa.

'I did not realize that your mother has had such a hard life,' the nun said. 'She was left a widow with three children and no income at all. And she was very brave to come here. And I can see the wisdom in what Núria suggests.'

'What does Núria suggest?'

'As you know, she thinks your mother should move into a small apartment close to Núria's. And she thinks you should find a job as your other two sisters did. And become independent.'

'In what way?'

'Find your own place to live. I know you are only sixteen but you look older, much more mature. You could pass for eighteen, maybe nineteen. And we'll all help you.'

Montse wondered if her mother or Núria had asked Sister Teresa to say this to her. Soon, her mother asked her to come shopping.

'You need to look older. Núria will pay for the clothes, but what we want to see is a change in your posture and deportment.

I want you to walk like a woman. We will get you shoes and stockings, but I want to see you change, and change quickly. As soon as you leave school, you can begin to tell people that you are eighteen.'

One day her mother came home from work flushed and excited.

'I spoke to the main boss,' she said. 'He is so busy normally, but I wrote him a note. And he is delighted at the thought that you will start learning how to do my job. And there is a commercial course you can do in the evenings. You can leave work early every day.'

The next day, as Montse prepared to leave school for the last time, she wished there was one girl to whom she would need to say goodbye. At lunchbreak, she spotted Sister Teresa moving towards her and suddenly turning away. She was sure the nun had seen her. She must have known it was her last day, the last time one of the Catalan girls would come to the school. Perhaps, Montse thought, saying goodbye would make the nun too sad. Or perhaps she felt guilty at letting Montse leave school so young.

On the way to work the first morning, her mother told her to answer to the name Núria as she had used Núria's documents to prove that Montse was twenty-one.

As soon as her mother sat at the desk, the phone began to ring. With each call, her mother transformed herself, becoming charming and reassuring and in control as garages from all over the province called looking for spare parts, and other garages that had been promised delivery phoned to find out what had happened.

'The rule is never say no,' her mother advised her. 'Take down the order and say that it should be no problem. And call them back to confirm. This means that you have the order and they will not go anywhere else. Develop a personal relationship with them so that they will not cancel the order.'

Montse noticed how much everyone admired her mother. When she was not taking orders, she was addressing the manager of the storeroom and the man who controlled deliveries, trying to get them to do things more quickly. These conversations were good-humoured, her mother making wild threats against the men for their failure to satisfy her customers, some of whom called in turn to tell her mother what would happen to her if the radiator or the brake pads for a particular model had not arrived by the end of the day.

'Sometimes,' her mother said, 'I take an order that I know cannot be delivered for a week, maybe more. Never tell them that! Realize that it will mean terrible phone calls. But never tell the truth! It is your job to promise and then keep them believing that the spare part is on its way. And the golden rule is never fall out with the storeroom or the delivery. Be nice to them, laugh at their jokes, keep them on your side.'

Neither Montse nor her sisters had ever known that this was what their mother did at work. When she said she was tired, Montse had no idea that their mother had spent a day promising, cajoling, laughing, and making sure never to lose a customer. Every time she put down the phone, it rang again.

In the evenings, Montse studied typing and secretarial work. Often, when she came home, her mother was at Núria's. Montse had something to eat on her own and went to bed.

At work, there were several young women who were secretaries and book-keepers. Her mother encouraged Montse to go out with them at lunchtime. When one of them came to her desk while her mother was on the phone and told her that a room had become vacant in her boarding house and it would be perfect for her, Montse was puzzled until she realized that her mother must have arranged this, her mother wanted her to find her own accommodation as she would be moving into an apartment near Núria.

But her mother gave no impression that she was involved. A week later, the girl approached her again, saying that if Montse did not show an interest someone else would take the room.

Montse remembered how long the name Núria had followed her. When they went to look at the boarding house, the girl called her Núria, and soon, after she began to take some of the calls from garages, men in search of spare parts for cars also called her Núria. It took Montse years before she could shed the name.

At the train station in San Isidro, she followed the directions to the Bustamantes' house that Conxita had sent. She carried a holdall with one change of clothes. It was lunchtime on a Saturday. She saw no pedestrians. In the Bustamantes' street, the houses became more opulent, the walls higher and the barking of guard dogs louder as she passed each high gate. Sometimes, a guard was standing proudly in front of a little hut outside.

It was typical of Conxita not to have alerted the guard at the Bustamantes' gate that her sister was coming. Since there was no bell, the only way she could gain access was by convincing this uniformed man that she was Conxita's sister. He stepped away from her to speak into his walkie-talkie and then, returning to where she stood, he ignored her. But when she made a dart for the gate so that she might peer into the garden, he moved quickly to block her view.

'There is no one home,' he said. 'Everyone is away.'

'My sister is home. She is Conxita.'

She called out Conxita's name. But that served only to cause the dog on the other side of the gate to bark more aggressively and other dogs nearby to reply strenuously to the first dog. Eventually, from the other side of the gate, in a sort of singsong Spanish, her sister Conxita told the guard to let the visitor through.

'This is my long-lost sister, fresh from the pampa. How dare you stand in her way!'

The guard moved sullenly aside, allowing Montse to get by.

Conxita, having embraced Montse effusively, showed her to her room in the guest cottage. The shutters were partly closed and the shadows hit against the white pillows and the white duvet cover and made the dark wood of the bedroom furniture look heavy and imposing. Proudly, Conxita showed her the bathroom with a separate shower and bath, with a white dressing gown hanging from a hook and massive white towels folded on a wicker stand.

'Is this normally your room?' Montse asked.

'No, I live in the big house now. Maria Luisa was lonely on her own there.'

Since Conxita was sixty-two, she calculated, her sister had been working here for well over forty years.

'Is it just you and Maria Luisa?'

'A cook comes every day and there is a maid and a cleaner, but at night it is just the two of us. Our night guard is the father of the guard you just met. He is even more protective. Maria Luisa says that the fact she sleeps at all is entirely due to this man.'

'The very thought of him would keep me awake,' Montse said.

'Then you are not Maria Luisa.'

They went first to the kitchen in the big house, using a side entrance. The cook was sitting at the table. A large woman in her fifties, she was introduced as Silvina.

'She did not eat a morsel of her lunch,' Silvina said. 'But she promises she will eat dinner.'

Montse presumed that Silvina was referring to Maria Luisa.

'If you cook rice with fish,' Conxita said, 'I'll make her eat it. Just don't put in too much salt.'

'Fish, chicken, carrots, chimichurri. It doesn't matter what it is. She won't eat it.'

They walked through the large airy rooms of the house, Montse marvelling at the size of the sofas and the opulence of the upholstery. She counted the chairs at the dining room table. There were twenty.

Under the stairs was a small room that Conxita showed Montse. It had a single bed, a few chairs and a tiny television.

'This is where I sleep,' she said.

'Why don't you stay in the guest cottage?'

'It is too far away if Maria Luisa is looking for me. I don't want to leave her alone in the big house.'

When it came to dinnertime, Conxita and Silvina whispered to one another anxiously. In the end, it was decided to put the food on dishes to be carried on trays to Conxita's room under the stairs.

'She will be more comfortable there,' Silvina said.

'If she sees me eating, she often follows suit,' Conxita said.

Maria Luisa appeared in a pink dressing gown and a pair of slippers that were too big for her. She was tall. Her grey hair hung over her shoulders. Normally, Montse imagined, she must arrange it with clips and combs so that it might add less to her bedraggled aura.

'I am suddenly very hungry,' she said, making herself comfortable in one of the small chairs in Conxita's room.

And then, as an afterthought, she greeted Montse.

'So lovely, lovely to see you. I asked your sister if we had met before, but I can't remember what she said. In any case, you have not changed, or so she says. And we have not changed either. Time just stays out in the garden. It never comes into the house. Now, should we watch something nice on the television?'

As Conxita busied herself switching from channel to channel, Montse sat down, her knees almost touching the knees of Maria Luisa.

Soon, Silvina came with the food.

'Dearest,' Maria Luisa said, 'could you close the door behind you when you go so that we can be more cosy?'

Montse could not understand why Maria Luisa did not want to have her dinner in the dining room. Instead, all three ate from plates held on their laps, with the television blaring. Maria Luisa did not speak but looked at a comedy on television with an expression of surprise mixed with satisfaction.

In the morning, Conxita came early to tell Montse that Maria Luisa wanted to see her.

'Don't ask me why,' Conxita said.

Maria Luisa received her in the upstairs library, a large square room with three windows on one side and a door that led to a bedroom. On all the free wall-space, there were books from floor to ceiling.

'The books are mainly my grandfather's,' Maria Luisa said. 'It was he who wanted a library upstairs. And we never got around to changing it.'

She waved at the books as if they were a garden grown wild. She was wearing a long black shapeless linen dress and the slippers from the night before.

'But some are my mother's. She collected French books. She loved anything that was French.'

Montse thought it strange to have a bedroom next to a library. And even the desk and chairs in the library struck her as strange.

'Biedermeier,' Maria Luisa said when she noticed her looking. 'My great-grandfather imported them.'

Maria Luisa left silence for a while and then sat up straight.

'Now, it's about your aunt,' she began. 'And it's about money. Your sister, Conxita, when she came here first, was paid in dollars. Not very much, but still. My father, I suppose, must have had a surfeit of them and I remember that he paid for everything at that time in dollars. And Conxita, bless her, continued to be paid in dollars. We have an accountant who looks after these things and he must have thought that was the arrangement. Then when my mother died, she left Conxita a small amount of money and we asked her for the name of her bank so that the money could be lodged there. But it turned out that Conxita didn't have a bank account, and it took weeks for her to admit that she had never, in all the years, actually changed any of the dollars into pesos. She had the dollars still in a case in her room, piles and piles of dollars. She doesn't need any money here. She is the same size as my mother was, even the same shoe size. So all her clothes come from my mother. All her food is provided. Even the dentist is paid for by some arrangement. She doesn't have any other needs. We sat for a day and counted the dollars. The accountant informed us that no bank would accept that amount of foreign currency without asking questions. Things are much stricter than they used to be. But we are working out a way of putting the money into a dollar account in Miami. Not that Conxita has ever been near Miami. In all her years here, she has never had any sort of holiday and I am sure that is criminal in some way. I mean, there are all sorts of regulations. So she has all this money and her legacy from my mother, and then the news comes that she has inherited a house in Spain.'

'She inherited it with me and my other sister.'

'Yes, and she wants to go and see it.'

'I imagine we will sell the house.'

'First, Conxita says she wants to go. So I am encouraging her to go. Then she thought that I wanted to get rid of her and said that she didn't want to go after all. But I know she wants to go. So, I said that I was going to be in Paris in September and maybe she would join me there, after spending some time in your aunt's house. And so that is what is happening.'

Montse wanted to ask Maria Luisa what was Conxita's status in the house. Maria Luisa had spoken of Conxita's whims and wishes as she might discuss a relative or a close friend rather than a servant.

And then it struck Montse that if Conxita were going to Burg to stay in Aunt Julia's house, she would like to accompany her. She would not wish to be left out of this.

'In the letter I wrote to you,' Maria Luisa went on, 'I didn't say any of this. I thought it better to invite you here so we could talk.'

'I got no letter from you,' Montse said.

'Of course you did! You replied to it.'

'That letter was from Conxita.'

'Yes, my dear, but I wrote it. It is in my handwriting.'

'Why didn't Conxita write it?'

'She can write some things, but not a whole letter. Writing is not her forte.'

Montse went over in her mind the fluent, witty letters she had received over the years from Conxita, all written in a beautiful hand.

'But some of the letters were about you,' Montse said.

'Yes, we always enjoyed adding private matters. I often came up with something unpleasant she would say about me. And how we laughed! There is nothing more amusing than insulting yourself. Conxita agrees. In fact, she was the one who said that first.'

Montse could make no sense of Maria Luisa. She decided not to ask anything more about the letters.

'I would like to go back to see our aunt Julia's house too,' Montse said, 'but we will have to ask Núria.'

'I have never warmed to Núria,' Maria Luisa said. 'She makes too much of an effort. She came here a few times when she was married first, as we all adored her husband and her mother-in-law. But then when Conxita was fully installed here, I wasn't sure what to do, until we all had the bright idea of making Conxita flaunt herself as the hired help. Núria pretended not to recognize Conxita at all. She looked through her. Well, I don't think I have ever enjoyed an evening so much. And Conxita also thought it was marvellous.'

Maria Luisa waved again at the books.

'Not one of those writers, great as they are, could ever have imagined such a thing. Núria Rojas pretending not to see her own sister, and Conxita making it all worse by serving at the table like a common maid. She even found a sort of uniform. And she developed a funny walk.'

'Núria has inherited the house too,' Montse said.

Two weeks later Montse, who had agreed reluctantly to come and spend a night in Núria's apartment, was being questioned by the *portero* in the hall of Núria's building with the same dismissive attitude as the security guard at Maria Luisa's. Once more, a guard had not been told to expect her, and, no, he would not phone the apartment as Señora Rojas did not like being disturbed.

'My sister is upstairs waiting for me.'

Eventually, when he did phone, he was told by a servant that Señora Rojas was out and no one knew when she was expected to return.

Montse sat on a cushioned stool just inside the door of the building and waited for her sister to appear. She rummaged in her handbag for her mobile phone, but then realized that she did not have Núria's mobile number. At intervals, the *portero* came and examined her disapprovingly and went out to get some air. She wondered if she did not look respectable. Was it her shoes, or did she need to visit the hairdresser's, or was it something that could not be so easily rectified?

She saw Núria alighting from a taxi and looked at her watch. Her sister was forty minutes late. Carrying a bag from a fashionable department store, Núria gave her no sign of recognition and almost pushed by her. When Montse tried to follow her to the lift, she was waylaid by the *portero* and forced to call out to Núria, who signalled that Montse should be let pass.

'Thank you,' Montse said when the lift doors were closed. 'That was really very kind of you.'

Núria was busy searching for keys in her handbag and did not respond. Even as they entered the apartment, Núria did not address her directly. It was only when they were both perched on uncomfortable armchairs in the sitting room that she began to speak.

'I suppose you think this apartment is too big for one widow?'

'I haven't put any thought into that.'

'Well, they will have to drag me out of here.'

Montse resisted the temptation to tell Núria that she did not care where she lived.

'Alejandro is the only one who defends me,' Núria continued.

Montse nodded and looked around the room.

At dinner, they were served several courses by two maids. Clearly, there was a cook in the kitchen. Montse felt that Núria had insisted she stay because she had run out of other people to impress and the need was overwhelming. The atmosphere in the apartment was frigid and formal.

Since her sister spoke incessantly about the small problems in her life, Montse did not know how she was going to introduce the subject of Aunt Julia's house.

In the morning, she finally managed to bring up the subject of the legacy.

'Oh yes, I got that letter. I am having Alejandro deal with all that,' Núria said. 'So none of us has to worry.'

Montse realized that flattery might work as a way of making Núria think about the house.

'Aunt Julia loved you best, of course,' she said.

'Did she?'

'Oh yes. Do you remember when she bought you that lovely yellow dress?'

'But that was only the last summer.'

'I often thought it was a pity that we missed all the summers after that.'

'I never thought about it again.'

'I think people in the village loved you. I remember how welcome you always were in everyone's house.'

'Yes, do you remember that family of boys?'

'The Puig boys? I remember Jordi and Miquel and then the two younger ones who used to call me names, Martí and Antoni. Jordi was the one you liked.'

'Yes, I liked Jordi. Aunt Julia often said that I would marry him. Since I am sixty-five, then he must be sixty-seven. Life has passed us all by.'

As Núria grew wistful, Montse thought she would take her chance now.

'It would be great to go back there just once. To see what happened to everyone. They would all remember us.'

'It was fifty years ago.'

'But I mean people like Jordi Puig and all the others we often played with. Jordi is still there.'

'How do you know?'

'Aunt Julia's letters always told me who died or who moved away and she never mentioned Jordi in that context.'

'You know, I liked them all.'

'It is the only place where people know us,' Montse said, and immediately regretted it, wondering if Núria might not feel that her own life in Buenos Aires was being undermined.

'Well, people know me here,' Núria said. 'Having grandchildren is a great joy.'

'Still, it would be lovely,' Montse said, 'to make one last visit to Burg. But maybe that's only a dream.'

'You are right,' Núria said. 'Now that you remind me of it, I would like to see it. And I can only say this to you but no one will really miss me when I am away.'

'Surely your grandchildren will?'

'Yes, I like to think that, but I would be foolish to set too much store by it.'

They had a few more hours together before Montse would return to Chivilcoy. Montse had to be quiet, letting Núria take the lead. She had to be careful when Núria quizzed her about how long Conxita and she could stay if they did travel to Spain.

In a flash, it occurred to Montse that if she made the journey, she would not return. Just as quickly, she decided not to tell

Núria. Instead, she told her that Maria Luisa Bustamante felt guilty that Conxita had never had a holiday in all the years and was ready to let her stay away for two months or more.

'Well, she must not be a maid then.'

'She writes beautiful letters,' Montse said.

'Doesn't she? So clever and with such beautiful handwriting. I showed one to Alejandro and he called her the clever one of the family.'

'Maybe she works as Maria Luisa's secretary,' Montse said.

Núria was so interested in Conxita and Maria Luisa that she asked no questions at all when Montse said that she, too, would be able to take more than two months' leave to accompany both of her sisters to Spain.

In a defeated tone, Montse then explained how much she and Conxita worried that, even though they would be able to get time off, they probably could not afford the plane fare. She tried to look both humble and grateful when Núria offered to pay.

'It is a big responsibility being the richest sister, indeed all the greater because the two of you haven't a penny. I don't know how you made that happen. But I will see what I can do.'

By the early afternoon it was arranged. Alejandro would call Oriol Mas in Sort and let him know that the sisters would come in mid-June and stay until the end of August in the house they had inherited. They would be able to give further instructions in person when they arrived.

On the bus back to Chivilcoy, Montse worked out a simple plan. She would sell her little house, explaining to anyone who asked that she wanted to move to a modern apartment. She would continue working at Facundo's until her last pay cheque arrived and then she would not turn up again.

In Burg, she would live on the money she had received for the house. It would last a few years. At least she would be rent-free. But she would have to convince her sisters that they should not sell Aunt Julia's house.

She remembered years before being shown the small room she was to rent by her colleague at work. It was dingy, the curtains were torn. She would have to share a kitchen and bathroom. And the price was much higher than it should be. That evening, she told her mother that she had seen it and didn't like it.

'You know,' her mother said, 'all I ever wanted when I was your age was my own room, my own freedom. When I went to Barcelona first, down from the mountains, it was after the Civil War, and no one would let a young woman live unsupervised. They put me in a terrible house run by a woman who demanded that every girl be home by nine o'clock. So I think it would be marvellous for you, and you can get a better apartment later.'

One evening, when she returned from her commercial classes, she found that her mother's possessions were missing. All the utensils from the kitchen were gone too. She waited for her mother to return, but at midnight, she went to bed. In the morning, there was still no sign of her mother. And, at work, since her mother did not appear, Montse had to start doing her mother's job, taking the calls and trying to arrange the movement of spare parts from the central depot to different garages. As she made promises that she knew could not be kept, she tried to sound as competent and cheerful as her mother had, and then, while trying to get accurate information from the depot, she worked on being firm and determined, but then laughed heartily at some flirtatious joke made by the store manager.

She found her mother at Núria's.

'Oh darling, you must see my new apartment,' her mother

said. 'It is tiny, but it is a jewel. I had to take it. I know I should have left you a note.'

It took Montse several hours to discover that her mother had not paid the rent on the old apartment for some time, and the landlord was demanding that it be vacated.

'So I think you should take that room you've been offered, just for the moment,' her mother said. 'As a stopgap.'

In her first week in the boarding house, Montse expected to hear from her mother or Núria, but they did not contact her. When she went on Saturday to her mother's new apartment, her mother invited her to lunch, insisting that she missed the office more than she had ever imagined and needed a detailed account of what had happened during the week.

'What we should do,' her mother said, 'is have lunch every Saturday in a place where we can talk. And then you will have shopping to do, and Núria will need me.'

Montse looked at her mother, realizing that she was being treated like one of the garage owners who were likely, if they were not humoured, to become difficult. Just as her mother knew how to calm them, she knew how to make clear to Montse that, while she was ready to have lunch with her on Saturdays, she did not want to see her at any other time.

Since she was called Núria at work and by the girls who shared her living quarters, she thought that she might follow her sister's example and move among people who were rich and exciting. At first, it was just something she dreamed about, imagining a boyfriend from one of the fashionable families and thinking of the expression of surprise on Núria's face were Montse to turn up at some country club on the arm of her fiancé.

Like Núria, she would go to Villa Gesell and Mar del Plata in the summer, but her husband and their friends would remain apart from Núria and Vicente and their set, thinking them dull and old-fashioned.

When her commercial course had finished, it was hard for Montse to know what to do when the day's work was over. By eight each evening, she had eaten and cleaned up after herself in the kitchen. She lay on the bed after supper until she began to fall asleep and then she would wake too early in the morning. The other girls in the boarding house had their own friends; some of them even had boyfriends.

She had one dress and one set of accessories that would allow her to go into the department stores or the posh hotels. She wore this for her weekly visit to her mother, but it struck her that she might linger some evening in the public spaces of one of the best hotels in Buenos Aires. She would sit in the lobby, as though waiting for someone, or find a discreet place in the lounge or the bar.

One Thursday, she decided to try the Alvear Palace Hotel. Having sat in the lobby for a while, she ventured into the bar. If she ordered an orange juice and sipped it slowly, it would not cost too much, especially if she came here just one night every week. Thursday would be a good night. On Fridays, fashionable people had other things to do, and they would be playing tennis or sailing for the rest of the weekend. And her aim was to meet someone fashionable.

If anyone asked her what she was doing, she would say that she was waiting for her sister, Señora Rojas, the wife of Vicente Rojas. But no one ever asked her. At first, she sat at the bar, but was too isolated and conspicuous. Even when the bar was busy, she felt she was in the way, uncertain where to look, with too many conversations going on around her.

It was easier to sit at one of the tables. In the early weeks, she saw a few men who interested her, but they were never alone. When, one evening, an older man turned a few times to stare at her, she looked away. She had not come here to meet older men.

She had a habit of not thinking for a long time and then making a decision in one second. After several Thursdays, the same older man appeared again and approached her table. Instantly, she put her hand up to deter him.

'I am waiting for company.'

As soon as he turned away, she was sorry. And, just as he was back at the bar, she realized that if she had any chance of meeting someone, then he would most likely be an older man.

It took her some time to settle on Rogelio Freitas.

Rogelio was impeccably dressed, with beautiful fingernails and light blue eyes. He was sitting one evening at a table near her, observing her carefully but discreetly. When he made a sign, as though asking for permission to take his drink to her table, she nodded. He confessed when he sat down that he had been waiting for a colleague who must have mistaken the date or the time.

Rogelio was not staying in the hotel, but lived with his family in a house in Tigre, not far from the centre. He was sixty, he said, and had been married for thirty-five years, had two sons and two daughters, and four grandchildren.

He asked Montse about herself and listened to the replies. She never thought of what had happened to her as something that could interest anyone else, but Rogelio paid attention to the story of her mother and her sisters, wanting to know more.

When he offered her another orange juice or even something stronger, she shook her head and looked at him directly. At first, this seemed to make him uncomfortable, but then he returned her gaze. She could see that he was working out what he should do.

'Can I see you again?' he asked.

'I would like that.'

'This day next week, at the same time?'

For the next two months, they met once a week in the bar of the hotel. Rogelio had a few beers and Montse had one or two orange juices. He told her about his business that imported medical precision instruments, supplying most of the hospitals in Argentina, and she told him about her work. It emerged that he was acquainted with Vicente Rojas and he nodded vigorously when she intimated that it might be best not to let Vicente know that they were meeting.

During their meetings, Rogelio never pushed her to do anything more than relax in his company. But one evening, he asked her if she would accompany him to look at an apartment he was interested in. As they drove towards Palermo Chico, Montse wondered if he was possibly planning to leave his wife.

The apartment was on the top floor of an elegant building. It was really just two rooms – a sitting room with three windows and a long balcony, as well as a bedroom. There was also a small bathroom and kitchen.

'We can put a dining table here,' Rogelio said.

Montse noted the casual use of 'we', as if he were asking her to share the apartment with him.

In the lift as they went to the ground floor, he handed her the key.

'You can start moving in at the weekend,' he said.

On the journey back to her lodgings in his car, she asked no questions but gradually ascertained what he had in mind. He would pay the rent for the apartment and cover the bills. He would visit her once or twice a week.

Often, in the nineteen years that this arrangement lasted, Montse imagined that Rogelio's wife would die and he would be free to marry her and she could go and live with him in the house in Tigre that he told her so much about.

He usually came to see her on Mondays and Thursdays, letting her know by the telephone he had installed if he had to cancel or if he was going to be late. Always, he was considerate, listening to what she said, noticing her clothes and making sure that she had enough money for her wardrobe. He made it clear that his visits to her were the most important time in his week. He whispered to her that he would not be able to live without her.

When he sat opposite her in the restaurant near the apartment that they favoured, he seemed kind, but could be sad. His wife, he said, was so involved in the house and the gardens, and in her social life, and now, in the lives of her grandchildren, that she barely paid him any attention.

'I could never talk to her in the way I talk to you,' he said.

Montse loved how he spoke to her with such frankness, but she could not tell him how difficult it was sometimes not to show her unease as he took his clothes off, letting her see his hairy back and his fat stomach. And she promised herself that when she found him in a good mood, she would ask him to shave when he came to the apartment so that she would not have to feel his rough stubble on her skin.

Her mother and Núria still believed that she was in the old lodgings and she saw no reason to inform them of the change. But she gave Conxita her new address because she did not want to miss one of Conxita's letters. Once, only once, did her world collide with that of Núria. It happened when she and Rogelio were in a restaurant they did not usually frequent. She spotted Vicente at a nearby table with some other men. When he saw her, he left his own table and approached hers. She noticed his surprise when he observed that Rogelio was sitting opposite her. Rogelio stood up, and the two men spoke for a few minutes about some social event they had both attended. And then Vicente returned to his friends without speaking to Montse.

She presumed that the following Saturday she would hear from her mother about the encounter and, even though she was sure that her mother would not believe her, was planning to say that the company often did business with Rogelio and they were in the restaurant waiting for others to arrive. But her mother did not mention the restaurant, and it struck Montse that Vicente might not have told Núria that he had seen her. She liked the idea that Vicente did not share everything with Núria.

Rogelio often spoke to her as if she were his wife. If she bought a new dress, using the cash he had given her, he said that he was proud to be with a woman who dressed so well. The happiest time, however, was the hour after he had gone when she remade the bed and tidied everything and looked forward to sleep. Sundays could be lonely, especially if she woke too early and thought too much about the life Rogelio and his wife must be having and how much he enjoyed it when his grandchildren came to play around the swimming pool, or when they had a big lunch with family and friends in the shaded area to the side of the house. But she was never lonely during the week. The evenings when Rogelio did not come were spent relaxing, watching television, cleaning the apartment and going to bed early with a magazine.

As he grew older, Rogelio walked with some difficulty and did not want to have a drink before they went to bed. He was less interested in sex and wanted instead to talk, complaining about his wife's indifference and his sons' interest in having him hand over control of the business.

Never once, in all the years, did she phone him at work, although she could easily have found the number. When her mother fell ill on a day that Rogelio was meant to come to her, she tried to be back at the apartment to meet him but was prevented from leaving her mother because Núria insisted that she stay until the doctor came.

When Rogelio did not appear the following Thursday, Montse believed that he was offended. She waited for him the next Monday and again on Thursday. On Friday, she phoned his business to be told that he no longer had an office there. When she enquired further, she was told that he had retired. She thought it strange that he had never let her know that.

Weeks went by without any sign from him until one evening when she returned from work, she found a man waiting at the front door who asked her if she lived in the apartment on the left-hand side on the top floor of the building. Before she answered, she saw that he had his father's eyes.

'Are you Alfonso or Dario?' she asked.

'Alfonso,' he said and gave his father's hesitant, melancholy smile.

Without speaking, he followed her into the lift and then, when they arrived at her floor, into the apartment.

His father had died three weeks earlier, Alfonso said. He had spent two weeks in hospital. In going through his father's papers, Alfonso had discovered a monthly payment for this apartment for a period of almost twenty years.

'And that explained something I never understood,' he said. 'It explains his absence on Mondays and Thursdays.'

'Does your mother know?' Montse asked.

'Nothing, and she won't be told.'

'And the others?'

'I will tell my brother.'

It was only when she offered Alfonso a drink that she became fully aware of his hostility to her. His refusal came with an irritated wave of his right hand.

'I came here to settle things.'

She had asked about his mother and his siblings as a way of trying to discover if Rogelio had made provision for her in his will. If he had, she thought, they would all have been informed of her existence. Since this was what she most needed to know, she thought it best to ask outright.

'No,' Alfonso said. 'His will is very straightforward. He was a very respectable man. There is no mention in his will of you or anyone like you.'

His effort to be openly rude was not lost on her. Once she found out what was to be done about the apartment, she would ask him to go.

'The lease states that the rental can end with three months' notice from either side. I will give three months' notice tomorrow.'

'And what should I do then?'

'That is no concern of mine or of anyone else I know.'

As he prepared to leave, he turned nervously towards her.

'There is something else I need to ask you.'

She could not think what this might be. Rogelio had given her jewellery, but she determined that she would deny that she had ever received it. She hoped that he had not noticed her bracelet.

'Was there any issue from the relationship between you and my father?'

'Issue?'

'Do you have any children?'

She laughed for a second and then became serious.

'No,' she said.

'That is a relief,' he said and moved into the hallway.

She held the door of the apartment open as he waited for the lift to come.

'Is there anything else?' he asked.

'You know, I loved him,' she said.

He glanced at her for a second and then looked at the ground.

'Yes,' he said. 'But where does that leave us?'

He smiled sadly and shrugged.

Afterwards, she asked herself whether he might have taken pity on her and found a way to look after her if she had detained him for longer and spoken about his father. But she did not think so.

In the weeks that followed, Montse realized that, since she had no savings and a small salary, it would be difficult to find an apartment for rent. When she asked some of her colleagues in the office about apartments, she discovered that prices had gone up and that all she would be able to afford was a room in a boarding house like before, where she would have to share a bathroom and a kitchen.

The Saturday after the visit by Rogelio's son, she found that there was no response when she went to her mother's apartment. When she went to Núria's, she was greeted by Vicente.

'Did Núria not get in contact?'

'No.'

'She was looking for your work number. Your mother has been in hospital since Wednesday. Conxita went to see her yesterday. If I were you, I would go there now.'

Her mother was in a private room. When Montse opened the door, she saw that her mother was laid out as though already dead. Núria, sitting on a chair beside the bed, did not stand up. Montse touched her mother's hands and her forehead and bent down to listen to her breathing. When she looked at Núria, her sister put a finger to her lips. She did not want her to speak.

For the next four days, Montse stayed as much as she could in the hospital room. A few times, when she took a break with Núria, her sister remained silent and did not respond to anything she said. On the day before her mother died, Conxita came when Núria had gone home for a rest. Montse told her about her sister's coldness.

'I have written her a long letter,' Conxita said. 'I will send it as soon as the time is right.'

'What does it say?'

'That she stole our mother and she should be ashamed of herself.'

'I don't think she feels shame.'

'She will, when she reads my letter. Maria Luisa and I have been awake all night writing it.'

Some days after the funeral, Montse received a call at work from Núria asking her if she could visit as soon as possible.

Vicente, when he let her into the apartment, indicated to Montse that she should exercise caution with her sister.

Núria had been crying. She had some sheets of paper beside her.

'Did you know about this letter?' she asked.

Montse looked puzzled.

'It is from Conxita and it is filled with vile accusations.'

Montse did not answer her.

'I did not take our mother prisoner,' Núria continued. 'I rescued her.'

Montse still saw no reason to speak.

'It was such a rash decision coming to Argentina. And she knew she had made a mistake. She was in such a state of shock and panic. I mean, she was traumatized. And so worried about you and Conxita. She could not think what to do. And so Vicente agreed that we should look after her. And that was best for everybody.'

'None of what you have just said is true,' Montse thought of saying.

'So, you did know about the letter?' Núria asked.

Montse did not reply.

'The apartment where my mother lived is in Vicente's name and we will be selling it,' Núria said. 'But we thought that you and Conxita might like to share the jewellery, there are some very good pieces. But I called Conxita, who told me that she wanted none of it. And she was very rude on the phone, quite obnoxious, I have to say. And then she wrote her vile letter. So we thought we would offer it to you.'

'All of it?'

'Well, some of it.'

For a second, Montse wondered if she could sound like Núria, or even like her mother or Conxita. She took a deep breath.

'I want all of it,' she said.

'I would have to ask Vicente.'

'Can you do that now? I don't have much time. And I would like to collect it now.'

'Oh, I am not sure where the key to the apartment is.'

'Could you become sure?'

When Núria left the room, Montse smiled at the thought that

this was the tone she used only when she felt impatient with one of the junior staff at the depot or when she was having difficulty with a recalcitrant delivery man. She had learned it from her mother, but she had improved on it, she thought.

One of the garages Montse dealt with was in the town of Chivilcoy, two hours from Buenos Aires. It was run by a man called Facundo, who had a way of letting her know when something was urgent. If she could not deliver it, he could entice her into telling him the truth so that he could go elsewhere. He did this by being friendly and charming, often phoning when he had no pressing business and sending her gifts at the end of the year. A few times, he had dropped by the office, ostensibly to pay a bill, but also to make himself known to the staff.

'If you ever come to Chivilcoy, there would be a great welcome for you,' he said to Montse.

On a recent visit, he had ascertained that she lived alone and was not married.

'I am doing a big expansion,' he said, 'and I need someone like you to run the office. My problem is that everyone wants the work done immediately, but no one ever wants to pay me. You would be good at getting money out of people. It would be an honour to have you in Chivilcoy. You could get a house for a quarter of the Buenos Aires price. And I would match your salary here, and maybe even increase it.'

She had told him that she was quite happy where she was.

Now, he came to visit again, apologizing for his dirty fingernails.

'I can't get the grease out of them.'

He was a large, cheerful man in his sixties.

'We got a girl in to do the accounts,' he said. 'She sent the wrong bills to the wrong people and then phoned up some of our best customers demanding payment of bills they had already covered.'

'So, you are looking to replace her?'

'Oh no! She has already gone. I am looking for someone to create an entire new system of accounting and inventory.'

'I could certainly do inventory,' Montse said.

'You could send out bills and pay bills as well,' he said.

Montse named an amount of money she would need as a salary.

'You were always a hard woman!'

'If you can't afford me, then call the girl and ask her to come back.'

'Are you serious?'

'What?'

'That you would move.'

'I might be. Are you serious about the offer?'

Often, once she was settled in her new job in Chivilcoy, Montse came to the city on a Saturday, arriving before the best dealer in old silver closed his shop. She had the pieces from her mother's collection examined by different dealers. Surprised at their high value, she learned that it would be wiser to sell them a few at a time. When she had sold most of them, she had enough money to put down a deposit for a small house near Facundo's garage, asking Facundo to write her a guarantee for the mortgage.

She had taken care of all the clothes that Rogelio had bought for her. She tried to be glamorous at work as she set about re-organizing the accounting and ordering system at the garage as well as the payroll and the inventory. When she sought to explain to Facundo what she was doing, he told her that he would look after the cars and she would look after the money.

'We are lucky to have you,' he said. 'And the best thing is to leave you to do your work.'

Soon, Facundo began to visit her sometimes on his way home in the evenings, parking his car a block away. He seemed to derive satisfaction from these encounters. He remained kind to her, and that made her life easier.

On the way between the house and the garage there was a small newsagent's shop that sold novels she liked. The stories were romantic, about women who had been unlucky in love suddenly finding happiness. In her first year she read all of the books the shop could supply. Afterwards, they let her know if a new book in the series had arrived.

She could see herself as a figure in one of the books, a woman who had married a man who was older. The man had now died, leaving her his estate, to the consternation of the four children from his first marriage. She was alone in the large house. Now, she imagined, she could live the kind of life she had always wanted.

The garage was busy and she enjoyed the job. In Buenos Aires, she had disliked the journey to and from work, especially when the bus was crowded. Now, she could walk. She was home in the evening in time for her favourite television programmes. When a video rental shop opened nearby, she bought a video player which Facundo attached to the television for her and showed her how to operate.

Facundo only called by on weeknights so Saturday and Sunday were quiet, often too quiet. Therefore, each Saturday morning, she rented two videos for the weekend, discovering that she preferred old American films, even Westerns, to anything modern.

Part of her job was to pay wages and overtime. Because overtime was paid at one and a half times the usual rate, Facundo asked her to be very strict with the mechanics, making sure that no one claimed more than they were due. The first row with Facundo Junior was when he claimed to have done the same overtime as the others, but she was certain he had not.

'I won't ask you twice,' he said.

'Don't ask me at all,' she replied.

'I don't want to have to complain about you to my father.'

'Your father is as concerned as I am that no one gets overtime pay unless they have put in the hours.'

Since then, Facundo Junior had made no effort to disguise his dislike for her.

When, twenty years after she had gone to Chivilcoy, Facundo Senior died suddenly, his son became boss. On his first day in charge, he asked Montse to stay at her desk after he closed the garage and everyone had gone.

'I need to make something clear to you,' he said. 'Everyone knows about you and my father and I don't want to hear any more talk about you and I don't want you flirting with men who come to have their cars repaired. In future, you will concentrate on your work.'

'How do you know about me and your father?'

'He told everyone. Give him one drink and he would recite the story. I don't want this establishment known for that kind of thing. So just do the job you are paid for.'

'I am sure I know how to do my job perfectly.'

'So it would seem.'

* * *

It would be a pleasure after all these years, she thought, not only to quit without notice and never see Facundo Junior again but to delete as many files as she could on the computer, including all the inventory files, and destroy invoices and bank statements.

The real estate office in Chivilcoy was run by a customer at the garage. When Montse told him that she wanted to sell her house and move into a modern apartment, he informed her that it was not a good time either to buy or to sell.

'But surely if it's bad for one, then it's good for the other?'

'Not now. At the moment, prices are low because no one is buying – no one has any money – but no one is selling either because prices are low.'

She asked him to put her house on the market; they could discuss what she might buy once there was a prospect of selling.

When a letter came from Conxita, she read it carefully.

> Alejandro says that our Spanish and Argentine passports will both have to be collected next week. We will be the three poshest ladies in the world, as we set out to conquer Spain, or maybe just Burg and some surrounding villages. Núria will be Don Quixote and we can both be Sancho Panza. Or maybe one of us can be a windmill. As I prepare for departure, things here are tense. Maria Luisa is sometimes a dog and sometimes a cat. She barks when she hears about my arrangements but then later she starts to purr when she thinks about going to Paris in September, and I purr too, so we are like a pair of cats. Núria says that we must come to stay in her apartment the night before we leave, but that is months away. Still, I thought I would warn you.

Montse imagined Conxita and Maria Luisa writing this together and laughing at the thought of Maria Luisa being like a dog and a cat. She wondered how she had ever believed that Conxita's handwriting could be as good as this and her ways of describing things as vivid.

A buyer was found for the house. Even though the price was lower than she had hoped, Montse accepted the offer, agreeing to vacate the house on the day before her flight to Spain. She asked, however, that the contract be signed some weeks before that. She would need time for the cheque to go through. When it did, she would withdraw some in cash and the rest in a banker's order that she would lodge in a bank in Spain.

She loved the idea that no one knew what her plan was. Núria had bought her a return ticket, presuming that they would both come back on the same flight at the end of the summer.

On her last day at work, she thought she would like to have a final altercation with Facundo. She told him that the office computer would soon need to be replaced.

'Just like yourself,' he said.

'It is on its last legs,' she said.

'Just like you,' he replied. 'Maybe we'll throw you both out at the same time and see if anyone notices.'

She scowled at him, but when he returned to the workshop, she smiled at the knowledge that he would be the one to notice on Monday morning. She set about deleting more files and carried a large pile of invoices and financial statements to the rubbish bin.

The following day she arrived at Núria's with a single suitcase and a handbag containing five thousand dollars in cash and a banker's order for fifteen thousand euro. The handbag also contained her jewellery.

Núria ushered her into a bedroom.

'Now, you have your own bathroom as before. I observed the last time that you didn't use the towel or touch the soap and this led me to believe that you didn't wash at all. This time, I want you to have a long bath now, and a shower before our departure. I can't have you smelling on the plane.'

In the morning, Núria announced to her two sisters that she had made appointments for them at her hairdresser's.

'They don't like dowdy women in Spain any more. All that is over.'

As the stylist worked on her, Montse realized that she had been given instructions by Núria. At the end, she saw that she and Conxita had hairstyles that matched Núria's.

'We look like those terrible women you see in Buenos Aires,' Conxita said.

'You mean, we look like Núria,' Montse replied.

Alejandro agreed to drive them to the airport and wait to make sure that they departed safely. Montse and Conxita had been told that they would not be allowed to check in more than one suitcase. But Núria, they noticed, had three.

'I don't want people in Burg to think we are all impoverished,' she said. 'So I brought my best things.'

In Barcelona airport, on arrival, they were met by a driver who had been found for them by Oriol Mas. Montse watched Núria deciding which was the best seat in the small van. She herself slipped quietly into the front passenger seat, but Núria soon decided that this was her preferred place. If she did not sit in the front, she told the driver, she would be ill.

On the journey, they spoke to the driver about the weather and asked questions about Burg. He had known their aunt Julia and expressed his sympathy at her death, saying that she was badly missed in Burg.

Montse wanted to ask if they were on the right road. She recognized nothing.

'All the roads are new,' Núria said, turning to speak to her sisters, and then turning back to ask the driver a question about the route.

What was strange, Montse saw, was that Núria spoke to her sisters in Spanish, using an Argentine accent, but addressed the driver in Catalan. In the airport, she was sure, and the night before in Núria's apartment, all three sisters had spoken to one another in Catalan, even when Alejandro was with them. Now, they had switched effortlessly, it seemed, into Spanish. In Argentina, when they were together, they had stood apart because they spoke Catalan, and now they stood apart again. She wished they would soon switch back to Catalan so that the driver might not think they were so foreign.

She remembered that there was a cafe in the town of Ponts where her mother traditionally stopped. And there was a grocery shop that had, her mother believed, the best range of goods. Ponts was halfway between Barcelona and Burg. Montse recalled the word 'Ponts' being shouted out by Núria and Conxita when they saw the sign for the town and her mother turning to smile from the front passenger seat.

Her father must have been at the wheel when this happened. Since she was four years old when he died, she had always believed that she had no memory of him at all. But in the image of her sisters shouting out the word, he must have been driving. She wished she could recall that moment more clearly.

After Ponts, there was a winding road over the mountain, and a moment at the end of this when, in a sudden panorama, it was possible to see the town of Tremp and beyond that the foothills of the Pyrenees. She knew the names of the towns between here and Burg – La Pobla de Segur, Sort, Rialp, Llavorsí, Tírvia. The journey was always too long. She remembered asking, 'Are we at Tremp yet?' always to be told that it was still some distance away.

Julia's tall house, she remembered, was in the middle of the village. It had a low-ceilinged storage space in the basement and then a large living space on the ground floor. On the floor above that there was a bedroom with a balcony, and a bathroom. In the attic, there were two bedrooms. During the day, the front door was always left open; a hanging screen made of lines of beads produced a rattling sound when anyone pushed through. The main room was dark. She tried to think where the single window was. And there was always a band of honey-coloured fly-paper hanging from the ceiling and flies circling around it. And there were cats sneaking into the cavernous spaces at the back of the ground-floor room and being shooed out by Julia or Núria or their mother when she was with them.

She tried to recall the sort of food they had eaten, but nothing came to mind. There was a small vegetable garden to the side of the house but she could remember only lettuce growing there, and there was a wired-in space for hens.

She wished that one of her sisters would say something about the house or the village or even about the years they had been away. Then, she saw that both of them were asleep. She could only talk to the driver.

'We have not been here for fifty years,' she said.

'So I understand.'

'But I remember it all, the house, the village.'

'Julia was a very nice woman,' the driver said. 'Everyone in the village will miss her.'

It struck her that Facundo would presume at first that she was ill but he would soon discover that she had left for good. The missing files and the invoices would be an inconvenience at the beginning, but it would not be long before Facundo forgot about them and about her. And in Chivilcoy, she would not be remembered.

She wished she had lived like Julia, all her life in the same place. It occurred to her how sad it must have been for Julia when her only sister and her nieces left for Argentina and never came back.

'Has much changed in Burg?' she asked the driver.

'Very little, I would say. Julia had the house decorated not long before she died. It was a pity she did not live to enjoy it.'

As they reached the town of Sort, Conxita woke up.

'I got the key as instructed on the way down,' the driver said. 'We don't need to stop, but you might want to go to the supermarket.'

Conxita prodded Núria.

'Núria, we have to go to the supermarket.'

In the supermarket, Núria took charge of the trolley, with Montse walking beside her. Montse noticed the ripe cherries, the peaches and the nectarines. When she found a plastic bag and began to fill it with cherries, Núria took it from her and emptied it.

'They will just attract flies,' she said. 'We need food that will keep. I am not sure that Julia has a fridge. She didn't have one before.'

'That was fifty years ago.'

'Yes, but other people had fridges then. It was not normal not to have a fridge. That is why the house was filled with flies.'

She put packets of rice and lentils and tins of vegetables into the trolley. She nodded in approval when Montse put two types of bread into the trolley and some fresh vegetables. Núria added bottled water and cooking oil.

'I am sure we can get eggs in the village,' she said.

'That might all have changed,' Montse replied.

Montse knew that they were now only half an hour from Burg. The excitement on this last stretch was the same as it had ever been. Before, she had looked forward to Julia appearing at the door. Now she would see the empty house. Because they said nothing and seemed bored, she believed that her sisters did not feel what she did. But they were not planning to live here, they were not thinking of the life they would begin in this village when the summer was over.

As they started the winding ascent to Burg, Conxita said, 'There's no going back now.'

Montse decided to reply in Catalan.

'We should have come when she was still alive.'

Neither of her sisters responded.

For a second, when the van stopped in Burg, Montse was confused.

Most of the houses were built on a set of terraces to get sun in the winter; she remembered that. They all looked out in the same direction. One of these houses had to be Julia's, but she could not work out which.

She heard Núria asking the driver if he could return for her on Monday when the shops would be open.

'I will need a day's rest,' she said, 'and then I will be ready to go shopping.'

Montse stayed behind her two sisters and the driver as they

walked up a set of steps and then into an alleyway to the left. Montse had no memory at all of this alleyway. She had been sure the house was to the right. They passed a barn and two small houses, and then, standing on its own, she saw the house she recognized as Julia's. It was narrow, as she remembered, with a balcony on the first floor. The driver tried a number of keys before finding the right one.

The main room was not the room she had known. The back wall had been replaced by double glass doors that opened onto a patio with a table and chairs. All the furniture was new, as was the tiling in the kitchen area. There was a large fridge and towards the back a cast-iron stove where the open fireplace had been.

The driver helped Núria carry her suitcases upstairs where she immediately made claim to the main bedroom, the one with the balcony, on the same floor as the bathroom, where the tiling and fittings were also new. Montse and Conxita climbed the next flight of stairs to the two attic bedrooms, each with a dormer window in a ceiling of brightly stained pine.

'I suppose these bedrooms are for us,' Conxita said.

Montse woke at four and waited until the dawn light crept into the room. In the supermarket, she had been too exhausted to work out the exchange rate between euros and pesos. She supposed that things were more expensive here than in Argentina. It must have cost Julia a great deal of money to put in all the fittings. Even the steps of the stairs seemed new and solid. The paintwork was fresh. She tried to think what age Julia would be if she were alive. She calculated that she would be ninety or ninety-one. Why would she spend so much money on renovation at that age?

She dressed as quietly as she could, but realized that the floorboards in her room, although new, were thin. Every time she moved, one of them creaked. She crept down the stairs and had some bread and cheese before slipping soundlessly out the front door.

The morning was cold, with a hint of ice in the air, even though it was mid-June. She should have taken her coat. She veered right and walked along a path that once, she was sure, had led to the road, but it was overgrown now. She went through an alleyway and walked around the small village that still, as far as she could see, had no shop and no cafe.

The sun was hidden by the hill behind the village, but, since the sky was blue, the day would, she imagined, become hot. When she turned, she was confronted in the distance by a massive wall of mountains. The sunlight showed clearly where the tree line ended and sheer rock took over. Montse could scarcely believe that she had no memory of this, the most imposing sight, the vista you could not miss. Even now, she could recall the names of some cats in this village from all those years before, and a few dogs too, and she could remember who had hens and who kept cows. But this jagged wall of rock had not lodged in her memory.

Montse had presumed that, as soon as their presence became apparent, people would call on them. Julia always had neighbours coming to her house, standing in the doorway, or sitting on a chair outside the front door. But on that first day, no one called. Perhaps it was because it was Sunday.

The next day, the driver came to collect Núria, who insisted that she wanted to go alone to Sort, where she had many things to do, she said, including replacing Julia's name with her own on all the utilities, as Oriol Mas had suggested.

'You will need to get chicken and eggs and fresh vegetables and more bread and cheese,' Montse said.

'And milk,' Conxita added.

'I am sure I don't need to be told what to get,' Núria replied.

In the afternoon, Núria returned, laden down with bags.

'The prices in the supermarket are outlandish!' she said. 'I was too tired to notice them on Saturday. And I don't like these euros at all. I don't know what was wrong with the peseta. The euro is just an excuse to make you spend more money.'

'Why didn't you take me with you?' Conxita asked.

'You would have been a nuisance,' Núria replied. 'But maybe you can come the next time.'

Montse made dinner for them, laying the table slowly while Núria and Conxita sat in armchairs. After a while, Núria went upstairs and Conxita wandered out onto the patio and then stood outside the front door. They could not settle.

When they spoke, they still used Spanish. It occurred to Montse that they had never spoken Catalan as adults, except when they met each other. It was not an adult language for them. For Núria, back from the shops, it was normal to speak about prices in an Argentine accent. That is what she had done all her life. For Conxita, it made sense to use her Argentine accent to describe a woman she saw that afternoon sitting precariously on a tractor driven by a man. Her accent made the scene foreign and strange.

She also spoke in an Argentine accent to complain to Núria that she had failed to get bread.

'They had none left,' Núria said.

'Of course they had bread,' Conxita replied. 'You just forgot. Admit you forgot.'

Montse watched them arguing as though they were still young girls and no time had passed at all.

* * *

The days went by, but no one came to the house. Conxita discovered a woman who sold eggs and returned home to get money from Núria to pay her.

'Ask if she knows any of the Puig brothers, especially Jordi and Miquel.'

When Conxita returned with the eggs, she had news of the Puig brothers.

'She says there never was a Miquel Puig here, but Jordi Puig lives beside her. He is the one who bought the land from Julia.'

'And what about Martí and Antoni?'

'Martí and Antoni what?'

'Puig.'

'I'm sure she's never heard of them either because I never did. But she remembers us. She says she is younger than we are, although she looks older. But she doesn't remember Montse at all. I said that Montse is the baby of the family, maybe that is why.'

Núria came across a walking stick in one of the cupboards and began to take walks in the afternoon.

'I stop anyone I meet. I thought I saw Jordi Puig on a tractor. I made the man stop, but he turned out to be someone else.'

Each of them rose at a different time, so there was no formal breakfast. Her two sisters took it for granted that Montse would cook and do the dishes afterwards. Conxita found a pack of cards in a drawer and played patience.

Núria expressed her disgust when she saw her.

'Is this what you have travelled all the way to do?' she asked. 'And on this, the most beautiful day of the year?'

'I am living on Argentina time,' Conxita said. 'I don't know whether it is night or day.'

Montse solved the intricacies of the washing machine. And the control dials of the oven that had appeared complicated at the start became easy to deal with. In the late afternoon, a corner of the patio caught the sun and she liked to sit there and take in the heat. When Núria and Conxita argued, she never joined in. Their accents grated on her ear and she had, in any case, other matters to contemplate.

She liked passing Núria's room and looking in at the double bed, the bedside lockers, the built-in wardrobe, the chest of drawers, the rocking chair that could be carried out onto the balcony. This would be her room when the other two left.

In the winter, she would use the patio to store the wood for the stove, maybe find a way of covering the wood.

Early each morning, when there was no sound except birdsong, she sat alone in the room downstairs dreaming up what it would be like three months from now, the long day ahead of her. She often moved to the chair outside the front door and went in her mind through all the houses in the village. Over the years to come, she would know all the people who lived in them. But she would not crave company, nor knock on people's doors if she believed she would not be welcome. Julia, she knew from her letters, had happily spent whole days without seeing anyone at all.

She tried to imagine what she would think about when she had the house to herself. She would not, she determined, go over what had happened with Rogelio or Facundo. No matter what, she would not sit alone at night letting her thoughts linger over what could have been. She would think other thoughts.

On their second Tuesday in Burg, Montse was coming back from a short morning walk when she saw a van pull up and several women getting into it. Recognizing the driver as the man who had brought them from the airport, she asked him where he was going now.

'Today is market day in Sort, and, for three euro, I can drop you there and collect you at lunchtime. It's a taxi service provided by the town hall.'

'Can you wait for two minutes?'

She ran to the house and went to her room, without checking if either of her sisters was awake. She fetched her passport, some dollars in cash and the banker's order. She did not have time to change her clothes or do her hair.

No one on the bus seemed to mind that she had kept them waiting.

'How are you and your sisters?' one woman asked.

Because no one had called to the house and since people passed her without stopping, she had presumed that the inhabitants of Burg must believe that she and Núria and Conxita were complete outsiders. This woman, however, knew who they were and when they had arrived.

'Julia talked a lot about you,' the woman said. 'She liked getting your letters.'

Another woman joined in the conversation.

'Which of the sisters are you?'

Montse thought she should find a bank in Sort before she did anything else.

In the bank, she explained that she wished to open an account. She showed the teller the banker's order. When asked for identification, she produced her passport. The teller shook her head.

'We also need a utilities bill and a letter from your previous bank and a certificate of tax compliance.'

'I have been paying taxes in Argentina.'

'Well, that won't help us here. You will have to apply for a certificate in this country.'

'Could I cash this banker's order?'

'Not without opening an account. And, no matter what, it would take time to process.'

Montse retrieved the banker's order and asked the teller to change two hundred dollars into euros, becoming irritated when she handed her a long form to fill in.

On the main street of Sort, just beyond the bank, she saw a sign for the office of Oriol Mas and decided that she should ask him what to do about the bank. He had seemed so kind on the phone in what felt already to her like a long time ago. When she went up the stairs, she asked for Oriol Mas, to be told that he was finishing a meeting in the next room. A few moments later, he appeared at the door. He was much younger than she had expected and more casually dressed.

'I know exactly who you are,' he said. 'Your sister was here yesterday. I have the mobile phone she ordered and it is charged, with fifty euro in credit.'

He ushered Montse into a smaller room.

'What can I do for you?' he asked.

She told him what had happened in the bank.

'Your sister had a similar problem. And I can sort out yours too. I even have a small cheque for you, from the legacy.'

He took out his mobile phone and was soon discussing her case with someone in the bank. His way of speaking Catalan was faster and sounded more modern than when he had spoken to her.

As she was about to leave, something else occurred to her.

'I haven't seen the actual will,' she said, 'but I wonder what would happen if not all of us wanted to sell the house.'

'I can get the will for you,' Oriol replied, 'but I am certain that Julia specified that if one of you did not want to sell, then the house could not be sold. I think she actually believed that one of you might stay. That is why she had the house done up.'

'Which of us did she think would stay?'

'Oh, I don't know that.'

When Montse returned to the bank, she had no trouble at all understanding the woman at the counter but, as with her earlier visit, she had difficulty finding the correct tone in which to respond, even sometimes the right words. The last time she had spoken Catalan to a stranger was when she was ten, but that was during the time of Franco, when no one spoke Catalan in banks, and no one spoke Catalan in schools. The language was used at home and in the street, with close neighbours and friends. But now all the signs were in Catalan, even the form she had filled in to change money was in Catalan. Her letters to Aunt Julia had always been in Spanish, as well as Julia's replies. She had never had occasion to write anything in Catalan before, and she could not even remember seeing the language written down.

She did not want to let the teller in the bank know that she was having difficulty with this new form, but she felt the woman guessed and politely took the pen from her and filled in each section.

'We will send you your card,' the woman said, 'and your PIN number will come in a separate envelope.'

Montse nodded her head vaguely.

The market, she had been told, was on the other side of the town. Since she did not want to be burdened for too long with heavy bags, and since she had two hours left, she thought she might walk around, maybe have something to eat.

When she saw the first narrow archway that led from the main street to the street that ran parallel to it, she remembered how frightened she had been when they came here once at night and she was convinced that she had walked into a cave. She ran into someone's arms, Julia's or her mother's. She demanded to be taken back to the bright main street. After that, on any visit to Sort, it was always a joke, Montse's fear of the archway.

She had forgotten how many shops were in the street behind. She decided to walk the length of it before going into any of them. And then she proceeded slowly to the market, savouring each sight, working out what ingredients she would need for meals she planned to cook over the next few days.

As she stood waiting for the bus to take her back to Burg, she knew that she had bought too much. One of the women mocked her gently.

'When you are here a while, you'll learn that the men can carry the heavy goods,' she said. 'We are all delicate souls.'

Glad she would be back in time to catch the late sun on the patio, she enjoyed the idea that the fridge and the larder would be almost full. The house was becoming more solid. Núria would be annoyed that she did not tell them where she was going or at what time she would be back.

Although the front door of the house was unlocked, neither Núria nor Conxita was there. In the silence, Montse realized that she had been looking forward to seeing them, and then began to resent that feeling.

Eight o'clock came, and then nine, and still neither of her sisters appeared. The chicken casserole she had made was ready. But there was no sign of them. She ate some bread and cheese. She even had a glass of wine, sampling the bottle she had bought in Sort.

She was in the armchair fast asleep when Núria and Conxita came back.

'Well, you missed the whole thing,' Núria said.

'We even met a woman from Tírvia who says she is our cousin,' Conxita said.

'But where did you meet her?'

'Señora Puig died,' Núria said. 'Jordi's mother.'

'She was ninety-four,' Conxita added.

'And I thought it was only right,' Núria continued, 'that we call at the house, since we knew them all those years ago.'

'Núria heard about it from a man she met on her walk.'

'Jordi looks old, but one of the brothers hasn't changed at all hardly. I think that is Martí.'

'No,' Conxita interrupted. 'It's Antoni.'

'But you said you didn't remember Martí and Antoni.'

'I do now.'

'And Conxita might have a job,' Núria said.

'It's just some work.'

'Where?' Montse asked.

'There is a centre for artists in Farrera and they had someone serving food and cleaning up in the evening, but she tore her Achilles tendon.'

'The people from the artists' centre are lovely,' Conxita said. 'They didn't think they could find anyone at such short notice. They are going to let me know tomorrow.'

'And then a woman came,' Núria said, 'who remembered all of us. She is a cousin on our grandmother's side. Her name is Tardà, but I don't remember her at all. She asked where you were.'

'And Jordi Puig's wife is dead,' Conxita added.

'Did she die today as well?' Montse asked.

'Don't be silly!' Núria said. 'She died a few years ago. And Jordi says that there were only three Puig brothers, but I am sure there were four.'

'Well, I'm sure that Jordi might know,' Montse said.

'Oh, and there was a man from Andorra,' Conxita said, 'and he is also a widower. He seemed very nice and he told Núria that he goes every evening to Font del Camp in Farrera and he meets friends and he invited Núria to join them.'

'And where was Jordi Puig's mother during all of this?' Montse asked.

'I told you,' Conxita said. 'She is dead. That's why we went to the house.'

'Her body was upstairs,' Núria added. 'She looked very peaceful.'

Montse knew that there was no point in showing them the casserole she had made.

At noon the next day, the three sisters went to the small church for the funeral mass. A few times, as mourners arrived, Conxita nudged Montse and whispered, telling her who they were. Some women came and shook their hands. Afterwards, they agreed that they should not go to the grave.

'We are still outsiders,' Núria said. 'Even if we're not.'

Montse saw her smiling at a well-dressed old man.

'That is the man from Andorra,' Conxita whispered.

Late in the afternoon, when she came in from the patio, Montse found both her sisters in Núria's room, where there was a full-length mirror. Conxita needed to see if her stockings were crooked. Núria wondered if her eyeliner made her look like an old woman trying to be young.

'When we were children,' she said, 'I thought women my age were as old as time.'

Montse examined them both. Even though Núria's clothes and her shoes were clearly more expensive than anything Conxita wore, Conxita appeared more refined and delicate and well cared for. If anyone speculated which of the two had led a pampered life, they would select Conxita. Her skin was softer, her eyes shinier. Núria had lines around her eyes and mouth. She had a hard expression on her face as she prepared to set out to meet the man from Andorra and his friends. Conxita, on the other hand, as she got ready to go to the centre for artists to find out about the job, seemed effortlessly ready to charm anyone she met.

Since their return the night before from the house where Señora Puig lay dead, the two sisters' voices had become louder, their tone more excited. They were like birds on a bright morning, Montse thought, chirping and singing and flying from one branch to another.

A few days later, when Núria was having her walk, Conxita approached Montse with notepaper and an envelope.

'I need to write to Maria Luisa,' she said.

They sat at the dining table, Montse with the pen in her hand. After many hesitations, Conxita dictated her letter:

Dear Maria Luisa
We have been here for two weeks now. The weather is nice. We had only one day of rain, but otherwise it has been sunny. Back with my sisters, it is really like being in Argentina when we went there first. Núria has her eye set on a man – this one is old and a widower and has a house in Tírvia, the village below us, and also a house in Andorra. He drives an old Mercedes. Montse is in a dream and hardly speaks and seldom goes out. I am in the middle and no one notices me. The biggest event so far has been the death of a woman called Puig who was in her nineties. At the wake in her house we met many people from the village and also

from Farrera, the village above, where there is an artists' retreat. They were desperately looking for someone to set the table for dinner, serve the food and clean up afterwards. Everyone they found could do it some nights and not others, or in July but not in August. As you know, I have never done any of these things before, but I pretended that this was what I had spent decades doing in San Isidro. No one has yet found me out. There is a sculptor from Chile in the centre and a painter from Barcelona. They both have black hair. The sculptor wears red lipstick. In my next letter, I will be able to tell you what the exact shade is called and what the brand is. It will change your life as well as your lips.

A few times, as Conxita dictated, Montse stopped and glanced at her quizzically. She was emphatically not in a dream. It was simply not true that she hardly spoke and seldom went out. But Conxita had ignored her and carried on with the rest of the letter.

Montse regretted that Conxita, now employed by the centre for the rest of the summer, had her dinner there each evening, because this meant that she and Núria had to dine alone.

Núria told her that the name of the man from Andorra was Jaume. His house in Tírvia was the one in the corner of the square beside the graveyard. He spent most of the year, however, in Andorra. He was seventy-eight and lived from the rents he received from various properties in Andorra. All this information was offered to Montse casually and not in one piece. Normally, Núria preferred to roam over many other subjects, including her children, her grandchildren, her late husband and her sister Conxita and her employer.

'Being so rich has made that Maria Luisa woman far too eccentric, of course. No one sees her any more. And there is a lot of talk about her.'

'What kind of talk?'

'I am sure you know what I mean,' Núria said and stood up from the table.

Montse took some sheets of paper from Conxita's pad and drew a map of the village, putting in a square for each house. She did this at first from memory but then took a walk every day, going to the very top of the village and finding buildings there that she could not see from the road.

While Farrera had many houses that were used only in the summer, all the houses in Burg were inhabited throughout the year. Montse tried to identify who was in what house in Burg, but there were still many squares on her map that she could put no name to.

She found that if she asked Tonia, the woman from whom she bought eggs, too many questions, Tonia became silent.

Each Tuesday, she took the minibus to Sort for the market. Before going, she discussed with Núria what supplies were needed, Núria giving her money to cover the cost. Since she could not carry heavy groceries on these outings, Núria paid the driver to take herself and Conxita to Llavorsí or Sort once a week, returning with many stories about people they had met and all the things that had changed.

Montse discovered that there was a place in Sort where older people could go during the day to relax, have coffee and read the newspapers. It was near the town hall and there was no one guarding the door asking for documents. She sat in an armchair in the main *sala* and began to read a newspaper, looking up when a young woman arrived and quietly moved from person to person to say that she was from the social services and was here to see if anyone needed help in securing the benefits that were due to them.

Montse explained that she had lived most of her life in Argentina so she did not think she was eligible for many benefits.

'Are you a Spanish citizen?' the woman asked.

'I have a Spanish passport.'

'If you are over sixty-five, then you are entitled to a pension.'

'How much?'

'About four hundred and fifty euro fourteen times a year.'

'How would I apply for it?'

'I could help you do it any Tuesday morning, I always drop in around this time. It's a good day because people are in the town for the market.'

'What documents would I need?'

'I think a passport would be enough to start with. Do you have a national identity card?'

'No.'

'Well, we could work on getting you one.'

By the time the woman left and she had returned to reading the newspaper, it had struck Montse that, though she herself would not qualify for another five years, Núria at sixty-five was eligible for this pension now. With Núria's Spanish passport, Montse could pretend she was her sister and apply. She did not look unlike Núria, especially since she had her hair done to Núria's specifications. She thought at first that she might take the passport some Tuesday and show it to the woman. But then she realized that she might be asked for it again. The only solution, she thought, was to wait until Núria was leaving and put her own passport in her sister's handbag and take Núria's.

* * *

In Buenos Aires when she went to work first, posing as Núria, no one had asked any questions then, and perhaps it was possible, once Núria was safely back in Argentina, no one would ask any questions now.

That night, as she lay in bed, she went over the plan, but it seemed too daring. It must have been the coffee, she imagined, that made her feel confident enough to dream of stealing Núria's Spanish passport.

In the morning, when she woke, she began to worry about what she would do if she ran out of money. As she calculated how much she had and how much she would require in this expensive new country, she came to see that she really would need this pension. Stealing Núria's Spanish passport was not such a preposterous idea.

In the third week they had been in Burg, Montse realized that no one had mentioned Aunt Julia's grave. She had thought about it on the first day, presuming that all three of them would go there. But she had let time go by, intending all the while to say something about it. When she finally raised the subject, neither of her sisters had any interest. So, one morning, she went on her own to the untended graveyard at the back of the church.

Some of the graves were marked with small, metal crosses, many of them rusted. Others had headstones that were crooked in the ground. There were graves not marked at all, including, she supposed, Julia's.

She walked around for a while and, meeting no one, decided to call on Tonia, who came to the door and took her in with a surprised glance. She had sold her a dozen eggs just the day before.

'Some day when I am not busy I will show you her grave,' Tonia said.

Montse was about to ask precisely what month Julia had died, but realized that Tonia might be shocked that she did not know.

'Was it a big funeral?' she asked.

'It was sad,' Tonia replied. 'Even though she was old, people were going to miss her.'

And then, as Montse prepared to turn away, Tonia asked her, 'How long are the three of you going to stay?'

Montse wished that she could divulge her plans.

'For the summer, I suppose. It's nice to be here.'

'And you'll sell the house?'

'We haven't decided that yet.'

In the morning, she became uncertain once more of her plan to purloin Núria's passport. She might be able to manage for a year or maybe two without that pension. But she would have used up all her savings unless she got a job. And she did not believe that a woman of her age, with no connections, would easily find a proper job. And even if she did, it would be in one of the other villages or larger towns. How would she travel?

One day a thunderstorm prevented Núria's usual afternoon walk and kept her at home when her habit was to sit on the bench at the entrance to Farrera with her new friends. She used the opportunity to complain about Burg.

'I am sure all my friends think I am living it up in Spain with great nightlife,' she said. 'How could I tell them that there isn't even a shop here in this desolate village, let alone a restaurant?'

'But the air is very pure and the views are beautiful,' Montse said.

'No wonder my mother wanted to get away from here!' Núria said.

'But Aunt Julia stayed. And she was always in good humour.'

'You don't remember her like I do. She was a very narrow-minded woman. She had cows when we came here first and she would make me get up early in the morning to milk them while you and Conxita were allowed to stay in bed. And the year before we left I stayed up late with some girls and Jordi Puig and a few of his friends came to talk to us. When Julia found out, she locked me in the cowshed for the day. And the whole village knew! Me and thousands of flies and piles of cow dung.'

'I imagine you didn't stay out late again,' Montse said.

'I couldn't wait to get to Argentina so I would never have to spend another summer here,' Núria replied. 'And I have been talking to Oriol Mas in Sort about putting a For Sale sign on this house. It would be lovely to get a buyer before we leave.'

Núria, it seemed, presumed that Montse agreed with her about selling the house. But she didn't stop to ask. She made clear that she would be the one to decide.

The next day, Conxita wanted her to write another letter to Maria Luisa.

Dear Maria Luisa
Núria is making progress with the man from Andorra. She has been to his house in Tírvia which she says is very nice. When he showed her the rooms upstairs, she noticed that he sleeps in a single bed with a crucifix on the wall above the bed. He is promising to take her to a classical music concert in the church in Rialp, which is another village near here. This will be their first date. She carried with her from Argentina some special perfume she says is French and says she will put some of this perfume on for the concert. While Núria is at her classical concert, it will be

all cha-cha-cha for me because there is going to be a party at the centre and I am going to dance until dawn with the sculptor from Chile, who is called Mariela. Her sculptures are abstract and shapely, mixing steel and wood, and she says that she is most inspired by the private shapes of women. When I asked her what this meant, she licked her lips and smiled.

'Did she really do this?' Montse asked.

'Maria Luisa is never going to check.'

'And did Núria really go upstairs in that man's house?'

'No, but she might have.'

When the letter was in its envelope, Montse asked Conxita what she would do, where she might live, if anything should ever happen to Maria Luisa.

'Nothing will happen to her.'

'But what if it did?'

'She is younger than I am.'

'But she is delicate.'

'That is just an act.'

'But where would you go?'

'Why do you ask?'

'Because it would be nice to have this house to come to.'

'Núria wants to sell it.'

'But she doesn't have the right to decide on her own. If one of us wants to keep the house, then it can't be sold.'

'Do you want to keep the house?'

'Yes.'

'Then tell her.'

'I can't. I need you to talk to her.'

'You tell her first and then I'll tell her!'

'She doesn't have the right to decide.'
'Try saying that to her.'

On the evening of the concert Jaume came for Núria at eight. They were to have a pizza in Rialp, like two young people, and then go to the concert. For a man living alone, Jaume was well groomed. He was sprightly, even if he did walk with a slight stoop. Montse wondered how much money he had.

In only seven weeks, she thought, Núria and Conxita would be gone. Jaume might be pleased to hear that Núria's sister was staying and the house was being kept in the family. Montse was glad she had met him, however briefly. In a year's time, he might call for her and they could go to a concert together. He would ask about her sister and she would say that Núria was well, that she had settled back in Buenos Aires and would soon be going skiing with her grandchildren.

In the morning, Montse realized that Conxita had not come back at all the night before. She told Núria that there had been plans to have a party at the centre and perhaps it had continued until late and it was more convenient for her to stay in Farrera.

'She is not like us,' Núria said. 'Conxita is very loose.'
'What do you mean?'
'In the inner circles of Buenos Aires, there is always a lot of talk about Maria Luisa Bustamante.'
'You said that before.'
'You see, no one knows that Conxita is my sister.'
'But what do you mean?'
'I mean that some people say that Maria Luisa has an attachment to one of her female employees that is irregular.'
'With Conxita?'
'That is what they say.'

'And you think that explains everything?' Montse asked.

'It explains nothing at all except perhaps why our sister did not come home last night. Up to further mischief, I suppose.'

The following Tuesday in Sort, having walked up and down the principal streets, Montse went to a cafe that she had noticed near the entrance to the town. On passing a real estate office, she looked in the window, checking the prices of houses in the area. Suddenly, she saw a photograph of their own house, the house in Burg, with a note below saying that it had three bedrooms and had been recently modernized. 'Price on Application', it said, and then below: 'Viewing by Appointment'. When she made an enquiry, saying that she was part-owner of the house, she was told that the estate agents were acting on the instruction of the family solicitor.

She went directly to Oriol Mas's office and found him once more on his way out of a meeting.

'I don't want it sold,' she said. 'I want the advertisement taken out of the window.'

'Your sister told me that all three of you are in agreement.'

'We are not.'

'Why did she tell me that, then?'

'Because she is under a misapprehension.'

'Well, could you let her know that you don't want it sold?'

'I would prefer if you would do that.'

He smiled broadly.

'I understand.'

When she arrived home, Conxita was in the room downstairs.

'Núria is in a fury,' she whispered. 'Oriol called her on her mobile phone. She is upstairs. But it won't be long before she comes down.'

Montse began storing the shopping, leaving the change that

Núria was owed on the kitchen table. Although she heard Núria coming down the stairs, she did not turn to look at her.

'Behind my back!' Núria shouted. 'You went behind my back!'

'So did you,' Montse replied, 'when you put the advertisement in the window.'

'We are selling the house. That is why the advertisement is there.'

'We are not selling it.'

'Why not? Who is going to pay for the upkeep?'

'I am staying here. I am not going back to Argentina.'

'When was that decided?'

'Did you really think I got two months' holiday? I never planned to go back. I sold my house and I left my job.'

'What is going to happen to your return ticket?'

'You can tear it up.'

'You are hardly going to live for very long on what you got for your house, I imagine.'

'I will get by. Julia wanted one of us to stay in the house.'

'Who said that?'

'Oriol Mas told me. And that explains why she decorated it.'

'All for you, I suppose?'

Since Núria had arched her eyebrows, Montse did the same.

'Well, she hardly did it for you!' she said.

'Are you going to pay us for our share of the house?' Núria asked.

'I don't have to. But, also, Conxita wants to keep the house.'

'Is she staying here too?'

'No, I am not,' Conxita said. 'I am going back to Argentina. And don't involve me in this.'

'You will freeze in the winter,' Núria said. 'And you will die of boredom. I can't imagine you here on your own. What if you fell or had an accident, who would find you? I can't bear to think of it happening all over again.'

'What happening all over again?' Montse asked.

'I mean, someone living on her own in this house all the year around.'

'I will survive, I imagine,' Montse said.

'Well, I am glad I won't have to witness it,' Núria said. 'On the first of September I am flying back to Argentina.'

'I am sure they will all be delighted to see you,' Montse said.

As July came to an end, Tonia warned Montse about August.

'There will be no peace. People from Barcelona will walk around this village wondering if they should buy one of our houses. They look at me like I am in the zoo. And try going down to Sort with all the heat and all the crowds! And try getting bread when the bakeries are all sold out in the morning. And then all the festas and the shouting and the staying up late! When I was young, I loved it then felt a terrible let-down each September. Thank God all that is over! People should pray to the Virgin to get them as quickly as possible into old age so they don't feel the urge to go anywhere at night except to bed.'

On the Saturday night of the Festa Major of Tírvia, Jaume invited Núria and Montse, as well as others from the group that he met with each evening, to dine at his house and then join the festivities in the square. Conxita would be coming later with some of the artists from the centre, including the Chilean sculptor.

Jaume's house was like a convent, with heavy furniture and sombre colours, and the walls left bare of any decoration. In the dining room, there was a table set for ten, everything perfect, the silverware gleaming, the napkins perfectly ironed. Montse wondered if Jaume had a housekeeper, but he appeared to have prepared the meal himself. It began with a salad and then lamb chops and sautéed potatoes. Jaume placed Núria at the opposite end of the table to himself. Montse was put between another man from Andorra, a friend of Jaume's, who had come to stay the night, and a woman from Farrera who, with her husband, went each evening to the bench at the entrance to the village.

'Your sister,' she said, 'always has the best stories. We will miss her when she goes. Indeed, we will miss you all.'

Montse was about to tell the woman that she planned to stay, but then she stopped herself.

'And we admired Julia,' the woman went on. 'She was such a private lady, and so dignified. Nobody likes to talk about what happened to her. People were really shocked that such a thing could occur.'

Montse felt that if she asked too direct a question the woman might not tell her anything more. She smiled sadly and nodded, leaving space for the woman to continue. Just then, however, Núria wanted everyone at the table to raise a glass to the host. Once that was done, the woman was distracted by her other neighbour, and the man from Andorra directed his attention to Montse, who listened to him intently, trying to think of questions to ask. She wanted to be able to finish with him definitively so that she could turn again to the woman next to her and try to learn what she could about Julia.

When the plates had been taken away, Jaume produced two pear tarts that came, he said, from the best *pastisseria* not only in Andorra or Spain, but better than any in France, and therefore, unless someone wished to contradict him, he would claim that this pear tart was the best in the world. And it would be accompanied by a Cava from a vineyard in the Penedès that was owned by a friend of his.

'I get six bottles a year and open two at Christmas, two for the Festa Major of Andorra and two for the Festa Major of Tírvia.'

When a further set of toasts had been completed, Montse turned to the woman.

'When did you find out that Aunt Julia had died?'

'The same time as everybody else. It's normal for people not to see one another in the winter in the villages. People stay at home. So no one noticed that Julia hadn't appeared. Everyone knew she had put in the wood-burning stove and had the chimney cleaned and they should have seen that there was no smoke coming from the chimney. Someone said that Julia had gone to Barcelona, but then no one could recall who had said that. It was only the driver of the minibus who missed her one Tuesday, and then, the second week, when he drove the bus back to Burg, he went to her house and climbed over the wall to the new patio. And he could see her through the glass doors.'

'How long had she been dead?'

'A week or two or maybe more, I think. Everyone was very upset. And no one knew where you three were. And then Oriol Mas was given the letter that came from you after she had died. It had your address. It was all very sad, especially when you think that she decorated the house just a short time before.'

They waited until they could hear the music from the square before going out to watch the dancing. Jaume offered to get drinks for everyone. As casual conversation and easy laughter went on all around them, Núria approached Montse.

'What was that woman talking to you about?'

'She told me how Julia died.'

'That's what I thought she was doing.'
'Does Conxita know?'
'Yes, we both found out at the wake we went to.'
'Why didn't you tell me?'
'We thought it might upset you too much.'

After a while, Jaume and his friend carried a bench from the house as Conxita and some others arrived. Montse sat quietly watching the crowd. If she could spend six weeks in the village without being told how her aunt had died, what else were they keeping from her, what else would they not tell her in the future?

Most people in the square were locals. She thought of all the things they knew that she did not know. So much had happened in her long absence, things people were hardly even aware they remembered. Not knowing them meant she was alone, sitting outside the circle.

Among the crowd, she spotted Jordi Puig in a white shirt with short sleeves. He had a beer in his hand and was laughing at some joke. Just then, she would have given anything for him to glance at her and look away and glance back. But the time for that was over, she supposed. He would be alone in his house all winter, as she would be in hers.

One evening when Montse and Núria were having supper, Núria wore a disapproving expression on her face.

'Conxita was seen cavorting with that Chilean sculptress in the swimming pool in Llavorsí after midnight. They had climbed over the gates.'

'Cavorting?'

'Don't ask me to go into detail.'

'Conxita says that the Chilean woman is very nice.'

'No one is very nice,' Núria said.

The following day, when Núria was out and Conxita asked her to write another letter to Maria Luisa, she wondered if there would be any reference to the swimming pool in Llavorsí.

Dear Maria Luisa
It is hot here and, now that it is August, the villages are full of people. The centre is full too and the heat is making people stay up late. Some people drink and others smoke weed, and that is a new experience for me. I think you would enjoy some weed as well. There was a festival in the village below which everyone enjoyed except my sister Montse who sat on her own looking like a ghost. On a more cheerful note, last Sunday night, when there was no dinner served at the centre, I went with Mariela, the Chilean sculptor, to Rialp for pizza. And then, on the way home, passing through Llavorsí, we thought it would be pleasant to have a swim in the pool there. This involved climbing over a gate and swimming without swimsuits. Mariela looked like a piece of sculpture herself in the moonlight before she dived into the water. When the men who run the pool caught us, we could not stop laughing. They threatened to call the police.

Conxita did not smile as she called out the words, but concentrated as though much depended on the next thing she would say.

'Are you not a bit old to be swimming naked with a Chilean sculptress?' Montse asked.

'I am only sixty-two.'

Montse asked Conxita if she could take her job at the centre when she left for Paris to meet Maria Luisa at the end of

August. Conxita said that she would enquire. When Montse asked her again, Conxita said she had forgotten all about it. A few days later, she told Montse that the people at the centre were not sure, but would be in touch with Montse if they needed anyone.

Núria asked her if she was still determined to stay.

'No one knows you. They know me and they know Conxita. What if you got sick? Who would look after you?'

'What if I got sick in Chivilcoy?'

'Surely you have neighbours and friends there? Jaume says that you don't know what the winter is like here.'

'It will be quiet,' Montse said.

'I'm sure Conxita could use the money if we sold the house. She has nowhere at all of her own.'

'I thought you said she was in league with Maria Luisa.'

'That could end as soon as it started and where would she go then?'

'She will always be welcome here.'

'The house partly belongs to her so welcome is hardly the word.'

'And it belongs partly to me too, and I am staying here.'

One morning in the middle of August, Jaume came to take Núria over the mountains to Andorra. She had booked a room for a night in a hotel there.

'Jaume said that I could stay with him, but I don't think that is quite proper.'

'Well, I am going for a long walk,' Conxita said, 'and having a picnic with Mariela by a lake. And we are also going to be quite proper. Montse, are you going to be quite proper?'

For some days before this there had been a chill in the wind, but now, as she made coffee and toasted some bread, Montse felt the heat of the day rising.

She had a shower and put on fresh clothes. And then she sat in front of the house.

Later in the morning, she walked up to Tonia's house to get some fresh eggs.

'I have nothing for you,' Tonia said. 'You should have put in an order. I have been cleaned out by the August crowd! In two weeks, you will be all gone and I will be begging the hens not to lay any more eggs.'

'I am staying,' Montse said. 'I am not leaving.'

'Staying where?'

'In the house.'

'For how long?'

'For good. I am not going back to Argentina.'

'You know, you are the image of her,' Tonia said.

'Who?'

'Julia. All of us think that.'

'In what way?'

'Your face. Your voice. The way you talk. Your sister, the rude one, is like her too, but you are the image of her.'

'Were you and Julia friends?'

'I lived beside her all my life. But we all have our own people. I have my brothers and my family and they are the people who look after me. But I suppose we were friends.'

In the days before Núria and Conxita were due to depart there were many visitors to the house. Conxita invited all of the artists at the centre for drinks on the last Sunday. Montse studied Mariela, who was a small, talkative woman, older-looking than Conxita. She tried to imagine her naked in a swimming pool after midnight. Mariela told Montse several times that she was looking forward to meeting Conxita and her partner when she was in Paris in a week's time.

'It will be a double reunion,' she said. 'I will be reunited with Conxita and she will be reunited with Maria Luisa.'

Jaume and his friends visited too; he spoke with delight about his hopes to go to Argentina.

'You will be welcome any time,' Núria said. 'More than welcome.'

'He will come back in our winter with a suntan that will make us all jealous,' his friend said.

Montse still wondered if it really would be wise to exchange her passport for Núria's. But receiving more than four hundred euro fourteen times a year would take some of the worry out of life. It was already agreed that the utility bills would be left in Núria's name but paid by Montse. To get Núria's pension, she could open a second bank account in the other bank in Sort. She could ask Oriol Mas again and, if he called the bank to tell them about Montse, she could declare in the bank that while she was known as Montse, her official name was Núria. Since this was just a detail, the people at the bank would hardly bother Oriol Mas with it. Surely, they would have more important things to do. Even if they did, Montse could claim it was a mix-up.

It was decided that Jaume would drive Núria and Conxita the four-hour journey to Barcelona. They would take a room at the Hotel Colón so they could have lunch and rest. In the evening, Conxita would then get the train to Paris and Núria would catch her flight to Buenos Aires.

'I feel very sad about leaving you here,' Núria said to Montse. 'I know we didn't see one another much over the years but it made a difference to me that you were there. We were always close, the three of us.'

Montse did not reply.

On the morning of their departure, Montse helped Núria carry all her luggage down to the main room, observing that Núria had left her handbag on the kitchen table before going back upstairs to the bathroom. When Conxita came down with her suitcase, Montse appealed to her to go back upstairs one more time and check that she had not left anything behind.

She stood at the foot of the staircase and watched Conxita ascend and listened to the sound of running water from a tap in the bathroom. She would have to move quickly. In her apron pocket, she had her own Spanish passport. She opened Núria's handbag. In one small pocket she found Núria's two passports. She took the Spanish one and put it into her apron pocket and replaced it with her own Spanish passport.

Then it struck her that life might be simpler if she kept her own Spanish passport, so she withdrew it from Núria's handbag where she had put it and placed it back into her apron pocket. Núria would just think that she had mislaid her Spanish passport. Her Argentine passport would get her back home.

It was now one minute to eight. Jaume was due at eight. If he was late, it would give Núria an opportunity to check everything again. But when Montse heard Jaume beep the horn of his car, she knew that Núria would not have time to find that one of her passports was missing. She called loudly up the stairs to her sisters to create an atmosphere of rush and alarm. When Jaume appeared, she went upstairs and banged on the bathroom door before calling to Conxita on the floor above to say that she should hurry.

Jaume took the suitcases to the car and Montse followed him with Núria's handbag.

'All your things are in the car,' she told Núria when she came downstairs. 'I put your handbag on the front seat. Now, if only Conxita would come down!'

Soon, as Jaume turned the car, all three sisters stood waiting for him.

'We have had such a great summer,' Conxita said. 'So maybe we'll be here next year again.'

'Exactly,' Núria said. 'I will be telling my grandchildren all about it.'

They embraced and kissed before getting into the car.

Montse waved until the car disappeared.

It would just take a second for Núria to check that everything was in order, beginning by looking into her handbag. Montse thought she might go for a walk and not be there should the car return.

Later, she would take the sheets from Núria's bed and put them into the washing machine. It would be her bed now.

This was what she supposed Aunt Julia did each year when her nieces left. She would begin washing and tidying in the silence of the house, knowing that another year had passed. She could look around the main room, quiet now, and remember her nieces who had filled this place with conversation and laughter just hours before.

First, Montse thought, she would clean the bathroom and put in fresh towels. On the ledge near the wash-hand basin she found the bottle of expensive French perfume that Núria had brought from Argentina, with a note beside it from her sister that said: 'I thought you might like this.' She lifted the bottle to her nose and smelled the perfume. For a split second she wanted to shout to her aunt Julia the news that Núria had left her the perfume. Immediately, however, she realized that there was, of course, no

Aunt Julia. She could not believe she had thought there was.

Montse did not believe that the people from the centre would offer her work, nor did she expect Jaume to appear in his Mercedes to invite her to a concert. She would be alone here. In Núria's bed, she could wake and, since she would soon be applying for a pension in her name, feel like Núria for a while and wear her perfume if she wanted to. Or she could walk up the stairs, as Conxita did, to the room where Conxita had slept and find her sister's notepad beside the bed and take it downstairs and sit at the dining room table and begin to write:

Dear Maria Luisa
It is still hot here, but most of the visitors have left. Soon, it will be all quiet. Soon, there won't be a sound.

In the meantime, she would do nothing except imagine her sisters on their journey to the city and then plan what she might do every day – go for a walk of course, using the stick that Núria had found, or venture to the edge of Farrera at the end of the day and join the company there that gathered around the bench. Or perhaps just stay here in the house, enjoy the silence that she had been looking forward to and maybe check the upstairs rooms to make sure that her sisters had not forgotten anything and then prepare dinner, but just for one, just for herself.

Acknowledgements

Acknowledgement is made to the publications where some of these stories first appeared: *The New Yorker* ('Summer of '38', 'Sleep', 'Five Bridges'); *All Over Ireland: New Irish Short Stories* ('The Journey to Galway'); *New Irish Short Stories* ('The News from Dublin'); *The Dublin Review* ('A Sum of Money'); *Marlene Dumas: The Image as Burden* ('Barton Springs'). And thanks to the editors: Deborah Treisman, Deirdre Madden, Joseph O'Connor, Brendan Barrington.

I am grateful also to my agent Peter Straus, to Mary Mount at Picador in London, Nan Graham at Scribner in New York, and to Cormac Kinsella, Katherine Monaghan, Katherine Stroud, Sabrina Pyun and Ebruba Abel-Unokan. Also to Catriona Crowe, Hedi El Kholti, Marlene Dumas, Veronica Rapalino, Ed Mulhall, Robinson Murphy and Steve Vopava.

I wish to thank Angela Rohan for her meticulous work on the manuscript.

'The Journey to Galway' takes images and phrases from *Seventy Years*, the autobiography of Lady Gregory.